Praise for
The McAvoy Sisters Book of Secrets

"The perfect read for a summer day."

—**Jill Shalvis, *Ne***...   ...**or**

"*The McAvoy Sisters Book of Secrets* is such a compelling story. It's filled with my favorite things to read about—sisters, secrets, surprises, and genuine, heartfelt sentiment. The talented Molly Fader will keep you turning the pages right down to the oh-so-satisfying final twist."

—**Susan Wiggs, *New York Times* bestselling author**

"Full of affection and wry wit, this is a surprising page-turner with a super-satisfying twist."

—***Woman's World***

"Fans of Jennifer Weiner will be pleased to have a new author to discover."

—***Booklist***

"Mothers and daughters, sisters and secrets... Molly Fader delivers a delicious summer read populated with spirited characters, a charming lakeside setting, and just enough mystery to keep the pages turning. A warmhearted delight of a book!"

—**Jamie Brenner, bestselling author of *The Forever Summer* and *Drawing Home***

"Mesmerizing and soul-searching. A story that makes you believe in the power of family."

—**Carolyn Brown, *New York Times* bestselling author**

"An emotional, tender, simply wonderful book. I loved everything about it, from the beautiful prose to the perfectly layered plot to the strong, compelling McAvoy women. Once you start, you won't be able to put it down until you discover all the secrets within."

—**RaeAnne Thayne, *New York Times* bestselling author**

"A riveting, emotional blend of family drama, mystery, and romance that you will not want to put down—but neither will you want it to end."

—**Jamie Beck, national bestselling author of *Before I Knew***

Also by Molly Fader

The McAvoy Sisters Book of Secrets

the Bitter and Sweet of Cherry Season

A NOVEL

MOLLY FADER

GRAYDON
HOUSE

GRAYDON
HOUSE®

ISBN-13: 978-1-525-80455-7

The Bitter and Sweet of Cherry Season

This edition published by arrangement with Harlequin Books S.A.

Graydon House
22 Adelaide St. West, 40th Floor
Toronto, Ontario M5H 4E3, Canada
www.GraydonHouseBooks.com
www.BookClubbish.com

Printed in U.S.A.

For Adam, Mick and Lucy. You have made my life so sweet.

the Bitter
and
Sweet
of
Cherry Season

One

HOPE

Night in Northern Michigan was no joke.

Hope had never seen a dark so dark. It had heft and dimension, like she was driving right into an abyss. She thought about waking up Tink in the back to show her, but the girl had finally fallen asleep, and she needed the rest.

And Hope needed a break.

Who knew traveling with a completely silent, angry and traumatized ten-year-old could be so exhausting?

Hope's phone had died when she got off the highway about twenty minutes ago. In those last few minutes of battery she had tried to memorize the directions.

Left on Murray Street.

Slight right onto County Road 72.

Your destination is five miles on the right.

But County Road 72 wasn't well marked and now she

feared she was lost. Well, for sure she was lost; in the grand scheme of things she was totally off the map.

But she was clinging to the one ratty thread of hope she had left.

And then just as that tiny bit of thread started to slip through her fingers, from the murk emerged a blue sign.

County Road 72.

The road took a long arcing right into the dark, and she unrolled her window, trying to keep herself awake. Adrenaline and gas-station coffee could only do so much against two sleepless nights.

Her yawn was so wide it split her lip. Again. Copper-tasting blood pooled in her mouth.

"Shit," she breathed and pressed the last of the napkins against her mouth. She was even out of napkins.

In the back, Tink woke up. Hope heard the change in her breathing. The sudden gasp like she was waking up from a nightmare.

Or into one. Hard to say.

"Hey," Hope said, looking over her shoulder into the shadows of the back seat. Her daughter's pale face slid into the space between the driver and passenger seats like a moon. "We're almost there." Hope sounded like they were about to drive up to the gates of Disney World.

Tink rubbed her eyes.

"Did you see the stars?" Hope's voice climbed into that range she'd recently developed. Dementedly cheerful. Stepford Mom on helium. She winced at the sound of it. That wasn't her. It wasn't how she talked to Tink. And yet she couldn't tune her voice back to normal. "There are so many of them. I don't think I've ever seen so many stars."

Tink ducked her head to look out the windshield and then

turned to cock her head at an angle so she could look out the passenger windows.

They'd gone to an exhibit about the constellations at the Science Center a year ago and Tink still talked about it. Pointing up at Sirius like she'd discovered it herself.

"Aren't those the pieties?" The constellation was called the Pleiades, but Hope got the name wrong on purpose, hoping for a snotty-toned correction from her miniature astronomer. Or at least a throat-clearing scoff.

But no.

"Sooner or later you're going to talk to me," she said. "You're going to open that mouth and all the words you haven't said all day are gonna come pouring out."

Silence.

"Do you want to ask me questions about where we're going?" They were, after all, heading deep into Northern Michigan to a place she and Tink had never been that Hope had never told her about until today.

Tink rubbed her eyes again.

"Or maybe what happened…tonight?" Her gaze bounced between Tink and the road.

When you're older, you'll understand. When you're a mom, you'll understand. She wanted to say that to her daughter, but she herself barely understood much of what had happened the last two days.

Still silence.

Hope tried a different angle. "I'm telling you, Tink. I know you and you can't keep this up much longer. I'll bet you ten bucks you say something to me in five…four…three…two…" She pulled in a breath that tasted like tears and blood.

Please, honey. Please.

"One." She sighed. "Fine. You win."

Her beat-up hatchback bounced over the uneven asphalt

and Tink crawled from the back seat into the front, her elbow digging into Hope's shoulder, her flip-flopped foot kicking her in the thigh.

The degree of parenting it would take to stop Tink from doing that, or to discuss the potential dangers and legality of it, was completely beyond her. She was beyond pick your battles, into some new kind of Wild West motherhood. Pretend there were no battles.

They drove another five minutes until finally, ahead, there was a golden halo of light over the trees along the side of the road, and Hope slowed down. A gravel driveway snaked through the darkness and she took it on faith that it had been five miles.

"This is it."

Please let this be it.

The driveway opened up and she saw a yellow-brick two-story house.

The Orchard House. That was what Mom called it in the few stories she'd told about growing up here. Actually, the words she used were *The Goddamn Orchard House.*

It was a grand old-fashioned place with second-story windows like empty eyes staring down at them. White gingerbread nestled up in the corners of the roof, and there was a big wide porch with requisite rocking chairs.

Seriously, it was so charming, it could have been fake.

The car rolled to a stop and Hope put it in Park. Her maniacal new voice failed her, and she just sat there. Silent.

Suddenly the front door opened and a dog—a big one, with big teeth—came bounding out. Cujo stopped at the top of the steps and started barking. Behind the dog came a woman in a blue robe carrying a shotgun.

Tink made a high panicked sound, climbing up in her seat.

Hope's impulse was to turn the car around and get out of

there. The problem was there was nowhere to turn around *to*. They had no place left to go.

"It's okay, honey," Hope lied. She went as far as to put her hand over Tink's bony knee, the knob of it fitting her palm like a baseball. "Everything's going to be all right."

More desperate than brave, Hope popped open the door. The dog's bark, unmuffled by steel and glass, was honest-to-god bloodcurdling. "Hi!" she yelled, trying to be both cheerful and loud enough to be heard over the barking.

"Get your hands up," the woman on the porch shouted.

Hope shoved her hands up through the crack between the door and the car and did a kind of jazz hands with her fingers.

"What do you want?" the woman asked.

"Are you Peg—"

"I can't hear you."

She stood up, her head reaching up over the door. "Are you Peg?"

"Never mind me. Who the hell are you?" She pointed the business end of the gun toward them.

Hope quickly sidestepped away from the car door, and Tink reached across the driver's seat and slammed it shut.

The heavy thud of the engaged lock was unmistakable.

"You don't know me—"

"No shit!"

"My name is Hope," she said.

The gun lowered and the woman's face changed. From anger to something more careful. "Hope?"

"Yeah. I'm Denise's girl. I'm… Well, you're my aunt?"

Two

Peg came down a few steps, the dog with her as if to get a better look, too. Hope turned, trying to keep the left side of her face in the dark.

At one in the morning, in an oversized bathrobe, with a rifle in hand, Aunt Peg looked like a version of Mom from an alternate universe. One without color rinses and starvation diets, Virginia Slims and wedge heels.

But, boy, the distrust in her eyes—that was familiar.

"Nelson!" the woman barked, and Cujo sat, then lay down on the ground and daintily licked a paw.

"That's a good trick," Hope said, relief and adrenaline making her head spin.

"It's training, not a trick." Peg was a tall woman, red hair going beige in a thick braid down her back. Her freckled face did not reveal even a hint of her age. She was broad-shouldered but thin, and everything about her, from the gun to the way the belt of her robe was tied, screamed, *I will not put up with your nonsense.* "What are you doing here?" She glanced at her watch. "At one a.m.?"

Right. What am I doing here?

Hope turned to the car, to Tink watching through the driver's-side window, hands pressed flat against the glass, fogging the windows around her pink fingers, then back to Peg. "I need help," she said, and then the kicker: "And I don't have anywhere else to go." The words came out with barely a catch. She'd gotten good at begging. Pride was a luxury she hadn't been able to afford in a long time.

Peg set the stock of the gun down by her feet. "Well, I suppose you better come on in, then," she said, far from welcoming. But Hope would take what she could get.

When Hope stepped toward the car, Peg lifted the gun again. "I'm…I'm just getting my daughter."

"You got a kid?"

Hope nodded and Peg peered at the dark car. Tink ducked back into the shadows.

"How old?"

"Ten."

For a still, breathless minute, Hope didn't have any idea what her aunt was thinking. Was she doing the math? Wondering when Hope had had a child? Maybe she hated kids. Ten-year-olds in particular. Maybe she wished she could rescind the invitation.

If that was the case, Hope wasn't going to give her that chance. She quickly pulled open the driver's-side door. "It's okay," she said to Tink. "I swear. Everything is okay. I won't let anything happen to you."

She coaxed her daughter out of the car like the wild animal she was, and then they stood there just on the edge of the pool of light cast by the bug-swarmed bulb in the middle of the porch ceiling, as if awaiting judgment. The silence stretched and Hope put a hand on her daughter's shoulder. *It's all right,* that hand was meant to say. *We don't need her to like us, we just need her to let us sleep here.*

Tink shrugged Hope's touch away.

"What's your name?" Peg asked.

"Her name is Tink," Hope said.

"She don't talk?"

"She's shy. It's been a long day."

"What kind of name is Tink?"

"Hers."

Hope hadn't said it to be funny, but Peg made a sound that might have been a laugh. Tink's name was actually Jenny, but Tony had given her the nickname Tinkerbell when she was born and it had stuck. A way to keep her daddy present in their lives when he never actually was.

"I'm Peg, but I guess you already know that," she said, and pointed to the dog. "And that's Nelson. Let her sniff you and she won't bug you."

Tink moved not one inch toward that dog, and so Hope did, just to prove it was all right. As she walked closer, the dog growled low in its throat, top lip curling to reveal those pink-and-black gums. White teeth an inch long.

"You sure she won't bite?" Hope asked.

"I guess I know my own dog."

Hope crept closer and the dog got up on her feet, tail slowly wagging. That was a good sign, right? Tail wagging?

She got to the bottom of the steps and Nelson stretched her nose out, tail wagging harder.

"Why'd you name a girl dog Nelson?" Hope asked.

"All my dogs are named Nelson," Peg said.

Denise had always said her sister was strange, but Hope never put a whole lot of stock in it, because Mom could find something sour to say about anyone. But up close and personal, strange seemed about right.

Hope reached out her hand, and Nelson sniffed her palm,

smelling yesterday's McDonald's, maybe. Gas-station soap. Every second she expected Nelson to open those jaws and snap her hand off at the wrist. But all she did was sniff. And once that was done, she licked the back of Hope's hand, like a stamp at a club.

"See," Hope said to her daughter. "Nelson's a good dog."

Tink did not budge.

"Tink," she whispered. *Please.*

"Come on now, girl. Before the bugs get you," Peg said.

Tink gave the light bulb a dubious look but still didn't move. Her ruling character trait was stubbornness, the kind of stubbornness that could keep a silent streak going for days.

"We ain't got all night," Peg said.

Hope hung her head. That tone wouldn't work with Tink. But then Nelson's thick tail started wagging again and Tink was there beside Hope with her hand out. Nelson gave Tink the same sniffing treatment.

"Come on in," Peg said. "No sense standing here."

Peg climbed the old stairs. There were four, not very steep, white paint flaking off. Yet to Hope right now they seemed like a mountain.

The familial tie to Peg was so thin it was nearly nonexistent. A stuffed animal on Christmas when she was a kid. An envelope of money every year on her birthday. It hardly seemed like enough to justify what Hope and Tink might bring to this woman's moth-covered door.

Hope just needed sleep. A few hours and then she'd think of something. She had half a tank of gas and a little bit of room on her credit card. The engine light was on, but that thing was always on. They might be able to get to Canada if everything went their way.

"You coming?" Peg asked from inside the house. Tink stood beside her, the screen door between them obscuring her face.

Hope nodded and somehow managed to get herself up the

stairs. Once she was under the full light of that bulb, Peg made a startled sound in her throat.

"Your eye."

Hope had forgotten for a moment and now that she'd been reminded, it ached again. All the way through her face to her teeth. Under the porch light, there was no hiding what had happened to her.

"You all right?" Peg asked.

"It's not as bad as it looks," Hope whispered, touching the bottom edge of her black eye, where it sat on her cheekbone.

"Bullshit," Peg said.

The buzz of a million Michigan bugs broke the awkward silence. Her mom told her once that for a biology project in high school, she'd gathered up all those bugs—mosquitos and house flies and white moths, and on the side of the barn even a brown moth as big as her hand—and pinned their wings to pieces of Styrofoam over tags with their scientific names. Mosquitos were called *Culicidae*. Hope remembered that. She'd forgotten so much, but for some reason that always resurfaced.

And that her mother had loved the project. And Denise Wright hadn't loved much of anything.

"Hope?" Peg had propped open the door again, watching her with those deep-set hazel eyes. Mom's hazel eyes. Tink's, too. Gold going to green going to brown. In the sunlight they'd probably glow.

"You all right?"

She held her aunt's stare from the other side of that screen. She was here. The door was open. Her daughter was inside. The monsters were miles away.

"I'm okay," she finally said. "Just tired."

"Come on. You need some ice on that eye."

Hope stepped into the old Orchard House and the screen door closed behind her.

Three

Everything was covered in crocheted blankets. A bright red couch and a pretty chair with splashy flowers and an ottoman cozied up in front of it. It was impossibly homey. Like a set for a family sitcom. At any moment an adorable family of four was going to come in and argue about the teenage daughter's skirt length.

Nelson trotted off across the living room and through a brick, arched doorway, nails clicking on the hardwood floors.

"Look familiar?" Peg asked, putting the shotgun back up on a rack over the front door. "Not much has changed since you were here."

Hope blinked hard. "I haven't been here."

Tink was staring at her with narrowed eyes. The entire drive Hope had said that she'd never been to this house. Never been to Northern Michigan. *What an adventure this would be*, she'd crowed like a maniac as she ignored the speed limit on her way up from Detroit.

A clock somewhere in the house ticked and hummed. "You were young," Peg finally said. "But you were here."

"I don't remember." She could feel Tink adding this to the column in her head. Things Mom Lied About. "I swear."

"Well, it's nothing to get worked up over." Peg watched them with an unreadable face. "Probably for the best."

"How is it for the best?" The solid ground beneath Hope's feet kept getting yanked away, and now it seemed like even her memory wasn't reliable.

Peg only shrugged.

"Mom brought me?" Hope asked, trying to sift through her memories, but there was nothing there. She stared at the ottoman, the brick entryway to the kitchen, the worn yellow wood of the floors. Her aunt's red hair and stern, freckled face.

Nothing. None of it was familiar.

"Denise was here with you."

"Was it summer or…"

"You know," Peg said. "It's late. Maybe this is a conversation for the morning."

Hope was so tired she could collapse on that couch. The floor would do. But still, it felt strange to be told something she didn't have any memory of.

She struggled to imagine what occasion would bring Mom back here, with Hope in tow. Mom didn't like going out to the country or across the river into Illinois if she could help it. She wasn't much of a driver, and in her lifetime they'd never taken a plane anywhere. A trip to Northern Michigan from St. Louis would have been a thing. A whole big thing.

"You hungry?" Inside the house, Peg seemed smaller, her shoulders still broad but rounded beneath her robe. "I've got some leftover ham in the fridge. I could make a few sand-wiches…"

Hope shook her head. Tink had eaten not too long ago and Hope was a million times more tired than hungry. "No, thank you," she said, her voice running out of steam. "We just need some sleep."

"That eye of yours," Peg said, and pointed toward the kitchen. "I got some painkillers around here somewhere. And ice."

"Really, it's fine—"

"Follow me." Peg ignored her and walked the same path her dog had taken through the living room, under the arch and into a big, wide kitchen with faded wooden floors. The cabinets were white with black pulls, and the countertops were thick wood butcher block. The kind of rustic farmhouse look people in cities tried to recreate a million times over. In the daylight it would probably be charming.

There were a bunch of windows along the back wall, and Hope stood by one, looked out. There wasn't another house for miles. The house was a little yellow-lit, bug-swarmed is-land in a sea of black.

"Here you go," Peg said, holding out an amber prescrip-tion bottle.

"What's that?"

Peg looked down at the label. "Vicodin."

"Oh my gosh, I don't need that. Just aspirin will do."

Peg said nothing, put the prescription bottle away and handed her generic aspirin. "Take the whole bottle," she said. "You need it."

With no strength to argue, Hope tucked the bottle into the pocket of her shorts. "Thank you."

From the freezer, Peg grabbed an ice pack, wrapped it in an old cheesecloth dish towel, the same type Hope's mother had used, and handed that to her, too. "Let's get you settled in, then," she said, and walked back into the living room. She opened a door that didn't quite fit the age of the rest of the house, revealing a set of steps. "You guys can sleep up here." Peg's body filled the narrow stairway as she made her way to the second floor. Tink followed her, Hope at the back. "It's not much," Peg said over her shoulder. "But you got your own bathroom."

At the top of the steps she turned right into a hallway and opened another door. Hope looked in to see a toilet and a claw-foot tub with a bright pink shower curtain.

"There's one bedroom." She stopped at a closet to pull out mismatched sheets and burgundy satin-edged blankets. "Two beds."

On the far side of a small kitchen, Peg pushed open another door. From the curtainless window, moonlight streamed in across two bare single mattresses. Peg pulled the chain on a lamp and began to make up one of the beds.

"Peg," Hope said, putting her hand against Peg's shoulder and fighting the sudden urge to lean against it. "We can do that. You've done enough. Go on back to bed."

Peg glanced at her watch and then back up at Hope, who tried to project the right amount of gratitude while hiding what she could of her bone-deep exhaustion.

Basically, she had no idea what her face was doing. Was she smiling? Snarling?

"We wake up early around here," Peg said. "Farm hours."

"Sure," Hope said, like she knew what those might be.

"Come on down when you get up. There'll be coffee on."

She'd had so much coffee in the last twenty-four hours her stomach was never going to be the same, but still she smiled. "Sounds good."

Peg glanced down at Tink, who in the overhead light had nearly purple circles under her eyes. Hope braced herself for

Peg to ask what the hell had happened to them but instead her aunt just edged out the doorway.

Then she stopped, her hand braced against the door frame. She had rough hands, thick swollen knuckles. A nail going blue.

"I got your letter," Peg said. "About Denise."

"Oh," she said, having sent the letter and the obituary from the paper when Denise had died a year ago. "I'd wondered. Not that I expected you to write back." Or come down for the funeral. But she'd hoped. A little. Someone showing up to help—even an aunt she didn't know—would have made those dark days less lonely. It might have changed everything that happened after.

"Was it…bad?"

Hope blinked away the memories that wanted to pull at her. "It wasn't good."

Peg hung her head. If Hope had the grace required for such a conversation, she might tell her that Denise had asked about Peg and that in the end it had been painless. And a relief.

But Hope failed the moment, like she had so many other moments, and the silence stayed empty.

"All right then. I'll let you two settle in," Peg said, and headed down the narrow staircase.

Hope listened for the click of the door shutting downstairs, and then as quiet as she could she crept down the steps, too, checking the door knob to see if there was a lock. There was only one of those bathroom locks, with the button in the middle of the doorknob. It wouldn't hold against someone who really wanted in. Someone with boots and a heavy kick.

But it would do for now.

The knob depressed with a click that seemed way too loud, and she tiptoed back to the bedroom only to find Tink already asleep on one of the beds. Curled up into a little Tink ball. No sheet. No blanket. No pillow. She had one flip-flop on and one off, her dirty foot white where the strap had been.

Hope stroked the hair off her daughter's face. She was sweating. She always sweat in her sleep, the first few minutes, like the effort of slowing herself down, of stopping the wild machinery of Tink, took work.

Fear and love clenched her body like a fist, and she couldn't breathe for the pain of it. She shook out a blanket to put over her daughter's tiny body and then collapsed in the bed next to her. No sheet. One blanket. No pillow. She swallowed two aspirin dry and placed the ice pack over her face.

She fell asleep so hard and so fast it felt like falling. Like something to be scared of.

My phone. I need to get my phone and check the news. I need—
She struggled for a second but got pulled under anyway.

Four

*S*he didn't remember.

That girl didn't remember the farm. The house.

She didn't remember Peg.

It didn't matter, of course. It didn't change anything. But Hope didn't remember her, and the pain was...well, it was something.

Peg tried the door to the apartment again. Locked. Like it had been when she'd checked this morning. She'd come in from the orchard at lunchtime and the house was silent. It was dinnertime now and there was still no sign of them.

She couldn't get over it—Hope had *locked* the door.

That girl had come down at some point, making sure those stairs didn't squeak, and pushed that button. That spoke to a lot of fear. A lot of distrust. It was plain as the black eye on Hope's face: those girls were running from something.

And Lord, Hope looked bad. Not just the beating she'd

caught. But she was razor thin. The same way Denise had looked when Jacob and the drugs had their claws in her all those years ago. Maybe that little trick with the prescription bottle earlier had been unfair, but Peg had needed to know what she was up against. And maybe Hope rejecting the Vicodin wasn't a definitive answer—because the one thing Peg knew was that addicts could be crafty—but it made Peg feel better for now.

She walked over to the big front window and stared out at the beat-up Camry parked cockeyed in the driveway. When she'd woken up this morning, she'd half expected to see the car gone and maybe the television. And, sure, that was unforgiving of her, but it was what it was. She'd learned those lessons from Denise too well.

Worse—she'd half hoped they'd be gone. Seeing that car crouched out there on nearly bald tires did not inspire relief. Nope. It felt more like dread.

What the hell was she supposed to do with those two?

Goddammit, Denise. This was her sister's fault. Had to be.

She'd gotten that letter from Hope. Grief, if she'd ever had any for Denise, faded quick. But the sight of Hope's neat handwriting had opened up all kinds of old wounds. She'd read only the obituary and thrown the letter away and put it from her mind, not once thinking about that girl managing all by herself. And with a kid, too. She might have known that if she'd read the letter.

Guilt was not a familiar sensation and Peg couldn't say she liked it any.

Fresh from her shower, Peg rubbed her head against her shirt to wipe off the water dripping down her neck. Were they still sleeping up there or were they just too nervous to come down?

Hank, she thought, the name rolling into her brain like a stone in a wave, tossed up from the very bottom of the ocean.

Hank, what should I do with these girls? Well, she knew what Hank would say. Because Hank was a soft-hearted fool. *Let them in. Forgive Hope for sins that were not hers. Love them.*

There might have been a chance for that a long time ago. But the years were all stacked up around her and Peg couldn't see over them. "And," she muttered to herself, because that was what you did when you lived alone, "it's none of my business."

She'd let the girls sleep as long as they needed. She'd feed them a good meal. Maybe a few of them. And then she'd see them on their way. There was a couple hundred bucks in an envelope at the very back of her underwear drawer. Peg would give Hope that envelope, a bunch of sandwiches. She'd make sure Abel gassed up her car and topped up all the fluids.

It was the right thing to do.

She checked her watch. Five minutes after five.

Dinner will wake them up.

Pleased with herself, she took a package of meat out of the fridge and put a big knob of butter in the cast-iron pan she kept on the stove. While the butter melted, she opened the cupboard in the corner of the kitchen. Like the women in her family had for almost two hundred years, she kept her carrots, onions and potatoes in there. It was cold inside thanks to a lack of insulation and a stone foundation and stayed that way even in the summer.

She chopped up one of the onions and tossed the pieces in with the butter. While they softened, she sliced up the last of her bakers. A puny soft thing, more eyes than flesh. She'd have to go to the market soon. She was running out of supplies. Sure, there was a garden out back with all the potatoes a woman living on her own could ever want, but she'd let that garden go too long. It was a wilderness now. Inhospitable to anything but blackbirds and bad memories.

As a matter of survival, she liked to pretend it wasn't there.

She tossed the cut-up potato in with the onion and everything steamed and popped, and soon the air smelled like a real good supper. A little garlic salt and some pepper to dress it up. The potatoes might be a tad crunchy in the middle but that never hurt anyone.

Hope sure was the spitting image of Denise, though maybe that was just the skinniness, the way Hope looked like she might jump right out of her skin. Denise had been that way, too, restless and wired to blow.

The first time Denise had left was at the beginning of cherry season, just like it was now. The Ulster cherries came in during the hottest, hardest part of the year. Days filled with so much work and so much heat, it was like walking around in a fever. Denise had taken Mom's jewelry and all the cash, slipped out in the middle of the night like a thief. Peg had woken up the next morning and, without even getting out of bed, knew she was all alone in the house.

Denise had not always been a good sister, but she'd been there. Right beside her, all day nearly every day. School. The farm. They'd even shared a bedroom. Her leaving had sent Peg off-kilter and it had taken a long time to get used to it. An argument could be made that she never had. Hank had liked to say she carried around the ghosts of that cherry season, tucked in her pockets like souvenirs.

That Hope was back here three days into the Ulster harvest, with the air smelling like sugar—well, it only made sense. In a way. Hank would say it was poetic.

Shit timing was what Peg said.

The pound of ground chuck made a big hiss when it hit the hot onions and potatoes. Peg glanced up at the ceiling, listening for the sound of movement upstairs, but it stayed quiet. She took down the Lawry's seasoned salt and hit it once against the counter to loosen up those clumps then gave it a good shake over the pan. "That should get them up," she said out loud with some satisfaction.

Plain as day she felt the eyes of another person on her back. She turned and wasn't at all surprised to see the little girl standing there. Fine blond hair twisted into a rat's nest on one side of her head. Creases along her cheek where she must have slept against the bare mattress. She was all bones and belly, that little one. Big white mosquito bites on her ankles.

Tink. Funny name. But since a woman named Hope had given it to her, maybe it wasn't all that surprising. Though how a baby girl named Hope came out of *this* house was a mystery.

"Hey there," Peg said.

The girl shrugged one shoulder. Shy, Hope had said, but there was more to the girl's silence or Peg would eat her hat. Not that she cared. Or was going to get too into things with these two. They'd be on their way in no time and it wasn't any of her business. "Hungry?"

This time the girl nodded with some enthusiasm, her eyes on the steam coming off the beef, onions and potatoes behind her. "It'll be a few minutes," Peg said. "Have a seat."

The girl didn't move toward the table but stood still in a shaft of sunlight that seemed to shine right through her.

"I can't read your mind. If you want something you're gonna have to ask for it," Peg said.

Tink turned sideways and slowly lifted her hand to point to something in the front room.

Peg stepped forward and saw that she was pointing at the gun over the door. "I'm not giving you my gun," Peg said, and actually laughed.

But Tink didn't smile. She didn't look away. She pointed at that gun with a heavy look on her face. An *old* look on her face.

"Do you want to see it?" Peg asked.

Tink nodded, and Peg walked through the house to the front door. She remembered when, during a string of break-ins all along Flagg Road, Dad had put up the pegs for the rifle. *Let 'em try*, he'd said.

"You ever touched one before?" Peg asked.

Tink shook her head no, and Peg took down the rifle. Tink lifted her hands up reverently, carefully. There were no bullets in the gun so there was no way the girl could get hurt, but Tink didn't know that.

Peg had learned to shoot about this girl's age. Dad had set up some tin cans on the back fence and she and Denise had popped them off.

"You want to learn how to shoot?" As soon as Peg had said it she wished she could take it back. She shouldn't be making plans. It was cherry season and she was too busy. And these girls wouldn't be staying.

But she'd said it, and the look in that girl's eyes made it real clear she wasn't going to forget it anytime soon.

Tink's enthusiastic nod sent her hair swishing over her shoulders.

"All right," Peg said, and then took the gun from her little hands. "Maybe after some food."

She put the gun back up on its pegs and led the girl back into the kitchen.

"Have a seat," Peg said, stirring up the meat and potatoes again. "Dinner's gonna be ready in a minute."

The wooden chair scraped against the floor as Tink pulled it away from the old oak table some ancestor had brought to Michigan on a covered wagon. It was lopsided and all the leaves were gone, but it felt wrong to get rid of something so historic.

Peg laid out one of her table mats and set down a glass of

milk and a bowl of fresh cherries in front of Tink before returning to the stove, where she shook in the last clump of seasoned salt, then tossed the empty jar in the trash. When she turned back to the table, Tink's lips were purple from the cherries. "Go slow," Peg warned. "They'll give you a stomachache if you eat too many too fast."

That didn't slow the girl down much. She ate the big black cherries like apples, little bites around the pits, her fingers stained purple, too. There was a fine spray of juice on the front of her dirty striped dress.

Laundry, Peg thought. *We'll work on that after some food.*

Or not, she reminded herself. They might have tons of clothes in the back of that car. *They don't need me getting involved. Touching their things.*

"Here," Peg said, setting down a bowl of the hamburger and a couple pieces of white bread, spread with butter so thick it was like cheese.

Tink fell on the food, barely chewing before shoveling another forkful in her mouth.

"You've got to breathe," Peg said, and Tink opened her mouth, took a breath and a bite all at the same time.

"Girl! You're gonna choke!" Peg laughed and, not thinking, put her hand on Tink's arm.

Tink froze. The fork was lifted halfway to her mouth, and a piece of potato fell onto the bare skin of her leg. Her eyes didn't move.

Peg lifted her hand away, and carefully—slowly—Tink put her fork down.

"I'm sorry. I won't hurt—"

The girl bolted and Peg got to her feet but was far too slow. The door to the upstairs apartment slammed shut, that doorknob lock clicked and her little feet thudded up the stairs.

Peg looked down at the half-eaten food. The small pile of cherry pits that had been sucked entirely clean.

It was very hard work not to care.

✦TINK✦

The not-talking thing was no big deal. It wasn't even hard.

Once, Tink had convinced her entire class that she'd broken her leg. *That* was hard, because Mom refused to get her a cast. A cast would have sealed the deal.

Without it, every morning Tink had wrapped her leg in an Ace bandage and limped to school. One day she'd wrapped the wrong leg and the kids didn't even notice. They kept helping her to the carpet and getting her snack for her.

Suckers.

Mom and her teacher and the principal had meetings about it, because she did it for, like, two weeks and they couldn't decide if it was just for attention. Or to get out of PE. Or if there was something else wrong.

Mom said Tink was a drama queen.

But the reason she did it—the real reason—was recess. With her broken leg, kids left her alone at recess and she could sit under the tree and read her book instead of having to play kickball or some other lame group game.

That made it all worth it.

Until Mom hid the bandage and said she had to stop, that if she kept pretending to have a broken leg the school was going to call a psychiatrist. And then recess wouldn't be under the tree; it would be in the teachers' lounge that smelled like microwave popcorn and coffee.

The next day Tink walked to school miraculously healed, and—side benefit—she still didn't have to play kickball at recess, because now the kids just thought she was weird.

Mission accomplished.

The not-talking thing was not a big deal. She could do that forever.

The touching thing, though…that was harder.

Since DeeDee had died, it was only her and Mom. (She wasn't counting those months with Daniel, because he didn't count for anything.) And ever since they'd stopped at the gas station two days ago and then the Motor City Lodge, it didn't feel right when Mom touched her. Or maybe it felt good *not to let* Mom touch her. That was the type of mean thing DeeDee would do, but Tink figured she had the right.

But when Peg had touched her shoulder for a second, Tink thought she might cry. She *wanted* to be hugged and touched and tickled.

Outside the bedroom, Tink leaned back against the wall and wrapped her arms around herself tight, feeling as much of herself as she could. As the hugger and the hugee. She squeezed her eyes shut and whispered, barely making a sound, "I am Tink."

Then she turned and walked into the bedroom. Mom looked like she was sleeping, but Tink got real close to make sure. Because after DeeDee died, Mom did a lot of lying in bed and staring up at the ceiling. Days of it. Telling Tink she didn't feel good and that she was real tired. That Tink could have hot dogs for dinner and sometimes for breakfast and it didn't matter how much television she watched. For a while that had been fun. But then it got kind of scary.

Mom's eye was all black-and-blue from her eyebrow down to her cheekbone. She had another bruise on her leg where she must have fallen. Tink had spotted it last night when she'd gotten up and moved to her own bed. Mom's lip was bleeding again, too. It looked puffy and sore. Tink kinda wanted to touch it, but then Mom would wake up and start lying to her in that awful voice, telling her everything was fine when it totally wasn't.

Little snores were coming out of Mom's mouth, so Tink went to the window to look out at the farm. All around the house were bright green fields. Across the driveway were trees, lots and lots of trees, and past the trees was a cabin. In the distance, at the end of the long gravel road the color of Tink's hair, was the dark deep blue of a lake.

From up here she'd be able to see if a man driving a blue car with Illinois license plates was coming up the road. And once she learned how to shoot that rifle, she'd be able to do what Mom couldn't—stop him from coming any closer.

Five

The dawn was oyster pink and cream. It was past time for her to be down in the orchard helping Abel with the harvest, but the door to upstairs was still locked. It was so quiet up there she might have believed she'd dreamed up Hope and Tink's arrival thirty-six hours ago, if it weren't for the Camry in the driveway.

And the fact that the cherries were gone from the fridge. As well as the mozzarella cheese and a two-liter bottle of Dr Pepper.

That kid. Hats off to the quality sneaking. Peg was a light sleeper and she hadn't heard a thing, and Nelson, that terrible guard dog, had been a church mouse all night. Tink must have come down, pawed through the fridge and gotten back upstairs without a peep.

But enough, really. What is Hope doing up there? Not showing her face down here after arriving on my doorstep like that?

Peg wasn't in the business of judging anyone—Lord knew she'd made her mistakes—but this just wasn't right.

She turned away from the coffeepot only to be brought up short by the sight of Tink. Worse today than the other day. Dirtier, though she didn't know how. Paler. Thinner. Her mouth was stained purple from the cherries. For a second Tink looked like a cat who'd been caught on the counter—guilty, sure. A little bit pleased, too. But then she folded all that up and went back to looking blank, an expression so familiar Peg felt like she was slipping around in time.

And looking in a mirror.

"Hi," Peg said. "I know you're not hungry after eating all my cheese and cherries." The girl didn't so much as blink. "Unless you gave that cheese to Nelson so she wouldn't bark."

Tink looked over at the dog, who sat in the long stretch between them, tongue out, and stepped away, biting her lip as she glanced back at the front door and pointed her skinny little arm at the rifle.

"You still want to learn how to shoot that thing?"

Tink beamed like a headlight.

Peg caught herself against the counter, a memory sliding over her like a chill. Hope—two years old maybe, standing at the front door, excited about something. Ice cream? An after-dinner tractor ride? She had liked those.

But she'd been smiling at Peg just like that, like Peg had made some small dream come true.

"All right," she said. She walked over to the cabinet where she kept the yellow box of cartridges. "We got a little time before I need to be in the orchard."

They went out the back door at the side of the kitchen. Peg usually used the external door in her bedroom, which was on the side of the house closest to the barn, but she wasn't walking that little girl and her eagle eyes through there. So they stepped out into the weeds and clover that crowded by the

old screen door and walked down to the back field that faced
the woods. The air smelled of the pine trees beside the barn.
Morning was the best time at The Orchard House, the world
damp and cool and just beginning.

The fence she and her sister would shoot cans off was now
crumbling and gray, covered with black-eyed Susans and milk-
weed.

"Where's your mom?" Peg asked, trying for a casual tone
she wasn't very good at.

Tink, predictably, didn't answer.

"She alive up there?" Peg smiled so the kid would know she
was joking. It didn't seem to work. "She sleeping or hiding?"

Tink blinked up at her.

"Both?" Peg asked.

Tink shrugged and put her hand against the gun for just
a second.

Peg got down on one knee, the way her father had when
she was Tink's age, pulled the bolt and showed her where the
cartridge went and how to load it carefully. There had been
so few moments of kindness with her father that the memories had a sort of sting to them. She found herself repeating
exactly what he'd said to her.

"It is never a toy," she said, and the little girl nodded sol-
emnly. "It's a serious tool and we treat it seriously. You never
touch it unless I'm with you. Do you understand?"

Tink nodded.

She explained how it worked. The base of the cartridge
filled with black powder. The bullet would come spinning out
of the end. The safety and what would happen once it was off.

"You ready?" she asked Tink, who again nodded.

Two things were going to happen when she fired this gun.
Abel would come running up from the barn, hell-bent for
leather, and up in that bedroom, Hope would jump out of
bed and go looking for her daughter.

Peg could put the gun away and go up and convince Hope to get up on her feet with words and patience, two things she wasn't exactly known for.

Truthfully, Peg didn't want to go up to that second floor again. The other night had been hard enough.

The second floor of The Orchard House had too many memories. Of her sister. Of Hank.

Of the life she'd thought she'd have.

"Cover your ears," she said to Tink, and fired one shot at the fence, taking a bloom clean off a black-eyed Susan.

She faced the barn, where, as predicted, she saw Abel running pretty good for a guy in rubber boots. At the sight of him, Tink crept behind Peg's legs.

"Coyote!" Peg yelled at him, waving her arm.

He stumbled to a halt. "What?" he yelled.

"Coyote."

Beside her, Nelson wagged her tail, all but calling her a liar.

"Everyone okay?" Abel asked. She knew he saw Tink, despite her trying to hide, just like he saw that dusty Camry parked outside the house, and he probably had a million questions, but their business arrangement didn't dip too far into personal matters.

"We're fine. Meet you in the orchard in a few."

From inside the house came a frantic scream. "Tink!"

"There you go," she said to the wide-eyed girl behind her. "Your mom's up."

✦ HOPE ✦

She'd woken up in a blind panic. Not sure where she was.

And that sound… She lay there, paralyzed, until she realized what that sound was.

A gunshot.

She threw the blankets off her body, tripping on a pillow as she ran toward the stairs. The door at the bottom was open, letting in a bright slice of morning sunlight.

"Tink!" she screamed and hurtled down the stairs. She slid across the hardwood floor and hit her hip on the chair just as a door in the kitchen squealed open and Tink came running in. Peg, behind her, entered at a more sedate pace.

But she was carrying a gun.

"What...?" Hope panted, light-headed.

"Coyote," Peg said and walked past her to put the rifle back up over the door.

"Coyote?" Hope repeated, because the word didn't make any sense.

"We get 'em sometimes."

"You shot a coyote?"

"No," Peg said. "Just scared it away."

Hope collapsed onto the ottoman, her head in her hands. Tink came over to stand by her, not touching, but standing there. Hope leaned forward slightly so her shoulder rested against her daughter's belly. Not a hug, but something.

"You okay?" she asked her daughter.

Tink nodded.

"Did you see the coyote?" she asked, and Tink shook her head no.

"You must be hungry," Peg said, as if everything were normal. As if Hope hadn't just almost had a heart attack. "I'll put some food on."

Peg vanished into the kitchen and there was the sound of pots being set down on the stove.

"Well, that's one way to wake up." Hope tried to smile for her daughter. Part of her very much wanted to crawl back into bed and pull the covers back over her head. But Tink deserved better. "Let's go get some stuff from the car and get dressed. Brush our teeth."

Tink ran her tongue over her teeth and grimaced.

"We'll be right back!" Hope yelled toward the kitchen.

"Okay!" Peg yelled back.

The fresh air was a blast to Hope's brain and she stopped at the foot of the steps like she'd run into a wall. Then she breathed deep, pulled that hot, sunshiny air that smelled sweet and dusty and alive down deep into her belly. The world out here was in Technicolor. The leaves and the grass were brilliant green, and the gravel of the parking area and the road were golden yellow. The sky was so blue it hurt.

"It's nice out here, isn't it?" Hope asked, forgetting for a moment that her daughter wasn't talking to her. "Smells good."

Tink kicked a piece of gravel toward the car. Before Daniel, she would have told her daughter that the air smelled like the color yellow. And then Tink would tell her that the air in St. Louis smelled like the color gray and they'd spend an hour trying to figure out what the color purple smelled like.

"Grab my phone, would you?" she asked Tink, who stood beside the driver's-side door while Hope went around to the back to grab their duffel bag. Tink didn't open the front door and Hope tilted her head so she could see her. "Please?" she asked, but Tink only grinned. "You already grabbed my phone? While I was sleeping? So you could play Temple Run?"

Tink nodded.

"Figures," she said. But that her daughter had grabbed the phone, and probably the charger, all without Hope noticing, was a little worrying.

How long was I asleep?

She had lost days in bed once before and that had not ended well for anyone.

Hope pulled the big duffel bag from the trunk and Tink retrieved her backpack from the back seat, and they headed back toward the house.

What seemed charming the night they arrived was even more so in the morning sunshine. The peeling white paint added character, and those windows that felt like eyes were the windows in their room. The farm looked welcoming and steady, like it had been here a long time and wasn't going anywhere soon.

It was impossible to imagine her mother here. Denise didn't even like going to parks.

Upstairs, Tink brushed her teeth, and Hope found her phone plugged into an outlet beside Tink's bed. It had been three days since the gas station and the hotel room. A day and a half she'd been sleeping. She took a deep breath and searched for Daniel's name and the Motor City Lodge on her phone.

Nothing.

And she honestly didn't know if that was a good thing. Or a bad thing.

They made their way downstairs, and it was like stepping right into a memory. The smell of coffee and bacon. The low hum of the news on a radio. The way the sun filled the kitchen with a pure yellow light. It was so familiar, and for no good reason really; her mom had never listened to the news. It seemed more like something that happened in the TV shows she'd watched after school, waiting for her mom to finish up at the shop. They were the kind of memories she wished she had. Not that hers were *bad*—because they weren't. It felt painfully disloyal to think that.

Or maybe it seemed familiar because *she'd been here*. Walked down those stairs before into a coffee-scented kitchen. Maybe it was the kind of memory that got buried beneath all the other memories of growing up: the apartment on Euclid, the women at the shop who took turns babysitting her. The smell of Eggos and Virginia Slims at the kitchen table.

"You coming?" Peg asked, poking her head around the brick doorway.

The dog came shuffling over and gave both her and Tink long, sniffing interrogations. "Nelson thinks we smell delicious because we stink. You especially," Hope said to get a reaction from Tink, but Tink only stared at the dog with her patented distrust.

The dog looked utterly crestfallen by Tink's indifference. *You and me both, dog. You and me both.*

In the kitchen, Peg was piling scrambled eggs and bacon on two plates, and Hope's stomach roared.

"Coffee?" Peg asked.

"Yes. Please."

There were big glasses of what looked like lemonade on the table, and Hope and Tink drank those down fast. The sweet tartness made her body buzz to life like a flickering lamp. Beside her, Tink's body did one long shake, like she was feeling the same thing.

Peg put a ceramic mug in front of Hope and sat down, another cup of coffee steaming in her hand.

"I need to thank you," Hope said. "For letting us stay."

"You already thanked me," Peg said, flat as a pancake.

"Right. Well. I guess, thanks again. And for this breakfast." She glanced over at her daughter, whose plate was practically empty, and set her own bacon next to what was left of Tink's eggs. "And the food Tink took. We will pay you back."

Peg made a sound that Hope could not decipher. *Yes, you will pay me back.* Or maybe *No, don't worry about it.*

"I wish I remembered being here," Hope said to fill the silence.

"You were young." Peg shrugged like it didn't matter.

"How young?"

"Hard to say."

"Was I a baby? Or—"

"Four," Peg said. "Or thereabouts."

"This morning, coming down the steps and smelling the

coffee and hearing the news, that…that seemed really famil-iar. Maybe I remember that?"

"Maybe." She took a sip of her coffee. "My guess is your mom didn't tell you many stories of your visit here. And if people don't talk about memories, they can disappear."

Well, that certainly felt like the truth.

"Were we here long?" *Did we drive? Why did we visit?*

"You know, I don't much remember, either," Peg said with a tight smile that said plenty about her desire for this conver-sation to be over. "No one around to remind me."

"Mom always called this place The Orchard House."

Peg hummed.

"Is there…an orchard?" she asked. God, she didn't have the energy for pulling awkward small talk from her aunt.

"A couple acres of cherries and apples. Some corn and soy beans. Our great-great-grandfather built the house after he started the orchard. People in town have been calling it The Orchard House ever since."

"It's been in your family that long?"

"Your family, too."

Right. It suddenly occurred to her that there was so much history behind her that she knew nothing about.

Growing up, when things had gotten real bad at home, Hope had been curious, eager to get away from her mother in the way lots of teenagers are eager to leave their parents behind. She'd wondered, *Seriously, how bad could it be in Michigan?* and had thoughts of going to find out.

Then Tink happened. And school. Trying to make a living. And then Mom got sick.

"She tell you anything else?" Peg asked, glancing up from her coffee for just a second.

"Your parents were strict. She told me that. She'd say, 'You think I'm strict, you should have met my father.'"

Denise had instituted early curfews and limited time away from the house. Hope couldn't spend the night with friends. In the summer, when kids were going to camp or the swimming pool, Hope was working in the salon, sweeping up cut hair. Or watching television alone in the apartment.

Peg looked out the window, and the sunlight coming in made the edges of her eyes glow gold. "My father was strict. My mother was just...unhappy." She tilted her head, as if inspecting the trees out the window. "And Denise pushed maybe more than she should have."

"That sounds like Mom," Hope whispered, and the two of them sat still in a moment of understanding. Denise needed to rattle and ruffle and push and push and push until there was some kind of wreckage. Maybe just because she could? Hope didn't think so. Or didn't want to think so. Instead, she thought her mother liked how secure other's insecurity made her feel. Seeing others so easily jarred and jolted reinforced her own wobbly edges.

But thinking that—*acknowledging that*—felt awful, so she stopped.

"Do you have pictures?" Hope asked.

"Of what?"

Hope nearly laughed. "Your parents? My mom as a girl? Anything like that?"

"Mom and Dad weren't big on photo albums," she said, and took another sip of her coffee.

Hope curled her toes against the hardwood, feeling foolish for asking. "Oh, well, I just thought it would be nice, you know."

"Hold on. I might have something."

Peg went through a big door on the other side of the kitchen. It was an old wooden door, probably original to the house, thick and dark with a large brass knob. Peg made sure to shut the door behind her, and when she came out again a second later, she slipped out like she didn't want Hope and Tink to catch a glimpse of the room.

"Here," Peg said and slid a picture onto the table.

It was a sun-blasted picture of a toddler with blond hair in a bowl cut, clutching at a stuffed animal owl, lifting it up to cover a good portion of her face.

Hope.

Next to a woman in cutoffs covered in freckles.

Peg. Younger, obviously, and wearing that wide transformative smile like she had no intention of becoming the serious, grumpy woman sitting across the table.

And next to her in the picture, looking young and out of place somehow with dyed blond hair, inch-long brunette roots, big black sunglasses and a scowl:

Denise.

Proof that Hope *had* been here and had not even a little memory of it.

"Oh my god," Hope breathed. "I've never seen a picture of her at this age."

"She was pretty," Peg said.

"She was," Hope agreed, but not in this picture. In this picture, next to Peg and all her incandescent happiness, Mom looked dark and bitter. A spider who wanted to ruin the soup.

Tink reached for the picture and Hope handed it to her.

"Why doesn't she talk?" Peg asked.

Hope looked at her daughter, telegraphing, *Help me out here, kiddo* as best she could. But Tink only sat back with her arms crossed over her chest, bacon grease shiny on her lips.

"Political protest."

"What's she protesting?"

"Me."

Peg's laugh was a rough bark that even startled Nelson,

who'd been waiting under the table for a dropped bit of bacon and now came out to stand beside Peg, tail wagging.

"Do you have anything else?" Hope asked. "Anything at all. School yearbooks? Your parents' wedding pictures—"

"No. Those are long gone. But you know... I think..." Peg stood, leaving her cup steaming on the table, and walked out of the kitchen. From the living room came the sound of furniture being pushed around. Nelson jumped to her feet, barked once and watched the doorway.

Peg came back in carrying a framed picture. The back was brown paper with a copper wire hanger crooked between its edges. "We had this on the wall for years. Mom had it done when Denise and I were in junior high." She turned the frame around and Hope could not hold in her gasp. Even Tink slapped her hand over her mouth.

"It's pretty bad, isn't it?" Peg smiled for the first time since Hope had met her. It was a good smile, bright and wide, and it transformed everything about her.

"No, it's just..." Hope was literally at a loss for words. It wasn't a picture. It was a painting. A heavy oil painting. Like something that might hang in a museum.

"A lot?" Peg asked, and Hope laughed. It felt good to laugh. "I haven't looked at it in years." Peg propped the painting up so it faced the kitchen, and then walked over to sit at the table so she could observe it, too. "Oh, lord. It's worse than I remembered."

The three of them stared at the painting of the family. Two adults in dark clothes with dour faces. The man in a suit and tie. The woman in a dark burgundy dress with a ribbon at the collar. Behind them stood two girls hovering in that place between girlhood and womanhood. Turtleneck sweaters and long curly hair out of the early eighties.

Hope took it all in. The unsmiling faces. Her grandfather

stern and her grandmother unhappy. Denise looking like trouble. Serious trouble. Even with the bulky sweater and unfashionable hair. And Peg looking... Hope tilted her head. Peg looked like she was waiting for something. Whatever was next, good, bad or otherwise, she seemed ready for it.

"We had to get a picture taken and then Mom took the picture to an artist in Charlevoix. Dad thought the whole thing was nonsense, but Mom was set on it. And she rarely stood up to him. So it was a big deal."

"Mom told me they died in a car crash."

"About six years after this painting was done."

"You took over the farm?" Hope asked.

"No one else to do it."

"You were so young."

"Twenty. Denise was twenty-two." Peg smiled with one side of her mouth. "Old enough, I suppose."

Hope studied Peg in the painting. The wide-set hazel eyes. The red hair. Hope knew she looked so much like Peg. And Tink looked like Marie, and Denise looked like Duncan. "The family resemblance is wild," she said.

"But watch," Peg said, darting out of the chair like a young woman. She lifted the painting and then walked it over a few feet to the left and then a few feet to the right. "See it?"

"They're staring at us," Hope said.

"Right. No matter where you put the damn thing, my parents are watching you. It's too much. I took it down two days after they died and put it behind the couch."

"It is a little..." Hope stopped, caught up in her grandfather staring at her with such disappointment, like he knew all of her sins without ever having known her.

"Depressing," Peg said, and put the painting down, turned away from them.

"So, that's...it?" Hope asked, smiling at her aunt. "My entire family legacy? A creepy oil painting."

"This house, I suppose," Peg said. "My orchard. The cherries." She swept her hand over the table like she was done with that conversation. "You said the other night that you didn't have anyplace else to go?"

"We don't." Hope felt like she needed proof, the names of friends whose welcome they had already worn out.

"Denise never got married?"

"No," she whispered. "She never married." There had been boyfriends, but they were few and far between.

It's you and me, kid, Denise had always said. Like they would be enough for each other. Hope had always worked so hard to hold up her end of that bargain.

"She was by herself all this time?"

"She had us," Hope said. Mom couldn't stand to be alone. When she and Tink moved out, she'd about had a fit. Hope joked that Mom had gotten sick just so she and Tink would move back in.

If that was true, I would have gotten cancer sooner, she'd said. A bad joke, but they'd both laughed. They'd been in the bad-joke part of treatment, when laughing about Mom dying had kept them from crying.

"What about your father?"

Hope casually took a sip of coffee, aware of Tink's utterly unblinking attention to this conversation. "I never met him."

Peg smiled like maybe that was a good thing. "She tell you about him?"

"Bits and pieces. He worked on the farm after your parents died. His name was Jacob and he...ah...played the guitar."

"That's all?" Peg asked. "That's all she had to say about Jacob?"

"He wasn't a good guy."

"No," she agreed. "He wasn't. And she wasn't, either, when they were together."

There was something in Peg's tone, something snide and

small, like Peg knew Denise better than Hope. But before Hope could defend her mother, Peg put her coffee cup down on the table so hard Hope jumped.

"Whatever you're running from…" she said in a low voice, but Tink heard everything. "Is it gonna follow you here?"

Hope shook her head and then said no loud enough for Tink to hear. She scraped half her eggs onto Tink's empty plate. Her daughter could glare all she wanted, but it wouldn't change how satisfying it was to watch healthy food disappear into her hungry growing body. There'd been too many Happy Meals on the road. Too much gas-station food.

If the cost of staying here for a few days, of keeping Tink safe, was telling Peg how she'd gotten here, with a black eye and silent daughter, she could do it. She could.

"You probably have a ton of questions and I can answer all of them," she said, straightening her spine, digging through the dark for the words to describe the last few days.

Weeks. Well, months, really.

Peg held up her hand. "It's none of my business," she said, and Hope got a little light-headed with relief. "That eye of yours tells me a pretty good story about what you've got in your rearview and I don't need the details." She stood up, and Hope noticed the overalls and gray T-shirt she wore were stained red and purple in places. She pulled gloves from her back pocket. "You can stay," she added.

"It's only for a few days," Hope said quickly.

"Doesn't matter to me," Peg said. "I imagine you might want to do some laundry?"

Hope nodded.

"I got a washer in the basement. A drying line in the back."

"I'd like to move my car," Hope said, looking up at her. "Where?"

"Somewhere…" *Hidden?* Did she really have to say it out loud? "Safe."

"Well, there's room in the barn." Peg pointed behind her at the cluster of buildings behind the house.

"Okay." Hope got to her feet. "Thanks—"

"Hold on," Peg said. "If you're staying, there are some rules."

She and Tink shared a look. Rules weren't really their thing.

"It's cherry season and we're real busy. You stay, you're gonna work. I'll pay you a fair wage. Both of you. You can take today to get yourselves sorted. But tomorrow, if you're here, you'll be in the orchard."

"Okay," Hope said. She would agree to just about anything if it kept a roof over Tink's head.

"If you go into town, don't tell anyone who you are. You'll wake up the grapevine and no one needs that."

No, she thought. *They very much did* not *need that.*

"I'll be across the road in the orchard if you need anything." Peg whistled and Nelson got out from under the table. She opened the back door and paused, and Hope found herself holding her breath. "One more rule." Peg pointed with a straight arm toward the shut door on the other wall of the kitchen. "You don't go in there. Ever."

Six

→HOPE←

Ten minutes later Hope and Tink stood at the top of the stairs leading down into the cobwebbed murk of The Orchard House basement.

"I will pay you a million dollars to go down there," Hope said to her daughter, who was emphatically shaking her head no. "Okay," she sighed. "I'll risk my life. You go find the drying line in the back."

Of course the stairs creaked, and there were cobwebs everywhere. Dim light came through the high windows over an ancient mustard-yellow washing machine. Hope put the duffel bag down on the cracked cement and found a box of detergent, chiseling a big clump of white powder and sprinkling it in the bottom of the washer, then turned on the water and started shoving their clothes in with zero care for colors or whites.

When the load was full, she shut the lid and turned for the stairs, grateful she managed to avoid getting eaten by spiders, but was caught up short by a bunch of baby stuff stacked in the far corner. A motorized swing and a high chair with owls on it. A crib in pieces, a mattress stacked up against it.

They sat forlorn and dusty, left to rot in the basement surrounded by rusted paint cans.

A chill chased down her spine and she sprinted for the stairs.

➤ TINK ⬅

Tink had a mission, and it had nothing to do with the drying line. She stood in front of the big wooden door that Peg said they were not supposed to go through.

What was in there that was such a big deal? Such a secret?

DeeDee had had a jewelry box she told Tink to never go in no matter what. So of course she had gone in there the second she'd been able, but there was nothing special inside. DeeDee had stood at the bedroom door and laughed at her.

Curiosity killed the cat, DeeDee had said, but Tink wasn't sure what that meant. Seemed to her, in this case, the cat just got bored by old jewelry.

The rule oughta be that if you made a big deal about something being a secret, there had to be a payoff. Though, really, adults were weird and their secrets were usually pretty lame. If Tink had a secret room it would be full of treasure. Money and gems. Tons of books. And chocolate cake. Escape tunnels. Booby traps.

Not a single dog.

Mom was making noise down in the basement, throwing clothes in the wash, and Tink knew her time was limited.

Getting in trouble wasn't really a thing with Mom. Tink had never been grounded or sent to her room. Mostly, Mom just sat her down on the edge of her bed and told her how disappointed she was.

You and me both, Mom.

Though the last few months there hadn't even been *that.* Tink went to bed without brushing her teeth. She stopped taking out the recycling or watering Mrs. Peterson's plants. She didn't vacuum on Sundays. And homework when school was still on? Yeah. Never.

Mom hadn't bothered to notice, much less be disappointed.

For a second she wondered how Peg would react, but Tink had no plans to find out. She'd be in and out of this room in no time.

With one hand she reached forward and tried the doorknob, but it didn't turn. Locked. Or maybe just jammed. She tried with both hands and then got her whole body involved, pushing against the wood. No good.

The door stayed shut.

→ HOPE ←

After they hung their wash on the line, all their underwear on display for the bees and bugs to see, Hope couldn't avoid it any longer. They needed supplies.

She wasn't sure how long they were going to stay at the farm, but truthfully, the opportunity to make some money wasn't one she was in a position to turn down.

A few days. A week tops. Her face could heal up and she'd get some cash in her pocket. If she could have, she'd have avoided going to town, but she needed tampons and they didn't have any shampoo or soap.

She didn't want to depend on Peg for every single thing they needed while they were here. No matter how short their stay.

She already felt like she and Tink were a problem for Peg; she didn't need to make it worse.

"We gotta go to town, kid," she told her daughter, who

didn't seem at all as scared about it as Hope was. She felt her mother's words in her mouth and worked hard not to say them: *You should be scared. You should be worried. The world is dangerous and we know that better than most.*

She didn't want Tink to live like that.

So instead of imagined dangers I brought real ones into her life. Nice going.

They hadn't moved the car into the barn yet and so they walked out the front door, toward the Camry, only to find the driver's-side door cracked open.

"You didn't shut the door when we got our stuff?" Hope asked. Tink looked guilty.

Hope got into the car, and even before turning the key she knew her battery was dead. Because that was her luck. She sighed and pressed her head to the steering wheel, rolling her forehead across the hard plastic. *Say you're sorry.* She projected the thought to her daughter, but Tink only climbed silently into the passenger side.

A dead battery wasn't a hard problem to solve; it just felt that way. She'd go find Peg in the—

Tink smacked her arm at the same time a man said, "'Scuse me?"

Hope jumped so hard she accidentally honked the horn.

"Hey, sorry." There was a man on the other side of her open door, leaning forward so he could see her through the window. She must have made a face. Or a sound. Something. Because he stepped back, his hands up. "You're having car trouble."

He was big, that was all she saw at first—muscled and tall. It triggered her fight-or-flight instinct immediately. The adrenaline made a hash of her brain and she couldn't do much more than take in one piece of him at a time. He wore a pair of gray coveralls with the arms tied around his waist, the legs tucked into a pair of high black rubber boots. His white undershirt was sweaty and stained purple and red. He had dark hair pulled back in a ponytail and tattoos up and down his arms. Part of a vine or a tree seemed to cling to the side of his neck.

"I'm Abel," he said. "Rodriguez."

"I'm sorry," Hope said. "You just…you startled me."

He smiled, a bright flash against his skin. "I see that. I'm sorry. I was going back to the barn and I saw you try to start your car. You need a jump?"

He was talking slow and keeping his distance like he knew he was spooking her, and that was a kindness she didn't know how to handle. She nodded and wiped her mouth with shaking hands that embarrassed her. And infuriated her a little. He was just a nice guy offering help.

"I do need a jump," she said, attempting to push that fear aside. "If you don't mind?"

"Pop the hood," he said. "I'll be right back."

He jogged off toward the barn as she fumbled around under the dash, trying to figure out how to pop the hood.

She finally found the button just as the barn door opened and a big mud-splattered pickup truck rolled out. Hope stood off to the side as Abel got out with the jumper cables.

"Do you—" he asked, handing her the clamps.

"I don't know what to do," she said honestly, feeling like a cliché. Useless, too. Neither of which she liked but she had grown used to.

"I can show you," he said, then carefully explained where the black and red clamps went.

She tried to listen, but the words just seemed to bounce around in her brain. The sun felt hot on her head and she wished she'd had a little bit more eggs at breakfast.

"Hey," he said, and he was suddenly right in front of her, his hand out as if he was going to catch her. "You all right?"

"Fine," she said, snapping her legs straight and her shoulders back. Her big dark sunglasses slipped down her nose and she pushed them back up. "So, do I start my car now?"

He nodded, and she sat down and cranked her car on. The engine turned over with a roar and she smiled with relief.

"Thank you," she said, getting back out.

"You need to keep it running for a while. Drive around for about thirty minutes."

"I'm headed into town, will that do?"

"Should."

"I don't...actually..." She turned left and then right as if there might be something she could see over the corn and trees. "Know where town is."

"That way," he said, pointing. "First stop sign, hang a left. Go for a few miles and you'll get spit out on Main Street. There's a big Kroger toward the highway if you go right on that street. But there's a little minimart in town. Next to the pharmacy. You'll know you've gone too far when you get to the harbor."

"Thanks," she said, her constant gratitude a little unruly at the moment. "I'm...ah, I'm Hope."

"Hope." He said her name with a smile. Most people said her name that way, and she'd long resigned herself to the fact that everyone liked hope and wanted hope—but that didn't necessarily mean they liked and wanted *her*. "Abel." He held out his hand to shake, and she stepped back involuntarily. His hand dropped and she felt the need to apologize, but when she looked in his eyes she caught him cataloging her bruises, the split lip. He shifted away, giving her plenty of room.

"How do you know Peg?" he asked, vanishing behind the hood as he unhooked the clamps from her car.

She shrugged. "I don't really. At all. But she's...she's my aunt."

His head popped back out from behind the hood, and she

would have laughed at his expression if she'd known him better.

"You're kidding. Aunt? I had no idea Peg had family." His brow furrowed like there were so many things rearranging in his head.

"We're not close." Obviously.

He slammed the hood down. "You sure you're able to drive?"

"I'm fine," she said, though he didn't seem convinced. "Really. And thanks. Again."

"Okay." He moved back toward his truck, and she found herself breathing a little easier the more the distance grew between them.

She got back in the car and drove away, watching him in her rearview mirror. He stood in the shadowed doorway to the barn, wiping his hands on a cloth as he watched her go.

Elk Falls was actually a cute town. Since it was close to the lake there was just enough tourism to warrant an elegant little main drag with a sandwich shop and a bar, a pharmacy and what looked like some kind of kitschy holiday store and coffee shop.

She wished she had sweet memories of this place. Getting ice cream at the ice cream stand. Walking down Main Street toward the beach.

"Tink?" she said. "What's your earliest memory?"

Tink did not take the bait.

"Like do you remember being four? What happened when you were four…" Tink's baby and toddler years all ran together in a sleepless, happy blur. "Oh!" The memory dawned on her. "We went to that carnival and you got your face painted like a rabbit and you wouldn't take it off, remember? You slept in the face paint for, like, two nights. Got it all over your pillow."

Tink was looking out her window, pretending she didn't care.

But she was smiling.

Hope couldn't remember being four. She was pretty sure her earliest memory was throwing up on Lincoln Logs and waiting for Mom to come and pick her up at preschool, but that was something *her mom* had talked about—she'd been called out of an interview at a ritzy salon in Clayton—not a fully formed memory.

There were a lot of fleeting impressions and sensations from Hope's childhood: a full moon out of a car window. The squish of green finger paint between her fingers. Crying at night until she fell asleep against a nappy pillow. She couldn't say how old she was in those memories. She couldn't even say if they were real.

Hope unrolled her window, and after a second, Tink did the same. The breeze whistled through the front seat, replacing the smell of old fast-food dinners with the cold, fresh smell of the lake. As Hope drove slowly around the parking area for the harbor, she took in two long docks stretched out into the blue-green waters of Lake Huron. Each dock was lined with sailboats and motorboats. She noticed a man on the back of a docked sailboat throwing a ball into the water and two dogs charging off the end to retrieve it.

Past the docks was a big rocky breaker. From her car, she could see kids out there with fishing poles, carefully crawling their way across the rocks, finding the best spot to drop their worms.

The lake itself was quiet. Still. The waves never broke, just quietly undulated their way to shore, where they rippled over the sand.

There was a sandy beach, dotted with bright umbrellas and beach towels and moms in black one-piece swimsuits, forcing their kids to stand still while they sprayed and rubbed in sunscreen. The kids wore goggles in the shapes of fishes and water wings that looked like shark fins.

"The beach looks good, doesn't it?"

Tink shrugged, which was something, and Hope grabbed it with both hands. "I remember once when I was little, my mom…" She stopped. Not her mom. Her mom hated being outside in summer. The sun gave her freckles and the heat gave her a rash. Kwanna. It must have been Kwanna from the salon.

"Anyway, we built a volcano." Ah-ha…that got Tink's attention. Hope knew her daughter liked a little destruction. "We built a big mountain. Huge. And we surrounded it with all kinds of castles and towns. And then we burrowed a hole down in the middle of the mountain and filled up all these buckets." God, the memory was coming back clear as day. That throat-catching feeling of filling up that hole as fast as she could. It had taken her a long time to get used to the sand on her feet and hands. In her butt crack. "And then we poured the water in the hole until it just ran right out and destroyed all the castles and towns we'd made." Tink was watching her, unable to hide her interest. Hope felt exposed in this town, but if it would bring her daughter back to her in some way, she'd risk it. "We should do it. We could go to Kroger right now and get all the—"

Tink looked back out the window.

"Maybe another time," Hope said lamely. She spent another minute watching a boy in a Lightning McQueen bathing suit talk nonstop to his mother, who nodded and smiled and probably wasn't listening at all.

Three days. It'd been three days since she'd heard her daughter's voice. It would probably already be different when she did talk again. She'd sound older, and Hope would have missed some incredible change in her. Some lost moment of development.

Hope pulled away from the beach and didn't look back.

As she drove back down Main Street, the cute businesses gave way to big houses, grand manors that told a story about past wealth, when railroad barons were a thing, brick with stained-glass windows and white porches. Or white houses with black trim and bright red doors. Houses with columns, even. Geraniums with brightly bobbing heads, planted in pots next to the front door. Slowly, the houses changed. Still big, but now they were split into apartments, with three TV satellite dishes hanging off the sides. Manicured lawns became overgrown gardens with cockeyed swing sets. Then there were no yards and houses with boarded-up windows or Michigan State flags instead of curtains, toed up right next to the cracked sidewalks.

They passed more fields, green corn high as the car, and the highway became visible, along with the stores and gas stations that always seemed to crop up around exit ramps. Hope turned the car around and headed to the small grocery store in town.

It was a tiny town, the smallest town she'd ever been in, surrounded by a sea of corn. But she still felt exposed. Like everyone would remember the car with the Missouri plates. The woman with the sunglasses who didn't hide her black eye or split lip.

She and Tink would put their heads down and try to stay invisible as they got their supplies and went back to The Orchard House—a tiny little needle in a giant green haystack.

And there, the only thing she could do was hope they were safe.

Seven

Farm hours were pretty lame. Farm hours meant going to bed super early and not being able to play on Mom's phone because she was worried about data. And there wasn't even a TV in their room and Mom said they couldn't go downstairs and watch the one in the living room because she didn't want to bother Peg.

Tink took a bath, just so she didn't die of boredom.

But because she went to bed so early, she woke up really early, which meant she could put her new plan into action.

The digital clock said six a.m., and out the window of their bedroom she saw Peg walking down to the barn, the dog right beside her. Right on schedule.

Mom was snoring in her bed. She'd set the alarm for 6:30 because today was their first day in the orchard.

Now or never.

Down the steps, through the kitchen. Tink checked the door to Peg's room just to see if it was still locked.

It was.

So she went out the squeaky screen door to the wild back-yard that was like no backyard she'd ever seen. She wasn't sure if she liked it—there were a lot of bugs. But there were butterflies, too. And birds. The sun was bright and hot and when Mom woke up she'd probably yell at her to put on a hat or sunscreen. Mom was obsessed with sunscreen.

Jumping with the crickets through the tall grass, Tink made her way around the side of the house to a white door. She'd spotted it yesterday when they had been hanging clothes on the line.

She thought it was another way into Peg's room.

Now. This was tricky. If Peg was looking, she might see Tink trying this door. But really? What were the chances of Peg looking?

Now or never. Now or never.

Making herself tiny, she eased around the corner and tried the doorknob. It was hot from the sun and turned in her hand. She pushed, just a tiny bit, and the door cracked open.

It wasn't that adults were dumb. It was that they thought kids were dumb. Every time.

Quick as anything she slipped inside and closed the door quietly behind her. She blinked, her eyes adjusting to the dark room. Whatever wonders she was expecting, it was just like DeeDee's jewelry box. The room was just a room. A bed, neatly made with sheets and a quilt. Bedside tables on both sides, one with a bunch of books and a laptop computer and a lamp with a crooked lampshade, and the other table clean as a whistle.

There was a television sitting on a dresser against a wall, blocking most of a painting behind it. There were a couple of windows with shades drawn. A bunch of shoes by the door that led into the kitchen. There was a bookshelf along one wall, filled with magazine and notebooks. The floor creaked under her feet at she crept over to it. The magazines were old *National Geographic*s about monarch butterflies and ice caps.

Boring. Though there was one about Vikings she liked the look of, so she grabbed it and hid it under her shirt.

There was an old and raggedy stuffed owl. Tink touched the black button eye that was hanging on by a thread.

Next to all the magazines was a jewelry box just like the one DeeDee had, made out of wood. Not expecting much, and a little bit disappointed with the whole adventure so far, Tink lifted the lid.

There were tons of pictures inside. Lots of them framed, some of them just loose. Peg said there weren't a lot of pictures around, but she'd lied. There was a baby in a bunch of them. Most of them, actually. A pudgy baby with food on her face. A pudgy baby in a stroller being pushed by a man with a big chest and a nice smile. The baby got older in some pictures but was still pudgy. And freckled. A woman that looked like Peg but younger and a lot happier helping a baby walk. And then suddenly the baby was a kid. Riding a bike. Standing in a garden holding a bunch of ears of corn with the man with the nice smile.

She went through all of them, hoping for something more interesting but never finding it. Until she lifted the last picture and beneath it, settled in the bottom of the box on worn red velvet, was a pistol.

→PEG←

First day of cherry season for those girls and she gave 'em a day. Two at most before Hope had a bunch of reasons why they should be moving on and that second floor would be empty again.

And life would go back to normal.

Peg opened the back door into the kitchen, having come from feeding the barn cats and checking on the new kittens. One of them had an oozy eye and Peg had a bright red scratch from their argument over the antibiotic cream. Nelson charged in the door behind her, nearly knocking her over.

Tink was sitting right there at the table, her hands folded in front of her like butter wouldn't melt in her mouth.

"You're up early," Peg said, hiding her surprise and her suspicion. It was almost 6:15. They didn't start work in the orchard for another half hour. "Sleep all right?"

Tink nodded. Peg walked over to the coffee she'd made before going to the barn and poured herself a cup. She waited as long as she could for the girl to say something. But Tink out-stubborned her.

"Girl," Peg said. "Unless there's a medical reason you're not talking, you're going to need to tell me what—"

"The rifle," the girl's voice croaked out, surprising both of them. Tink clapped her hand over her mouth, her eyes looking toward the stairs.

"What about the rifle?" Peg asked.

"You were going to show me how to shoot it."

"I did. Yesterday."

"You shot it."

"But I showed you."

Tink scowled and Peg smiled.

"We got some time, I suppose." The girl lit right up and Peg felt that old joy that came from making a kid happy. They weren't going to actually fire the gun—she didn't need to give Abel or Hope any more heart attacks. But there'd be no harm in learning some safety.

Peg went and got the old rifle and a cartridge from the box in the cabinet above the oven.

"Let's go, kid," Peg said, and Tink and Nelson followed her out the back door and into the tall grass behind the clothesline. The sun hadn't burned off the dew and the grass was still wet.

Tink walked on one side of her and then dropped back to walk on her other side. Peg realized she was trying to avoid Nelson, who was trailing her like a shadow.

"You don't like dogs?" Peg asked.

"I don't know any dogs," she said.

"Your grandma didn't have a pet?" Now, why did she have to go and ask that question? She didn't care one way or another if Denise had had a pet. It was just surprising to hear. Denise had been such an animal lover as a kid, fighting with Dad over the fate of the chickens all the time, trying to get the outdoor dogs indoors.

"She said she was allergic."

Peg didn't bother hiding her surprise this time. "She wasn't allergic," she said.

Tink shrugged. "That's what she told me when I asked if we could get a kitten."

Well, Peg didn't even know what to think of that. So she decided not to think. "So you've decided to talk today?" she asked, and the question seemed to push the girl right back into her silence. "Whatever your mom did, it must have been bad."

"It was," Tink said. "It was bad."

She hadn't expected the girl to answer.

"Yeah?"

But the girl didn't respond and whatever bad thing happened was not going to be talked about this morning.

"Well, I'm glad you decided to talk to me." As the words came out of her mouth, Peg realized that for a woman who wanted to stay squarely in her own business, she was doing a terrible job.

✦ HOPE ✦

"Umm…hi," she whispered into her phone.

"I'm sorry, miss, I can't hear you."

"Right. Sorry." She spoke up a little louder, not even sure why she'd been whispering. Tink was downstairs with Peg. She'd woken up to find Tink gone, and her heart about burst out of her chest. But then she heard Peg in the kitchen saying Tink's name, asking her what she wanted for breakfast, like Tink was going to answer.

"Can you hear me now?"

"Yeah. What can I do for you?"

"I…ah… I'm wondering if you have any John Does?"

"John who?" the woman asked, and there was the clacking of a keyboard.

"D-O-E. John Doe. I was wondering if you have any men there without ID? Who might not be conscious or…remember who they are?"

"Yeah. Honey, I know what a John Doe is. Are you looking for a relative?"

"Yes." The word was sticky with lies and revulsion. "About thirty years old. A white man—"

"Didn't you call yesterday?"

"Yeah."

"Sorry, hon. Not here."

"But, maybe—"

"We have five John Does. All of them over sixty. None of them white. Try County. Or the cops."

"The cops?" she asked.

"Yeah. Maybe your guy is in a drunk tank somewhere. Or been arrested for something."

Four days. It'd been four days. Nothing on the news and no John Does.

She couldn't breathe. It was hard to breathe. *Where is all the air?*

Daniel was alive. He was alive and he was out there somewhere, looking for her and Tink. Because he wouldn't stop. He'd proved that, hadn't he? Showing up in Chicago the way he had?

Did I tell him? she wondered for the millionth time. What were the circumstances that would make her say something like *I have an aunt I've never met who lives on a farm in Michigan.*

She couldn't imagine them. And even if she *had* said something, there were probably seven hundred farms in Michigan. Seven thousand, maybe?

But that didn't make her feel any better. Every day it was getting harder and harder to hope they were safe.

She slipped the phone in her pocket and went into the little kitchen to make peanut-butter-and-banana roll-ups for her and Tink.

Today was their first day in the orchard, and Peg had made it sound like they'd be engaging in hard labor. Hope had her doubts that she and Tink were really up for it. They weren't really hard-labor kind of gals. They were Netflix-marathon kind of gals. Starbucks-frappuccino kind of gals.

But part of her was excited to lay down all those terrible weights she carried and just work. Just do the thing that needed to be done and then the next thing and the next.

She just wasn't sure if the next thing she needed to do was pack up Tink and run.

Again.

"Morning," Peg said when Hope made it downstairs, and pulled a coffee mug the size of a thimble from the cupboards. It was a holdover from the days before venti sizing. How did anyone even survive? "Hungry?"

In her hands Hope had a sandwich bag full of the peanut-butter-and-banana roll-ups she'd made in the kitchen upstairs, but Tink looked like she'd already finished a plate of eggs. "I'm okay," she said.

"I haven't seen you eat a meal once," Peg said, handing Hope the cup of coffee.

"I'm all right. So?" she asked, changing the subject. "What are we doing today?"

"Well," Peg sighed. "Hard work mostly."

"Great," Hope said. She was excited about working. About *doing* something. "For how long?"

Peg stared at her for a long moment. "As long as you can, I suppose. A few hours, maybe."

A few hours? That didn't seem so bad.

"No, I mean, how long in total?" Hope asked.

"Cherry harvest takes about three weeks. We're a few days in already. Used to be less when we had more people helping us out."

"What do you do with the cherries?"

"Most go to a processing plant in Lawton. Some we keep."

"To eat?"

"No. We sell them around town."

Peg and Hope drank their coffees in big burning gulps, Hope at the table, Peg standing near the kitchen sink, like medicine they needed to face the day.

"Hey," Hope said. "I remembered something—"

"About the farm?" Peg asked.

"No. Not really. About you." Peg blinked, her face blank. "You sent me money on my birthday and stuffed owls at Christmas. I had them all up on a shelf in my room for the longest time."

"I didn't send you anything."

"Yeah…you did. I mean, when I got older, you just sent the money. But when I was a kid—"

"I didn't send you anything, Hope."

"But—"

"I didn't know where you were," Peg snapped. "I didn't send you anything for your birthday because I didn't know where to send it."

Peg put her mug down in the yellow enamel sink, so hard it sounded like it cracked, and then left, the back door slamming behind her.

Eight

Hope pushed out the kitchen door into a morning that was already damp around the edges, the sun hot on her skin.

Ahead of her, Peg whistled between her teeth and Nelson showed up out of the bushes, running right to Tink, who tried to veer away.

"Peg," Hope said, jogging to catch up with them. "What do you mean—"

"I don't suppose you got any boots," Peg said, eyeing their beat-up tennis shoes over her shoulder.

"No," Hope said. "No boots."

Peg humphed under her breath and kept moving.

"Did you not know where we were because Mom didn't tell you?" Hope asked.

"How else would that work, Hope?"

"But I just don't know…why?"

"Because she was mean? Spiteful?" Peg spat out. "Because she didn't care—" Her voice cracked.

"Peg—"

Peg turned, her eyes glittering, her anger unable to mask how upset she was. "*Why* is a question you should have asked her. I don't know why my sister did half the things she did."

"But what about...the owls? There was money on my birthday from you..."

"Not from me. Not sure why she said it was." Peg stomped through the high grass, like it was her job to mash it. "The bees get bad in the orchard. But remember if you don't bother them, they won't bother you."

"Peg. I just want—"

"I know what you want. But apologizing for Denise is a waste of time. So don't do it. I did it half my life and it got me nothing and nowhere."

Hope stopped in her tracks. She never took it well when people didn't accept her apologies. She was one of those people who really wanted everyone to get along, which was hilarious because her mother got along with like ten people. And Tink didn't get along with anyone.

Peg stopped, too, and turned. "I'm sorry," she said. "None of that is your fault."

"I know she could be mean," Hope said. "But she was a good mom."

"Was she?" Peg asked dubiously. "Did she feed you good food and make sure you got to bed on time? Did she read you stories at night and take you to the beach? Help you with your homework? Did she pack—" Peg stopped and Hope stood there stunned.

"Sorry," Peg whispered into the silence.

"It's okay," Hope said. "And yeah, she did those things." Some of them. A few. Actually, as she thought about it, not really. But did bedtime stories really matter? She glanced over at Tink and thought about all those nights with Harry Potter. All that spinach and avocado she hid in smoothies and muffins. The digestive-tract science project they'd worked so hard on.

But then she thought of Daniel and wondered what made a good mom.

Denise hadn't made her healthy dinners, but Hope had been safe. Denise had kept the bad guys out.

It was more than Hope could say for herself.

"Good," Peg said, but Hope wasn't sure Peg believed her.

"I'm sorry, too. I wish I'd known you. It would have been nice to have an aunt."

Peg looked over at the barn, silent for so long Hope was embarrassed by what she'd said, felt her edges curling up.

"I should have written back to you," Peg said. "When you sent the letter that Denise died."

"It's all right," she said, because it was a thing she was used to saying.

Peg stared at her, at her split lip and the eye that was turning black and green, the edges of the bruise halfway down her cheek, and she sighed real hard.

Nothing is all right, was what her sigh said. *Not one thing.*

But then just as the twitchy uncomfortable feeling nearly became too much and Hope was about to laugh, because she was a stress laugher, Peg smiled. With teeth and wrinkles around her eyes and even a dimple in her left cheek.

"Better late than never, I suppose," Peg said.

Tink came up beside them and put her hands on Hope's butt, shoving her into motion.

"Okay, okay," she laughed, and they crossed the dirt road toward the big field of trees.

In the orchard, the air smelled like sugar, and just underneath that something burning. The hum of whatever machinery was deep in the belly of this orchard was matched by the hum of bees and blackflies that hovered over the ground in search of the cherries that had fallen off the branch and sat in the dirt.

Hope looked up at the trees and the sky. The trees weren't tall, but the canopies were wide. The leaves and the fruit reached over the aisles to meet nearly in the middle of a cloudless bright blue sky. The shade of the orchard was spotty, and the sunlight came through in chunks, like she could just grab it in her hands.

"Hey!" Peg yelled, startling Hope. "We've got cherries to harvest."

They turned a corner in the orchard and up ahead were two old tractors. The big red one had some kind of machine attached to it that clamped around the tree.

"That's the harvester," Peg shouted, pointing to the machine. "It literally shakes the cherries off the trees and onto the tarps. The tarps are attached to my tractor." She pointed at the second tractor, yellow with a series of chains off the back all connected to the black tarps beneath the tree.

"When Abel has cleared a tree, I drive the yellow tractor and drag the tarps to the end of the row." Peg pointed to the end of the row, where there were stacks of white coolers. "I put all the cherries that are in good shape in the cooler and then drive the tarps over to the next tree. Arrange 'em. And then we do it all over again."

That all seemed simple. Loud, but simple.

Abel was sitting in the tractor with the harvester attached, and once he saw them, he turned it off and the buzz of the flies and bees filled the sudden silence.

"Morning," he said with a smile.

Hope smiled but it was kind of a wince, and then she tried to make it better with a super awkward hip-high wave.

"I brought help," Peg said. She bent and picked up cherries, tossing them gently onto the black tarps.

"I see that." He nodded his head at Hope and waved to Tink, a slick two-fingered thing that looked so cool. "I'm Abel."

"She's Tink," Hope answered, real fast. "My daughter."

Tink gave Abel the same slick wave and he grinned at her. "Good to meet you, Tink. You ready to pick some cherries?"

Tink shrugged.

The tarps were thick with cherries, some in bunches attached to stems, others on their own. A few were split. Most were shiny and perfect.

Hope's stomach growled and she laughed, embarrassed. "So?" she asked. "What do we do?"

"Well." Abel took a red bandanna from the back pocket of his coveralls and wiped his face. It wasn't even seven a.m. and his skin was slick with sweat. "I run the harvester," he said. "We shake the tree clean and then you and Tink will go around the tree picking up the cherries that don't land on the tarps and putting them on the tarps. When Peg drags the full tarps to the end of the rows, you guys will go through them, putting the good ones in the cooler and getting rid of the ruined ones."

"Ruined?"

"Split or rotten."

"No eating the cherries," Peg said in a sterner voice, pointing at Tink, and everyone laughed.

And then the work began.

✦ PEG ✦

They'd cleared two trees before the sun was fully overhead. Back when her parents ran the farm, seasonal workers would come help out—mostly high schoolers and a few migrant families that Oscar had known—and they'd be able to harvest the whole orchard in a week even without the shaker. At night, Oscar would host big cookouts at his cabin, and she and Denise would listen to the party through their room's open window.

After her parents were killed in a car accident, Peg and Denise hired Jacob to help with the harvest. Oscar told them they were making a mistake hiring Jacob, and when they didn't believe him, he left.

Nothing was the same after that.

No parties at night. No orchards full of people. No help.

It was surprising how good it felt to have more people out here now. They didn't talk. That was too hard over the sound of the machinery. But it felt communal. The way she remembered the farm used to feel.

She walked over to Abel, who was climbing off his tractor. "You want to start on the west—"

"You got some reason for not calling a break?" Abel interrupted her in a low whisper. "They do something to you that needs to be punished?"

She glanced back at the two girls, who were lifting cherries into the ice-water baths. "No," she said. *Punished?*

"We stay out of each other's business," Abel said, sounding like his father, Oscar. "And that suits us both. But Hope looks like she's gonna drop."

"They'd say if they were tired."

"The whole world's not like you, Peg," he said, shaking his head. Then he yelled out so Hope and Tink could hear, "I need a breather. You guys want some water? And I've got some food."

Peg felt her face grow red. She'd forgotten to tell them to bring water, and she knew Hope always gave half or most of her serving of any food to Tink. An hour ago, she'd watched as Hope had given Tink one of the banana roll-ups she had in her pocket, and then, a few seconds later, after Tink had inhaled it, she'd broken her own in half, offering Tink the larger of the two pieces.

Still, there had been something in the way Hope had been working, something in the set of her face, that had made Peg keep her mouth shut. And who was she, really, to tell people what their limits were? She didn't know Hope.

"I'll be back," Peg said, and hopped on the yellow tractor that for the moment wasn't attached to the tarps. "You guys take a break."

Nine

"Come get a drink," Abel said, waving Hope and Tink over to his tractor. Hope's butt and legs were sore from all the squatting and lifting. She hadn't done a workout like this since that DVD she used to do with her mom a decade ago when she was in high school.

Shaun T. would have approved.

Tink didn't seem too bothered, and Hope imagined her legs must be made of rubber bands and stretchy cords. "I'm proud of you," Hope said to her as they walked through the high grass at the end of the row of trees.

Tink looked up at her for a long second, and Hope stopped walking, her heart lifting into her throat with the careful but steady hope that this moment, right now, Tink would end her silent streak. But then Tink broke into a run toward Abel's tractor, leaving Hope to wrestle with disappointment and grief that had nowhere to go.

At the tractor, Abel filled a mug from a thermos of water. Tink drank it down and then held it out for an immediate refill.

"Let's give your mom some, too," he said.

"I'm all right," Hope said, waving it off.

Sweat ran down Abel's neck. "Drink," he said, firm, offering the mug with water so cold that the outside had condensation on it.

The thirst and hunger she'd been pretending not to feel roared to the surface. She was famished. Her hands shook when she reached for the water, and when he handed her the mug, half of it spilled out.

"Careful," he murmured in a low voice, holding on to the cup, his fingers brushing over hers. "Go slow."

The touch of his hands embarrassed her even more, and she could feel herself go red-hot all over. She guzzled the water, dripping it down her chin and T-shirt.

"More, please," she practically gasped. "Unless—"

He filled the mug for her, and as the water did its work, she was aware she was causing a bit of a scene. Abel watched her with soft and worried brown eyes. Her daughter watched her with hard and worried hazel eyes.

"I'm okay," she said to them, wiping her mouth with the back of her hand. "Totally fine. Just thirstier than I thought."

"Sit down." Abel shifted away from the footrest of the tractor and gratefully Hope took the spot. From the cooler, he pulled a tin-foil-wrapped sandwich and began to open it, releasing the smell of steak and cheese and something limy. "Here," he said. "You guys can share this."

"We can't take your lunch," Hope said, even as Tink was reaching for it. "Tink," she said and pushed her daughter's hands back into her lap.

"I don't know what you're doing," Abel said. "But if you

don't eat something you're going to fall over. You're hungry and I'm offering you food. It's fairly straightforward."

She had about ten things she could say about how none of this was his business, but the smell of his sandwich was too damn distracting.

"Hope," he said. "You don't need to make this hard."

No part of this was hard. She was sitting on a tractor with her daughter on a beautiful day. Hard had been three months ago. Three weeks ago. That hotel room.

This was sweet relief.

She took half the sandwich and tried to pull it into pieces to give to Tink. The soft bread tore but the stuff inside resisted and so she gave up and just took a bite, a big one, then handed the sandwich over to Tink, who also took a big bite.

The flavors were explosive. Bits of grilled steak, cold salty crumbled cheese. Big slices of tomato and a thick layer of re-fried beans. There was something spicy in there, too, that woke up her whole mouth. Tink handed the sandwich back and Hope took another bite.

Abel watched them pass the sandwich back and forth a few more times and slowly started to smile.

Hope wiped her face, thinking she had a piece of tomato or something hanging off her chin. "What are you smiling at?"

"My mom's favorite thing in the world was feeding hungry people," he said with a shrug. "Never really understood it until right now." He unwrapped the second half of the sandwich and started to eat. "I like your name," he said to Tink between bites. "Short for Tinkerbell?"

Hope acted real casual, fishing a piece of grilled meat from the folds of the tin foil, but she watched intently from the corner of her eye as Tink nodded.

"How old are you?" he asked. "Wait...let me guess." He narrowed his eyes and tilted his head. "Twenty-four."

Hope rolled her eyes but Tink smiled, that little twist of her lips.

"Twelve?" he asked.

Tink pointed down.

"Three?" he asked and then shook his head. "Don't be ridiculous."

She pointed up, and he took a bite of his sandwich and leaned against the tractor. "Between three and twelve, huh?"

Honest to god, she could feel the words in her daughter's throat. She could feel the laughter. This was some mid-grade-level teasing, but coming from this man with his tattoos and muscles and big, tall boots, well, it was effective. Tink was charmed, and she did not charm easily.

"I'm gonna say ten," he said, and for a second Tink sparked right up. "I'm right!" Abel held out his hand for a high five, and Tink closed down, looking down at the sandwich, leaving him to figure out what to do with his unslapped hand.

"Thank you," Hope said into the silence. "For the sandwich. We'll know to pack a lunch for tomorrow."

"And some sunscreen," he said, and touched his nose.

Hope put her finger over her own nose and felt how hot it was. It was probably red and freckled. Perfect.

"How long have you worked for Peg?" she asked, crinkling up the tinfoil and stretching out her sore legs.

"Well, my dad used to be the foreman, but he left after Peg's parents died. And then came back about…" He grimaced. "Six years later? After she sold off a bunch of her land. And once I was old enough I came with him every summer until I joined the army. I came back full-time when I got discharged a few years ago."

"She doesn't own all this land?" Hope asked.

"Nope. She sold the corn and soybean fields years ago.

She held on to the cherry and apple orchards for as long as she could."

"Who owns everything now?"

"Corn and soy are owned by one of them big conglomerates. The orchards—" he glanced around and swatted at a blackfly that was dive-bombing his head "—are mine."

Hope shook her head. "You… This is yours?"

"Yep. Well, we split the cherries. She wasn't ready to sell those and I didn't have enough money when I got back. But I own the apples on the far end of the property," he said, pointing behind him. "I've been trying to buy the rest of the cherries for a while, but she's not budging."

Hope glanced around at the cherries, the latticework of sun and shadow on the thick grass. All she'd ever owned was the Camry, bought with the money her mother left when she died. It hadn't occurred to her she could own something like this.

"How old are you?" she asked him.

He laughed. "How old are you?"

"Twenty-seven."

She watched all the familiar reactions cross his face. The quicksilver doubt and then shock. The smiling glance at Tink, who didn't even realize he was doing the math in his head.

"I'm thirty," he said.

Thirty and he owned all this? It wasn't his fault, but she felt small all over again. So many bad decisions. So many things she would do over.

He tilted the thermos to drain the last of the water into the metal cup and handed it to Tink, who took only a sip but smacked her lips after like it tasted delicious.

He offered it to Hope but she declined. "You know," he said after he drained the cup himself. "My mom used to do what you're doing."

She bristled. "What's that?"

"Turn down things like her not having any would mean more for us kids."

Before Hope could deny that was what she was doing, the yellow tractor came roaring back to their row. Peg turned off the engine and held up a small cooler and a bag. "Brought some food. It's not much."

"Abel just shared his lunch with us," Hope said, stuffed. She hadn't eaten that much in ages. Even Tink, the bottomless pit, seemed satisfied. She was sitting, drowsy and droopy, in Abel's tractor seat.

"Oh." Peg stopped, the plastic bag slapping into her leg. "Well. Maybe a snack later on, then."

"Whatcha got?" Abel asked.

He ate a few of Peg's ham sandwiches and took a slice of watermelon, eating it in big bites and spitting out the black seeds.

"So," Hope said, fighting back a yawn. "What's next?"

Peg and Abel had a whole silent conversation. Peg shook her head, he shrugged. She shrugged back.

"For you," Peg said. "A nap."

"No. Come on," Hope protested. "We're fine."

She looked over to see Tink with her head in her arms, if not asleep, close to it.

It would seem the first day of their first cherry season was over.

They walked back at a slow shuffle, the aches and pains of the day's work settling into her muscles. Her eye and the bruise on her hip throbbed, and sweat ran into the cut on her lip, making it sting.

"That wasn't so bad, was it?" she asked Tink, who gave Hope a you-must-be-kidding look. "Yeah, it was pretty bad. You did great."

Tink was silent.

"I'm super proud of you."

Tink looked back, her hair falling over her eyes. She wasn't talking, but she was listening. That had to count for something.

"A shower," Hope said to her daughter. "And then you can have a nap."

Tink nodded, her cheeks pink, her nose even pinker.

Hope was tired, but she didn't want to go in the house. Or lie down in the bed. The work had felt good. Not in her body so much, but in her head. She couldn't think when she was working that hard.

The decisions she'd soon need to make faded into the distance. And so did the fear.

The sound of the harvester starting up again in the orchard startled birds from the bushes between the barn and the house, revealing a fence. Tentacles of sweet peas and weeds pulled at its chain link. The bloody hearts of strawberries beat inside leaves so green they appeared black. Bees and butterflies hovered over the white-and-yellow flowers. Gigantic sunflower eyes watched over the whole of it. The fence could barely contain the monster of greenery.

"Tink," Hope said. "There's a garden back here."

Hope strayed off the worn yellow path between the house and the barn and into the knee-high grass that got taller as she approached the garden. It looked like no one had touched it in years. It was huge, too, at least the same size as the barn.

"Remember DeeDee's garden?" Hope asked. It had been part of her rental agreement: one well-tended and organized raised box in a sunny bit of the backyard. "All those tomatoes. And those pumpkins you grew?" The pumpkins made great jack-o'-lanterns but terrible pie. After Mom died, Hope had let the garden go. Just like she'd let everything go. She imagined the Euclid Avenue squirrels and raccoons enjoying the buffet.

She reached over the bent and twisted chain link and picked a strawberry, bright red and tiny, warm from the sun.

"Tink!" she said.

Soundlessly, Tink appeared beside her.

"If you're not going to talk," Hope said, "I'm gonna put a bell on you like a cat."

Tink plucked the strawberry from Hope's hand and popped it in her mouth.

"Good?" she asked, and Tink nodded, reaching for another. "Why do you suppose they let it go like this?" Once upon a time, someone had worked hard on this garden. "Seems a shame. You want to help me—"

Tink shook her head and walked away, uninterested in either the garden or helping her do anything. Maybe both.

Ten

Peg thought the girls were gonna quit on the second day, and she was wrong. The third day went by, and rain that night broke the heat wave, so the fourth day was cooler. And still those girls worked. In the orchard, they were well ahead of schedule, clearing more trees in a day than they had in years.

Tink was taking to the work like a duck to water. She got up early every morning for their lessons with the rifle first, clearly still frustrated that Peg didn't let her actually shoot the thing. Some mornings she talked. Some she didn't.

Hope was…well, Peg wasn't sure. But somehow after four days of cherry season, of steady meals and good sleep, of sunshine and healing for that eye, she looked worse. Thin and manic, with a wild look on her face whenever Tink was out of her sight that she did her very best to hide.

Hope had said that whatever she'd been running from

wasn't going to follow her here, but something had. It was grinding that girl down to nothing.

Every morning Peg still woke up thinking they might be gone.

"Well," Peg said when the coolers at the end of the row were full on the fourth day. It was three in the afternoon and there was still more work to do. But she felt bad making the girls do it when they looked so worn. "I think that's it for the day. You two can go back and clean up—"

"No," Hope said. "No. We're fine. We'd like to keep working."

Peg looked down at Tink, who didn't argue, and then over at Abel, who, she knew, was as skeptical as she was.

"You sure?" Peg asked. "You look—"

"I'm sure," Hope said resolutely.

All right then, she thought. *If we can't avoid it, we're just gonna run right at it.*

"Then I'll get the girls back to the barn," Peg said to Abel. "Have them do some washing and sorting."

Abel lifted his eyebrows and glanced over at Tink and Hope as if assessing their abilities for a difficult mission. Tink straightened and Hope smiled down at her daughter. "Sure," he finally said.

Peg unhooked the chains that held the tarps, and Hope and Tink hauled over a small, wooden flatbed trailer that Peg attached to the back of the tractor. Then they lifted the big white coolers, filled with cold water and dark, shiny cherries, onto the flatbed. Once the coolers were all stacked up, Tink and Hope hitched a ride across the road back to the barn.

It was cool and dusty inside the barn, and smelled like motor oil and dirt. Attached to the wall on one whole side were the drying and sorting racks. Peg wasn't sure who'd built them, but they'd been there as long as she'd been alive.

"So," Peg said as she hauled one of the white coolers toward the closest rack. "You take this." She picked up one of the dozen or so sieve baskets attached to handles. "And you use it to scoop out the cherries and put them on the drying racks."

She dipped one of the sieves into the cherry coolers, scooped out a heaping basket of dripping sweet cherries and dumped them out on the wire-mesh drying racks. Water trickled down onto the dirt beneath the rack. She ran a hand over the small mound of cherries, getting them all spread out, and then did it again. And again.

One cooler filled the racks with pounds and pounds of cherries, dripping and drying onto the floor.

"Once all the cherries are out on the racks and drying off, we do one more sort."

"Another sort?" Hope asked.

"The processing plant down in Lawton doesn't want any weird ones. No deformities." She plucked a little mutant cherry that had two stems and a strange bulge on the side, grabbed a plastic bag and put the mutant cherry in the bag. "But there's a baker in town that uses the outcasts for jam. She buys them in bulk."

"You do all of this by hand?" Hope asked.

"Some of the big operations have machines. But we've just always done it this way."

"I think we can handle it," Hope said, and Peg looked around as if to make sure she wasn't forgetting anything. But really she was just assessing the girl's ability to stay standing.

"You…you both worked real hard these past days," Peg said.

"Sure," Hope said. "Thanks. We're happy to help. Tink—"

Tink was crouched over by the wheels of the truck.

"Tink? What are you doing?"

"She probably heard one of the barn cats," Peg said. "The one with half his ear gone, stay away from him. He's mean. But the calico just had a bunch of kittens and they're real sweet."

Tink's face went wild with delight and then she was on the hunt for kittens.

"Well," Hope said ruefully. "That will be the end of her usefulness."

"She's been plenty useful." *Tell her they* both *have been real useful. That they've worked so hard and that you're proud of her. Tell her.*

But those kinds of words never came easy for Peg. Hank had been able to throw around compliments and kindness like he had them coming out his ears. But Peg was always so stingy with hers, like she only had a tiny, meager supply to get her through life and she meant to take some with her to her grave.

"Hey, Peg?" Hope asked. "What's the deal with the garden back there?" She pointed with the dripping end of the strainer toward the back window. The garden was barely visible through the skyscraper cobwebs.

Peg got busy fiddling with the key to the tractor. "What about it?"

"Why was it left to grow wild?"

"Because I only have two hands and so many hours in the day."

"Peg," Hope said quietly. "I'm not judging you. It's just… it must have been an amazing garden."

"When Hank was here, he took care of it. God. Treated that garden like a child." The words just spilled out of her, like they'd been waiting. Like Peg had been longing to say his name out loud.

But now that his name was out there she wanted to suck it back in, keep all those memories behind the locks she'd been using for years. Because talking about him hurt. Remembering him hurt.

"Hank?" Hope turned. "Is that who lived in the apartment before us?"

"No."

"Was he a hand here?"

"No—"

"An employee?"

"No. Hope. No. He was none of those things. And I'm not talking about him with you."

Hope nodded, her face red from the sun and from being chastised by Peg like she was a girl.

Peg was embarrassed that she'd talked to Hope like that, the way her father would have.

"I'm sorry," Peg said. "I shouldn't have snapped at you."

"It's okay."

"It's not," Peg said. "It's not okay at all. And you don't have to pretend it is. Hank was my husband, I guess. Though we never made it official. He always wanted to go down to the courthouse and I always found a reason to put it off." She sighed, looking down at the drops of water on her boots. "I don't know why I did that." Her voice revealed more than she wanted of old deep wounds. Regrets.

"Where is he now?" Hope asked.

"Petoskey."

"What happened?"

"You know, I think I need to get back to the orchard to help Abel." She got back into the tractor and drove out of there like she was being chased.

Once Peg was back, Abel turned off the shaker, looking at her like he wasn't expecting her.

"What?"

"They okay?"

"Yes. Maybe?" She shrugged.

Abel shook his head. "There were guys like that in my unit—"

"I know," she sighed.

"Like they were going to twitch right out of their skin."

"I know, Abel!"

"Then, what are you going to do about it?"

This was the sort of stuff Hank knew how to handle. He was the one who kissed bruises and dried tears and made things better. She just didn't have the touch.

I should call him. He should know that Hope's back. He would know how to help her.

But she wouldn't.

She couldn't.

✢ HOPE ✦

Hope was emptying the white coolers of their pink-tinged water outside the big doors of the barn and Nelson was lapping at the puddles when the two tractors climbed the ditch on the other side of the road and made their way over.

Peg lifted her hat and waved. Nelson barked a greeting but went back to the water.

"Hey," Hope said, shielding her eyes from the sun as they pulled in and then turned off the motors. Peg had taken additional white cooler boxes out into the orchard and now lifted two of them onto the wooden shelf where the others had been. "How'd it go?"

Abel grinned at her with half his mouth. "We got another two trees today."

"Is that a good day?"

"It's an amazing day," he said. "Where's Tink?"

"She's sleeping in the truck."

Hope finished cleaning out the metal grate built into the shelf, tossing the wet stems and leaves onto the ground so she could dry and sort the new batch, but Abel put a hand on her arm to stop her.

She twitched out from under his touch fast and quick and placed her hand over the spot like he'd hurt her. Not that he had. But it felt like any touch would split her skin like those cherries.

"I'm sorry," he said quietly.

"Don't worry about it. I'm just a little jumpy, I guess. What...what happens next?" she asked.

"Well. I'm gonna load up the truck and drive the cherries down to Lawton. You and Tink want to come for a ride?" he asked with a smile. The bees had followed him in from the orchard, buzzing around him like he was some kind of sweet-smelling flower. His power to ignore them was superhuman. "There's a dairy down by Lawton. They make their own ice cream. We could drop the cherries off and stop there and get a scoop."

"Oh, no," she said. The memory of that exposed feeling the day they'd been in town made her stomach sour. She'd been working so hard not to worry, to hope that they were safe. Going into town felt like it might jeopardize all that. "You guys go. Tink and I will stick around here. Finish up this sort."

"I'll finish the sort," Peg said. "You go. Tink would like it. They've got a playground and everything."

"That sounds..." *Dangerous. In a lot of ways.* "Nice. But I think we're gonna stick around the farm." Her efforts to sound casual were pretty awful, and he smiled at her kindly, like he knew what she was doing, which was funny considering she had no idea. "Let me just wake Tink up and get her out of your truck."

She opened the driver's-side door, expecting to find her daughter curled up with kittens.

Only to find the front seat empty.

↠TINK↞

Mom hadn't let Tink out of her sight for days. If she woke up at night to go to the bathroom, Mom was right there asking if she was okay. But now Mom was down at the barn and Peg and Abel were in the orchard, and no one was paying much attention to her. This not-talking thing was sort of making her feel invisible, and she wasn't sure if she liked it. Mom had stopped trying to trick her into talking, didn't try to touch her anymore.

If she didn't talk to Peg in the mornings, she would think she was vanishing.

Tink went up to the bathroom and decided to have a little look around Peg's secret room. She found some bullets for the pistol, took two and put them in her pocket. The owl had tipped over and she set it back up. Touching it, she realized the wings were made out of velvet.

The pistol was still in the bottom of the jewelry box. Peg would notice if it went missing or Mom would notice it in their room, so she didn't dare take it. But Tink liked looking at it. She tried to imagine Daniel with one. That was what he'd said that night in the gas station. That he had a gun in the pocket of his blue jacket.

Sounded like all the rest of Daniel's bullshit to Tink, but Mom had believed him.

Even settled against that faded velvet, the pistol looked dangerous. A ferocious animal waiting for its chance to bite.

When she went to close the lid of the jewelry box, she saw next to the pistol two letters all tied up with string. The envelopes had DeeDee's handwriting. Tink recognized it right away because she'd tried to copy the flourish with *y*s and the big fancy *t*s for years.

The envelopes were addressed to Peg. Before Tink could pull out one of the letters to read, she heard her mom yell from the barn.

Crap. Time was up. She grabbed a magazine about space and the bundle of letters and ran upstairs to stash the stuff in her pillowcase.

That giddy, happy feeling of knowing Peg's secret made her skip down to the barn.

Eleven

P eg and Abel had humored her panic, telling her in calm voices that everything would be okay, trying to make her think she wasn't overreacting, until Tink came strolling down from the house, wiping her hands on her shorts, skipping every third step. She'd said earlier she had a stomachache, Hope remembered. Not everything had to be code red.

Hope knew she was compounding the damage Daniel had done to them every day by not letting Tink be a ten-year-old kid, by being so scared and making her daughter scared, too.

"Hey!" she yelled, running over to Abel's truck, where he'd been idling, waiting for Tink to show up before he drove off. "That offer to go for ice cream still open?"

"Hop on in," he said.

"We can follow you," Hope said, predictably making things awkward.

"Follow? We can all fit in the truck."

Could they, though, with all this baggage she had? Daniel and her mom. A fading black eye and a lip that kept splitting. How could there possibly be room for all of that *and* her stubbornly silent, traumatized daughter?

"Hope?"

"Yeah?"

"It's just ice cream."

Dropping off the cherries at the processing plant took about fifteen minutes, and the dairy was only a few miles farther along a dirt road, winding its way between cow pastures and barns.

Tink wrinkled her nose at the smell of manure coming into the truck on the breeze.

"It takes a lot of cow poop to make good ice cream," Abel said, and Hope laughed as Tink shuddered.

"Why didn't Peg come?" Hope said over the wind.

Abel glanced at her and then Tink and then back at the road. "You a chocolate kind of person?" Abel asked Tink, changing the subject. "I am," he said. "Chocolate or chocolate peanut butter. If they don't have that I'll settle for rocky road. If they don't have *that*? Well, what's even the point?"

"She's a free agent," Hope said, referring to Tink.

"And you?" he asked Hope with a quick grin. "Are you an ice cream free agent?"

"Nope," she said. "Mint chocolate chip every time."

"Well, I have it on good authority, the mint chocolate chip here is the best."

"I will be the judge of that," she said, looking out the window, unable to bear how casual all this was.

They turned the corner in front of a low red barn with wide-open windows where ice cream was being served to crowds of people.

So many people.

Hope stiffened, her hand up by her face to hide what was left of the black eye around the edge of her glasses.

Abel parked in the far corner and hopped out. Tink scrambled out the driver's-side door after him, but Hope couldn't do it. She felt raw in front of all these people. Profoundly and terribly unsafe.

It was ridiculous; she knew that. But knowing it didn't change her fear one bit.

"You coming?" Abel asked.

"I... No. My eye..." she said with a wan smile. "If I go in with you people might think you did it." She was aiming for a joke, but his entire face went taut.

"I'll bring you a scoop," he said through lips pressed thin.

"You don't—"

But he slammed the door and led Tink into the dairy. Tink looked back and Hope waved.

Ten minutes later, which felt infinitely longer, Tink returned with a waffle cone piled high with what looked like strawberry and chocolate ice cream. It was so big she couldn't climb up into the truck without help.

"Holy cow, Tink, look at that," Hope said, taking it from her hand so she could get up on the seat.

Tink gave her a very stern "don't eat it, Mom" look.

"How about if I just clean it up—"

Tink snatched the cone back.

Behind her Abel laughed. "The old 'I'm just going to clean it up' trick. My father would do that and eat half the cone."

Abel sat down and handed Hope a sugar cone with a perfect ball of pale green ice cream flecked with bits of chocolate. He kept a waffle cone the size of Tink's filled with chocolate.

"So," Hope said, trying to project a calm she absolutely did not feel. "There's a playground around here?"

"I've got something better than a playground," Abel said.

He was good at this. Good at being kind. And easy.

They pulled out and bounced down a gravel road until the truck finally came to a stop in a cul de sac. Together with their ice cream cones, they walked down a dirt path through scrubby bushes to a rocky stretch of shoreline along the lake. The beach was made up of bits of blue and green and purple sea glass that gleamed like diamonds among small flat rocks.

Tink went hunting.

"It's a nice spot," Hope said, watching her daughter collect bits of glass between licks of her cone. "How'd you find it?"

"My dad used to bring me out here to skip rocks. The sea glass is fairly new. A clean fill dump on the spit about five miles south of here."

He sat down on a fallen log that looked like it had been placed here for adults to sit while an eager child combed the beach. She sat down on the other edge of it, aware of every inch of distance between them.

"I'm sorry," she said. "About that joke—"

"I know."

"It was a bad joke," she said with an awkward laugh that drew a sideways glance from him.

"You're really working yourself up over this," he said.

"I'm a stress laugher. When things are really tense and awful, I sort of... I can't help it. I laughed at my mom's funeral."

"Yikes."

"I know, right?"

"In the army you learn to joke about everything," he said. "Not sure if it's healthy, but it got us through some bad days."

They ate their ice cream in silence. *Does this feel awkward to him?* she wondered as she watched him eat his ice cream from the corner of her eye. He didn't seem bothered.

It's just me, she thought. *It's always just me.*

"So," he asked, "how are you liking the farm?"

"More than I thought I would," she said. "I've lived my whole life in St. Louis. Never thought I'd like living on a farm so much."

"In a few weeks it will be even better. You came in during the hardest part of the year."

"Actually, I like the work. A lot. It's nice being useful. It's nice being done at the end of the day and seeing what you've accomplished." She hadn't really realized that before the words came out of her mouth. It was so busy every day there wasn't a whole lot of time to think about whether she liked what she was doing or not. It was kind of a surprise to realize she did.

She really did.

He nodded like he got that.

"And living with Peg?" He grinned at her.

Hope could make a joke about being used to living with emotionally unavailable women, but that didn't seem kind. Or fair, really. "Peg's been very good to us."

"Her bark is much worse than her bite," he said.

"So? Why doesn't she go out for ice cream?"

"She doesn't go out for anything," he said with a steady look.

"Come on." Hope laughed. "What about groceries or gas or I don't know…" What else was there in Elk Falls? "The beach?"

"We have a gas pump in the barn," he said. "And once a month in the middle of the night she goes to Gaylord for supplies. But other than that she doesn't leave the farm."

"What about friends?"

"I think you're looking at him."

"Come on," she said. "That seems—"

"Odd?"

"Sad."

"When I go into town to deliver cherries to the stands everyone asks about her," he said. "And I never know what to say."

"She told us not to talk about her when we go into town because it would 'wake up the grapevine.'"

"It's Peg's business. And as Peg's business partner, if there's one thing I've learned, it's to stay out of Peg's business. But I've been working with her for years and I swear every year it gets worse."

"She has a bunch of baby stuff in the basement," she said. "A high chair and stuff. Did she... Do you know if—"

"If Peg had a baby?" He shook his head, his eyes wide like she was presenting him with information that was just too much to be believed. "No. I don't know."

Tink came running up, pockets full of glass that she emptied at Hope's feet, and then dashed off again.

"When my mom died I started to hate to leave the house, you know?" Hope said. "All those people asking me how I was doing. Asking what they could do to help. It was exhausting trying to make *them* feel better."

"You're saying being a recluse just got to be a habit for Peg?"

"Maybe?" she said. "Or maybe that baby stuff isn't Peg's and she doesn't leave the farm because it's a Wright-family thing. Apparently, her parents were like that. My mom kept to herself. Didn't like people knowing her business. She had a lot of rules about what I could do and where I could go. She kept telling me that the world was a dangerous place."

Oh god. It *was* a Wright-family thing. She blew out a long breath, so disappointed in herself. "And now... I'm doing the same thing to Tink."

"Telling her it's a dangerous place?"

"Showing her," she said with a bitter laugh. "Giving her real proof. That ice cream place," she said. "I didn't want to go in there, not just because of my eye, but because I don't want to be recognized. I don't want Tink to be recognized. If anyone asks about us, I want to be completely unmemorable. That probably sounds paranoid, but—"

His hand brushed her arm. He did it on purpose, like pressing a stop button on her blabber. Predictably, she froze, colder than the ice cream. She controlled the urge to leap to her feet and forced herself to just be there, present and still.

"After I got out of the army nothing felt right. Not my home. Not my family. Not my own head. But the farm... It felt good. Safe."

"You're telling me we're safe at the farm?"

"Yeah," he said. "I believe that you are."

Oh, if only belief and hope were enough.

Hope had gotten them to The Orchard House, to the roof over their heads and the comfortable beds. The good food. The needle in the green haystack. She'd thought, stupidly, so stupidly, that if she just got them here, that what she'd been telling Tink all this time would just magically be true: that everything was going to be okay.

"I can't hide there forever. Tink's got to go to school and I need to find a job. I don't want to be like my mother. Or Peg."

"You're not."

She laughed. "Did you miss the part where I was scared to go in for ice cream?"

"No," he said. "I didn't miss the part where you were scared to leave the farm today to come for ice cream, either. But you did it."

Minor victories, she guessed.

"So, you're thinking you'll move on after cherry season?" he asked.

"Yeah."

"That's too bad. It's been good having you around."

"I just…" *Could be making things dangerous for all of you.* "I don't know how I can stay."

"Before I came to the farm. I lived at home for a while, after I left the army," he said. "I was wild. I was angry. I made trouble with my family and my friends and I blamed them for the mistakes I was making. My friends stopped calling. My dad kicked me out of the house. My mom went to church to pray for me every day."

"Sounds bad," she said, trying to reconcile this calm, capable man with some wild-eyed version of him.

"It was, and I made all these noises about going back to the army, because it was the only place I knew where I felt normal." Abel shook his head. "Dad told me it didn't matter where I went. I was always going to be angry."

"You don't seem angry."

"Yeah. Thanks, therapy."

She glanced away, attempting to hide her reaction to his honesty. She couldn't imagine anyone she knew admitting they'd gone to therapy. Another Wright-family thing, maybe.

"I'm just saying, if you leave, Hope, are you going to be any safer? Like, is there someplace out there that's magically going to make all the stuff you're running from go away?"

She didn't say anything, because the answer was obvious.

"Elk Falls and The Orchard House are better places than most," he said.

Their eyes caught and the moment stretched, full of bugs and sunlight.

Interest and attraction sparked and sputtered in the darkness that had been inside of her for so long, she'd grown used to feeling nothing. How long since she'd wanted someone? Tink's father, certainly, that mad dash into lust that had started so sweet and gone so wrong. Daniel, no. Whatever she had felt for him had not been attraction, had not been this sudden heated awareness.

It felt so pure, this feeling.

"Can I ask you something?" Abel looked away, became very focused on unwinding the paper from around his waffle cone. He twisted the cone one way, pulled the paper another, the small muscles in his arm flexing and relaxing as he went.

"Shoot," she said.

"The guy that did that to your eye—" She went so still her heart might have stopped beating. "Never mind," he said. "It's none of my business."

"No," she said. "What's your question?"

"Was it Tink's dad?"

"No. God, no. Tony and I dated in high school. He was two years older than me and when I got pregnant he joined the army."

"Yikes."

"At the time it really didn't seem like he was trying to get away from being a father or whatever," she laughed. "In hindsight, though, it's pretty obvious that he was getting the hell out of Dodge."

"I'm sorry."

"Nothing to be sorry for. We tried for a while. He wrote letters and I sent pictures. But over time it just seemed like work and not at all like love."

She'd been young enough and naive enough to think that love didn't come with work. That if it was love, it should be easy. She knew better now. Funny, the auxiliary lessons of motherhood.

"So if it wasn't Tink's dad, who was it? Who hurt you?"

"He was..." She bit her lip and chose her words carefully. "A very bad mistake I made."

"Where is he?"

"I don't know." That was the truth that really scared her.

"Well, if you find out, tell me, would you? I'd like a few minutes with him."

✢ PEG ✢

The day was done. The work over. Abel and the girls were still gone, so the house was empty. Just the way she liked it.

Except she didn't right now. She didn't like it at all. The house felt too big. Quiet. Like she was rattling around inside of it in a bunch of broken pieces.

Somehow in the days the girls had been here, she'd gotten used to them. To the shoes at the back door and the sound of Tink's footsteps coming down the stairs. Hope's raspy voice in the morning as she asked for more coffee.

They were little things, but it was always the little things that rubbed a person raw. That hurt the most.

How she missed the sound of Hank's snoring, when she'd despaired of it for years, and the way he'd come in at the end of day with something from that garden of his, and she would have to fawn and fuss like she'd never seen an eggplant before.

They'd been real good eggplants, though.

Peg wiped off her neck and chest, bits of leaves and tiny parts of branches and twigs stuck to her skin. Little black-flies, attracted to the salt of her sweat, trapped there. The farm was all over her, seeping down into her skin. It felt like if she stood still too long, she might look down and see a vine creeping up her leg.

A shower, she thought. *You just need a cool shower and a tomato sandwich and everything will be fine.*

She opened the door to her room and stood in the entry-way. Normally she kept the doors open, and the breeze cleared out all the ghosts and the smell of the lotion she used on her

hands and feet before going to bed. But since the girls had arrived, she'd kept the room shut up tight.

Once her father's office, the room was large, with a door
that led outside to the remains of a narrow yellowed path cut
through the grass, the path that Hank used to take to the garden. Her bed was in the corner, messy and unmade, and she
had a recliner and a lamp nearby. The old sewing box was full
of the photographs she'd taken off the wall, too, the night Hope
and Tink had showed up. Pictures she didn't want Hope to see.

She'd already shown her the old one of Denise before she
left the second time. But there were others. Pictures of Hope
at the beach, a white stripe of sunscreen on her nose. Hope
and Hank on the tractor. Peg with Hope in her arms, one of
the Nelsons at their feet. Hope as a baby wearing a bib covered in mashed bananas.

What she couldn't hide was the wall with the growth chart
beside the door to outside. The careful lines, pencil and pen,
drawn over a growing child's head, the dates next to it. Of
course because Hank was Hank, the growth chart he'd made
took up a whole wall, with little handprints to go with the
height markings. *I need to paint over it*, she thought for perhaps
the millionth time. But she wouldn't. She knew she wouldn't.
It was one thing to pretend it wasn't there; it was another to
erase it like it had never happened.

The wall closest to her was filled with bookshelves, old farm
records and her father's books, moldering *National Geographic*
magazines. When they thought Denise was going to come to
the farm to stay, Hank had split the big room upstairs back
into two bedrooms and turned her father's office into their
bedroom. It was never supposed to be permanent, sleeping
among all her father's old magazines and books. But then Denise had left. And then Hank had left. And this was just how
she lived now.

Suddenly it seemed so outrageous that she'd left the magazines and books, that she'd been sleeping in the room with the disapproving ghosts of her father lingering in the corners. She'd gotten rid of his desk and that big chair, but those books…

She dragged in the big plastic garbage bin from the kitchen and started to throw away the old books and magazines, feeling not at all better with every handful. Sweat was running down her back, over her face. She was dizzy and dry-mouthed, but she kept tossing until the garbage was piled high and only her things were left.

Her mother's jewelry box.

The ratty stuffed owl with the button eyes and the patchwork feathers made of red calico and velvet.

Since Hope and Tink had arrived at her door, she'd warded off the shame, crushing and all-consuming. But now she felt her arms growing weak against it. Maybe she deserved this room. She deserved the ghost of her father, the mural she couldn't cover up.

She started to put the old magazines back. The books, bibles and theology, *Farmers' Almanacs*, they all went back into their spots on the shelves, and with each one in place she felt better. The shame put away again. Her arms strong again.

Peg didn't want to think about why, but there was something about her father's mistakes and great cruelty that made her own feel bearable. He'd been an awful parent. Mean and miserly. She was just a coward.

The books and the owl sat side by side on the shelves. The Wright family legacy.

⇥ HOPE ⇤

The next morning started wrong. Peg was in a bad mood, and Tink was hurt by Peg's bad mood. Hope tripped over

Nelson and accidentally broke a coffee cup, which made Peg sigh heavily and stomp out the squeaky screen door.

In the orchard things got even worse. One of the nets that covered the unharvested trees got blown off in the night. The nets protected the ripe fruit from the birds, and without it, they had one big cherry-eating party. One half of a tree had been picked clean, and the other half had been aggressively pooped on. It wasn't pretty.

Peg and Abel stood beside that half-eaten, pooped-on tree like it was a funeral.

"How much do you think this is going to cost us?" Peg asked, defeated.

"Too damn much," Abel muttered.

But that wasn't the end of it. Once everyone started in the orchard, the shaker broke down every ten minutes with whining and a smoky smell. Abel would work some kind of magic, but it would only last a few minutes and then the cycle would repeat.

"I think that's all we're going to get for today," Abel finally said, turning away from the shaker machine like a parent walking away from a child pushing their very last button.

Tink and Peg were at the end of the row of trees, circling the other tractor and bringing it back around, and so for the moment it was just Hope and Abel, staring down at the silent machinery.

Abel was...very un-Abel today. The normally unflappable and outrageously capable guy was angry. There was no blaming him, he was having a shit day, but the charge around him was electric.

"What are you going to do with it?" she asked.

"Drive it into the lake?" he joked, but not really. "I need to take it apart, and that will take the rest of the day."

"I had no idea the cherry business was such an emotional roller coaster."

A gruff laugh broke his scowl, and she was glad she could give him that. It lifted her heart up higher in her chest.

Abel rubbed a hand up over his beard stubble and into his hair. "Jesus," he said with the kind of sound people made when what they really wanted to do was scream or cry. "What have I done? I mean...who gets out of the army and buys a goddamned orchard?" He said something in Spanish, and her Spanish wasn't great, but she knew every curse word he'd muttered.

"How can I help?" It wasn't just a polite offer. She did want to help. She'd been breaking her back helping make this season successful, but more than that, she couldn't stand by and watch as it got derailed while knowing the real consequences for Abel and Peg.

He shook his head. "Never mind. We'll figure it out."

"Figure what out?"

"It's too small a load for the processing plant. I guess we could get some of the cherries we did harvest and deliver them in town."

"Peg doesn't go into town," Hope said.

"I know. I'll do it."

The sound of Peg and Tink's tractor preceded them as they made their way back into the orchard. Peg cut the engine, and Tink hopped off the running board where she'd been standing, holding on to the back of Peg's driver's seat like she'd been riding tractors her whole life.

"No luck on the shaker?" Peg asked.

Abel shook his head. "I need to take it apart. Hopefully I can get it up and running for tomorrow."

"That's gonna put us behind."

And that was when Hope did it. She decided not to be afraid. Or maybe to be less afraid.

"We'll take the cherries into town. Me and Tink," Hope said, trying to be helpful.

Tink looked happy at the news even as Hope's stomach tied itself into a bow. She could feel Abel's gaze on the side of her face where the bruise was turning yellow.

"Hope," Abel said. "You don't have to."

"Why are you trying to talk her out of it?" Peg asked, wiping her neck with the back of her hand. "You can fix the shaker and they can deliver the cherries. Seems win–win," Peg said. "Come on, Tink. Let's go clean up." She got back up on the tractor, and Tink jumped onto her spot on the riding board like some kind of diminutive sidekick, and the two took off again.

"So what…what do we do with all this fruit?" Hope asked, looking down at the mountains of half-eaten and rotting cherries that had come from the bird-ransacked tree.

"Leave it for now," Abel said, glancing up from the engine, a new streak of grease across his chin. "We'll rake it up after harvest so we don't get rot."

"Is that how it works? Rot prevention?"

"Yeah," he said, glancing again at her over his shoulder. "You gotta clean shit up or it will all go bad."

"Here's the key to the truck," Peg said, coming back into the barn with a blue foam fob that said First National Bank of Elk Falls.

It all seemed very simple: they were supposed to take the truck and drop off bags of cherries at the three fruit stands Peg and Abel had set up around town: one out by the highway, another down by the beach and the third right on the edge of the cute shopping area in the parking lot of a liquor store.

"We just leave everything?" she asked.

"There's a money box," Peg said. "People pay what they can."

Hope shook her head. "We leave the cherries and a box of money and hope no one steals them?"

"How many times have we been robbed?" Peg asked Abel.

"Never."

"You've got to be kidding me," Hope said, and Peg shrugged.

"Some people might not spend the recommended amount, but most people are honest."

There was simply no way this worked. *Most people are honest.* Were they delusional? The shop where Mom did hair and the books had been broken into three times. Mom's apartment on Euclid had bars on its windows, and Hope refused to live on the ground floor of any apartment building so people couldn't climb in her windows at night.

"The signs are up?" Peg asked Abel.

"I didn't take them down after last cherry season," he said.

Peg scowled and he shrugged. "You could have done it anytime," he said.

"Leave ten bags with each of the stands. More if there's a line," Peg said to Hope.

"A line? There might be a line?"

"Sometimes. Take five into the pharmacy."

"The pharmacy?"

"Yeah. Carole sells them in her side of the store. But if anyone stops you while you're driving around and asks for some, take them out of her stash."

Was there some kind of wild demand for cherries that Hope just didn't know about? These cherries were good, but waiting in line for them seemed extreme.

"Okay, and the rest?"

"Swafiya, at the bakery. Now, it doesn't look like a bakery. It's a commercial thing she does and sells her stuff wholesale. I got it all written down."

Peg handed her a piece of lined paper torn out of a little notebook. There was a frayed edge across the top.

"I don't..." Hope stopped because she didn't want to sound scared or in any way ungrateful.

"Hope," Abel said once again. "You don't have to do this."

"What's the problem?" Peg asked, looking from Abel to Hope.

"Why don't *you* drop the cherries in town?" Abel asked Peg. "If it's all no big deal."

"What are you getting mad at me for?" Peg asked.

"It's fine," Hope said with a laugh because that was what she did when things got unbearably tense. "It's totally fine."

Twelve

➜ HOPE ←

Ten minutes later they were in the big pickup truck with the cherries in the back. Tink clutched a hand-drawn map with x's to show where the stands, the bakery and the pharmacy were located. Hope clutched her courage in one hand and her fear in the other.

"Tink," she said. "This is going to sound ridiculous, but I'm serious. Don't talk to anyone."

Driving into town, Hope noticed a wooden sign on the side of the road that she hadn't seen the day she'd come into town with Tink. A series of them actually.

"Sweet cherries," the first one said.

"Ten dollars a bag," said the second.

"Washed," said the third.

She pulled into the sandy parking area of the first stand, by the beach. By the time they got out of the truck, there were two cars parked behind them and a group of mothers in swimsuit cover-ups holding toddlers by the hand.

"These Peg's cherries?" one of the drivers asked.

In an old baseball cap she found under the bench seat and her big sunglasses, Hope was practically invisible, but it was still hard to force out the word. "Yep."

"Two pounds," the driver said, holding out a twenty-dollar bill without leaving his car.

Hope wanted to make him wait a little, because she didn't like his bossy tone and the lack of a *please*, but Tink bounded right over, two bags of cherries in her arms. The guy grinned and gave her an extra dollar, and Tink turned to Hope with wide eyes and an open mouth, clutching that dollar as the guy left.

"Give me the twenty," Hope said. "The one is all yours."

By the time they had gotten to the stand in the liquor store parking lot, there were already cars waiting, people milling about. When they drove up, people actually cheered.

They were good cherries, but this seemed ridiculous.

Tink hopped into action, handing out cherries and taking money, lingering a little when people didn't catch on to the tip part of the program.

"The cherries are back!" cried a woman with long black braids and some serious workout gear. She'd arrived at the parking lot with a group of women who looked like they were power walking across town.

"Abel made noises last year about selling apples at these stands in the fall. Is he still thinking of doing that?"

"I...don't..."

"And is he planning on selling them himself?" one woman asked in a very dirty-bird fashion. The others were divided between rolling their eyes and laughing into the water bottles they were handing around.

"I don't know what the plans are," Hope said, keeping much of her body averted. This group of women seemed like the kind who might want to know her name just to know it, the kind who would remember her, no matter how hard she tried to be forgettable. "I'm just delivering cherries."

"Well, we appreciate the cherries," the woman with the braids said, her eyes seeming to take stock of everything about Hope, especially the green-and-yellow tendril of bruise slipping down past her sunglasses.

The group parted and Hope found Tink standing over by an SUV, where a woman with a notebook in her hand and camera around her neck was talking to her. Hope broke the land-speed record getting over there.

"Can I help you?" she asked, taking Tink by the shoulder and pushing her back a little as she stepped between them, wondering with an adrenaline-spiked fear what she was going to have to do to get that camera. She was aware this could backfire, alarming this woman and making her and Tink memorable for no good reason.

"Yeah, I'm with the *Elk Falls News-Leader* and I was just taking a picture of your beautiful daughter."

"Why?"

"Just a little feature on cherry season for the front page—"

"No picture," Hope said, shaking her head.

"It's a tiny little paper," the woman said, like it was just between them. "I mean, four people will see it."

"It will be online, won't it?" Hope asked.

"Well, sure, but still—"

"No picture. Please."

Something in Hope's shaking voice must have finally registered, and she nodded. "Here," she said. "You can watch me delete them." She lifted the camera and called up the five images of Tink. They were good photos. Cherries and freckles and a little girl with blond hair.

Hope wondered if everyone else could see the fear in her eyes.

"Thank you," Hope said.

"No problem. I hope…ah…" She looked between Tink and Hope. "I hope you have a good day."

When the woman was gone, Hope turned on Tink. "You can't do that, Tink. You know that." She blew out a long breath and put her hand to her nose, squeezing on the bridge, pulling the skin taut across her face so her bruise hurt. "I need you, Tink. I need your help on stuff like that. I can't…"

Protect us on our own. That was what she'd been about to say. But she hadn't protected them at all. Tink glared at her like she was thinking the same thing.

Back in the truck, they bounced down Main Street and found parking in front of the building that was supposed to be a bakery.

Tink opened the door and was out of the truck in a flash, pounding on a heavy metal door until it seemed to rattle the whole building. Hope scrambled out after her.

"Wow, kid, you don't need to knock the place down," she breathed, horrified and impressed at the same time.

But it did the trick and the metal door was thrown open by a woman wiping her hands on a white apron, spotted with flour and chocolate. She wore a long-sleeved gray T-shirt and a bright blue-and-yellow hijab. "Hi," she said with a bright smile. "Is this my cherry delivery?"

Hope was distracted for a second by the smells wafting from the door behind her. Sugar and baking bread and butter and all the good things.

"We…ah, we are. I mean…we have your cherries."

"Excellent," she said, eyes wide. "I'll help you bring them in."

The baker put a wedge in the door and walked out to the truck to help.

"Oh, look at them! How many bags do I get?" she asked like it was Christmas morning.

"I have thirty for you."

"Wonderful," she said. "More tomorrow?"

"I don't… I'm not sure," Hope said, again looking away, wanting to be unmemorable.

They loaded up their arms with as many bags as they could carry, and it still took two trips into the back room of the bakery. Inside, the stainless-steel countertops and tables seemed to be covered in a fine dusting of flour and sugar. Tink pressed her finger to the sugar and slipped it into her mouth, glanced around to check the baker wasn't watching and did it again.

"You'll give this to Peg? Or Abel? I'm never sure who to pay?" the woman said, giving Hope a check. "And remind them I need an invoice. I know they hate it, but I need something for my books."

"I'll tell them."

She really didn't know when Peg or Abel would have the time for invoicing. It wasn't a hard job, but it could be time consuming if they didn't have any systems in place. And she kinda doubted they had systems in place.

"I'm Swafiya," the woman said, holding out her hand.

Hope didn't move. No one had asked her name all day, just the way she wanted it. But she couldn't avoid it now. "I'm Hope," she said quietly and a little mumbly, then immediately wished she'd thought of an alias. Sue. Sue would have been good. Jane?

"Nice to meet you, Hope. And you?" She turned to Tink.

"My daughter… Jenny."

Tink raised her eyebrows, but of course said nothing.

"Are you working with Abel and Peg for cherry season, or the whole summer? I've been telling them for ages they need to get some help. It's too much for just the two of them." She said it with such an openly intimate tone that Hope had to stop herself from agreeing and telling her how hard they were working and that there was still tons more to do. Then maybe Swafiya would offer them tea or one of those cookies over on the counter, and Hope would sit down on that floury stool and drink tea and eat a cookie and talk, the way women did on television shows and in books.

But not only did she not know *how* to do that, she couldn't. She was supposed to be lying low. Making friends was the opposite of that.

"We're just passing through," Hope said quickly. "And we need to deliver some more cherries to the pharmacy."

"Sure!" Swafiya said. "Of course. Would you like to take something with you? My strawberry-pistachio brioche is just out of the oven." Tink nodded with such enthusiasm Swafiya laughed and clapped her hands together. "A girl after my own heart." She pulled one from the cooling racks, a golden yellow loaf, round and fat and glistening. "I brush the outside with rosewater syrup and butter," Swafiya said and held the loaf out for Tink to smell, which she did—rapturously—accepting the loaf of bread like it was a gift from a queen.

"Thank you," Hope said, and hustled her daughter out the door.

Once they were in the car, Tink tore the bread in half. It was creamy and flakey with a thick river of pink and green throughout.

"Wow, it's beautiful," Hope said, and Tink took one of the chunks and handed it to her.

Stunned by the gesture, for a moment Hope just stared

at the steam rising from the fragrant and beautiful brioche. Tink pushed it forward, until Hope felt the heat of it against her arm.

"Yeah," she finally said. "Thanks, Tink."

Tink took a bite of the bread. She made a face, a couple of them. Skeptical and then happy and then skeptical again.

Hope laughed. "Is it good, or not? I can't tell by your face."

Tink took another bite, positioning the bread so she got the most of what she wanted, which seemed to be the sweet glaze on the top.

Hope took her own bite and froze at the unexpectedness of its flavors and textures. The bright tang of the strawberries tempered by the rich ground nuts, and then the sweet hint of roses. It was like nothing she'd ever eaten before, and absolutely perfect.

They gobbled up the loaf, and for once Hope ate her full share, trying not to feel guilty about it as they both sat there licking their fingers.

"We're gonna need more of that bread," Hope said, and Tink emphatically agreed.

Hope started the car and drove down the main street toward the next stop, the pharmacy and Carole's store. As they drove by the liquor store parking lot, Tink pointed out the window at the cherry stand; the green shelf where there had been a small stack of bagged cherries was now bare, big flakes of green gone to reveal the yellow wood.

"Huh," Hope said. "Let's go see if anyone left any money."

They jumped out of the truck, leaving it running with the doors open. Inside the cashbox she found a bunch of crumpled-up ten-dollar bills. A couple of fives. One twenty.

The exact right amount for the cherries.

"Wow," she said, turning to Tink with the wadded-up bills in her hand. "Maybe people aren't as bad as we thought."

✦TINK✦

That was it. She was never going to eat again, just so she could keep that nutty strawberry taste in her mouth. And when she was forced out of starvation, she would only go back to that bakery and get the same bread. She had twenty bucks in her pocket in tips. That could probably buy a million loaves of that stuff. She'd keep one loaf under her bed and another in the back seat of the car just in case they had to up and leave in the middle of the night again. She'd crumble that bread up and keep it in her pockets. She'd give a loaf to Peg. And another one to Abel. Abel would love that bread.

Tink watched her mom out of the corner of her eye, thinking about Abel and Mom on that beach, eating ice cream.

On the weekends Mom and Tink used to stay up late, eat Sour Patch Kids and watch old horror movies. She liked the old ones because they really weren't that scary. The blood looked fake and the special effects were terrible. So it was scary but not *scary*.

"It doesn't even *seem* real," she would say to Mom when Mom would jump or hide her face in a pillow.

One of the old movies was about people being replaced by aliens. The aliens looked the same, did all the same stuff in their life, but they *weren't* the same, like zombies without the decomposing flesh and brain eating. With Daniel, Mom had been like that. Herself, but not. Saying "yes, Daniel" and "no, Daniel" without ever really hearing what he was saying. Or seeing what he was doing.

And that had been *scary* scary.

Thank god that version of Mom was gone.

The everything-is-fine version of Mom was going away, too. Which was good. She just didn't know what new version was coming next.

She wondered if Mom knew Abel liked her. She was always a little dumb about that stuff. DeeDee would tease her about it until she got super upset.

The pharmacy was in the middle of the busiest block on Main Street. There was no parking in front so Mom went around the block, turning the steering wheel so hard the tiny little muscles in her arms popped up. Behind those buildings was a big parking lot and, across the road, a school.

Elk River Elementary School. It looked like any other school, but in the playground off to the side, surrounded by a ginormous field, was a spaceship.

"Look at that, Tink," Mom said. "That's got to be the coolest playground I've ever seen."

It was just a spaceship, and maybe when she was eight she would have loved it. But she was ten now.

"What do you think—"

Tink opened her door to get out, but Mom grabbed her hand. Tink froze, trying not to feel her mom's calluses and the way she gripped her fingers, but unable to feel anything else.

"I miss the sound of your voice, Tink. And I'm scared I'll never hear it again. Please, Tink." Mom's voice broke. "It feels like you're slipping away from me and I don't know how to fix this."

Tink didn't know what to say. Sometimes she forgot why she stopped talking, but then she would remember how she'd screamed no as loud as she could, using every muscle in her body.

And still her mom had let Daniel in the car.

Tink pulled her hand away and climbed out of the truck.

They walked around to the front of the building. When the door opened it made a bell chime and then another one and then another, until it seemed like there was a bell ringing in that place for, like, five minutes. And inside was really strange.

The store was cut straight in half. One half was a pharmacy, with rows of toothpaste and tampons and medicine to make your snot go away. The floor was white and the walls were white, and there was a man sitting behind a window wearing a white coat.

The other half of the store was like an…explosion. A holiday explosion. There were Christmas ornaments and those skeletons people put in their yards on Halloween that seemed like they were rising from graves. There were Easter bunnies and flags with trees on them that said, "Don't forget Arbor Day."

In the back was a coffee shop. An old lady stood back there with long gray hair and glasses. She looked like that witch in *The Princess Bride.* Another movie she and Mom would stay up late to watch.

"Can I help you?" A different woman came out from behind the window on the pharmacy side of the store. She was real tall and pretty with long blond hair. She was carrying a baby and, as she stepped out of that little back room, it seemed like twenty kids came out after her. Cannonballs of kids in shorts and skirts. Kids Tink's age and some younger.

They stopped when they got to the edge of the white half of the room and stared at Tink. There weren't twenty. There were three. Two girls and one boy. The baby still in his mom's arms. Tink hadn't seen other kids in…ages. Like weeks and weeks. And usually she wouldn't care. She didn't like other kids. They wanted to do dumb things like play with dolls or watch shows about teenage vampires who made out all the time.

But it had been so long.

Before she could stop it, she had that feeling, the same one she had at the beginning of every school year, or the first day of every camp, or when a new family moved into the apartment building. *Maybe*, she thought. *Maybe these kids will like me.*

They never did, but it didn't stop her from hoping.

She wanted to ask them about that spaceship in the school-yard, the witch in the back and the way the store was divided up.

"Hey," said the oldest girl, who looked like she'd recently fallen off her bike and caught herself with her face. Her whole chin was one thick scab. Tink had had one like that when she fell off DeeDee's porch and scraped her knee on the concrete. It had itched. Tink wanted to ask the girl if her chin itched.

"I've never seen you," the boy said.

"Where are you from?" the other girl asked.

Instead of answering, Tink walked toward the back of the store, staying on the wild side of things. The kids followed but on the opposite side of the line down the middle of the store, made by the different floors, like they weren't allowed to cross from the white tile onto the wood.

Mom had said no talking. Tink had done that for, like, weeks and *now* it was hard. Figured.

She turned to look at the kids and took a sidestep toward the coffee shop. The kids did the same. Their toes pressed up tight against the edge of that white tile floor.

"Don't tease them," the old woman said from the back of the store. "They're not allowed over here."

"Nana!" the oldest one cried. "We promised."

"Yeah, you promise all the time and it never works. You stay on that side of the store until you're twenty-five. That's the rule. Is there something you need help with, honey?" she asked Tink.

Mom came up from behind her and put a hand on Tink's shoulder.

"We're here delivering cherries," Mom said, and the old woman did a double take, like Mom was a ghost.

"Holy shit," the woman said. "Hope?"

Thirteen

→TINK←

The old lady was weird and she swore around kids. Tink liked her already.

Mom blinked. "I'm Hope. Do I know you?"

"My god," the old lady said, her hand to her chest. "I can't believe it. You did know me, when you were little."

"Really?" Mom cried. "I'm sorry, I don't remember."

"Well, you were pretty young. You both were," the old lady said, pointing to the blonde woman. "You two had your first birthdays together."

Mom and the fancy lady looked at each other.

"In fact…" The old lady went back behind the counter and started pulling things off shelves, rummaging around until she found an old gold picture frame. "Look!"

Mom and the fancy lady walked over to the counter. The kids stayed stuck right where they were, their toes pressed up against the wood planks of the floor.

"Oh my gosh," Mom said.

Tink crept up to Mom's side, and she tilted the picture down so Tink could see it. Two women sat on a red blanket with babies in their laps. The babies were covered in chocolate cake and frosting. They even had it in their hair. The two moms were laughing, squeezing those babies close.

It took her a second to realize one of those moms was Aunt Peg.

"That's me," Mom said, pointing at the baby in a red dress.

"And that's me," the fancy lady said and stuck her hand out to shake. "I'm Janice."

"Hope."

They shook hands, smiling at each other.

"I'm Carole," the older lady said, and there were more handshakes.

"Sorry I can't stay and catch up," Janice said. "I mean, I'm guessing a lot has changed since the last time I saw you."

Mom laughed. "Well, I still eat chocolate cake with my hands, so not that much." She had made a joke. An actual joke. Everyone laughed.

"Are you living out at the farm?" Janice asked.

"Peg must just be…" Carole shook her head, like she couldn't figure it out. "Over the moon."

"Well, over the moon might be a stretch. And we're just visiting."

"I'm sorry, I really do have to run," Janice said after checking her watch. "We should catch up sometime."

"Sure!" Mom said in that voice that Tink knew meant "absolutely no way."

"I'll help you unload the cherries," Carole said, leading Mom out a back door to the truck.

"Let's go, kids," Janice said.

The younger girl and the boy took off after their mom, who

went out the front door and set off all those chimes again. But Tink and the oldest girl stayed put.

"I'm Avery," she said.

Avery, Tink thought, rolling the name around on the back of her tongue. *Avery.*

"What's your name?" Avery asked.

Mom wasn't there to answer for her. She couldn't hear her breaking the rules.

"Tink," she said.

"That's a good name," Avery said.

"So is Avery."

"Avery!" the mom yelled over the chimes.

→ PEG ←

Peg was real busy pretending she wasn't waiting for the girls.

And she was doing it in a rocking chair on the front porch. Which was ridiculous. She never sat out here. The chairs had been uncomfortable when she'd bought them and they were still uncomfortable. Her butt was going numb.

And as if that wasn't enough she knew Abel was in the barn, pretending not to be waiting, too.

Lord, she thought. *What have we come to?*

Finally, the old truck made the turn into the driveway and headed down to the barn. Hope lifted her arm out the window and Peg called herself all kinds of foolish. It was cherry season, there was more work than time and she'd been sitting here answering emails on her phone just so she could see them coming up the road.

In time, the girls walked up from the barn and Nelson put up a big fuss like she'd been dying without that little girl who scowled at her whenever she came over with her tail wagging. They climbed the old steps of the porch, sunburned and a little wilted, and it hit Peg somewhere in her belly how lonely she'd been. Not just alone—alone she could handle. But *lonely*. It was like they'd arrived with a big light that revealed just how dark the shadows in her life were.

"Hey, Peg," Hope said and stopped on the top step. "It just occurred to me, do I call you Aunt Peg?"

"I...I guess I hadn't thought about it."

"Me neither. Aunt Peg," Hope said as if trying it out. She tried it in a terrible British accent, looking down at her daughter like she was trying to make her laugh.

It was an absolute marvel that Hope still had her humor. She reminded Peg of the sunflower growing behind the house in that wilderness of a garden. No reason that flower should flourish among all those weeds.

But maybe no one had told that flower it wasn't supposed to be growing. That it had no business tilting its head toward whatever sun it could find.

"Peg is fine," she said, tired of the fuss. "So, how'd you do?"

"Here," Hope said, pulling tens and twenties from her pockets and handing them over to Peg in tidy stacks. "You were right. No one stole anything and people lined right up for the cherries."

Goodness, Peg thought, looking down at that stack. They hadn't done so well in a long time.

Hope jostled Tink with her elbow. "Cough it up, kid," she said, and Tink rolled her eyes but held out a crumpled five-dollar bill.

"I said she could keep the tips she made," Hope explained. "But she snagged that from the glove box when she thought I wasn't looking."

"Keep it," Peg said. "You earned it." She separated out some twenties, too, and handed them back to Hope.

Hope stared down at that money and then up at Peg. "What's that?"

"I said I'd pay you."

Hope smiled with the half of her mouth that didn't have a cut and Peg could see her warring with her pride. But Peg also knew half the reason they'd stayed this long was because they didn't have a lot of money.

"Take it," Peg said. "You worked hard."

"We did." Hope pushed the money back over to Peg. "And we were glad to help."

Tink looked absolutely appalled. But Peg understood.

"This is from Swafiya at the bakery." Hope took a check from her back pocket and handed it over. "She says she needs an invoice."

Peg sighed. Invoicing was the devil.

"I can help," Hope said. "I was a bookkeeper."

"Was?"

"Am, I guess. I am a bookkeeper. I mean, I went to school for it and everything, but I could probably email some old clients and get recommendations."

Peg needed nothing of the kind. There was a warm, willing body here to take over invoicing. Sold.

"I don't need any recommendations," Peg said and went inside the house. She slipped into her bedroom, making sure to shut the door behind her, grabbed her laptop and stepped back out to the kitchen, where the girls were waiting. "It's all in here. I got a program but everything is really behind."

Peg held it out to her, the cord falling on the floor with a *thunk*.

"I should tell you," Hope said. "I don't know how long we're staying."

"So, you're leaving?" Peg asked, sounding gruffer than she intended.

Hope looked down at Tink. "Can you run upstairs?" she asked.

Of course the girl had the good sense to shake her head no.

"You don't like it here?"

"No. We do."

"Is it the work? Because you don't—"

"It's not the work. I'm just… I don't know if it's safe. For us. Or you."

"Well, it's my farm," she said, sounding like her father. "I guess I know if it's safe."

"Peg," Hope whispered, clearly miserable.

What's wrong with here? Peg thought. *What's wrong with this farm? And this land. The work. Me. What's wrong with me?*

But she swallowed those words right back down and clutched the laptop to her chest. "Well, then, I guess, there's no sense in giving you this—"

"I'm happy to take a look," Hope said. "I can sort things out and get a couple of systems in place. Make it easier for you, you know…when we leave."

"And when will that be?"

"End of cherry season. I suppose."

Tink was glaring at her like she would start a fire in her hair, if she could.

"Peg," Hope said, reaching for the computer. "Let me help. While I can. I really want to."

Well, Peg wasn't going to say no to that just out of spite, so she handed over the ancient laptop. Hope scooped up the cord and draped it over her arm.

"How was it?" Peg asked. "You know…in general." She'd felt bad after they left, having been blind to Hope's reluctance to go out in public. Abel had explained it all to her and then walked away, giving her the impression both that he thought Peg was an idiot and that the man was starting to care for Hope.

I wonder if he knows she's going to leave.

"I met Carole today. And Janice," Hope said, glancing up at Peg and then away, as if she were trying to hide how eager she was to talk about this. How curious.

"I heard Janice was in town," Peg said carefully.

"Carole showed me a picture of the four of us celebrating first birthdays."

Peg held herself very still as if the floor might break out from under her if she so much as breathed. *Of course she did.*

"It looked like fun," Hope said.

"It was." It had been one of the most beautiful days of her life.

"So, that's when I was here? When I was one?"

Peg nodded.

"Did my mom take the picture?"

This was the moment she could tell Hope the truth. She *should* tell Hope the truth. But when she looked up into Hope's face, damaged but still so beautiful, so kind and soft and, despite knowing better, open, Peg could see the pain the truth would cause.

In that moment, lying wasn't just about protecting herself from the pain of drudging up all those old memories, of revealing the mistakes she had made. It was also about protecting Hope. The truth would hurt this girl who had been hurt enough. And to what end, really? Who was served by the truth? And soon she would drive away from The Orchard House, and life would go on.

"Yep," Peg said. "Your mom took the picture."

Hank had.

"You and Carole look like you were really good friends," Hope said.

"I suppose we were."

"What happened?"

"I don't know, what usually happens? You get busy. You fall out of touch."

"You should get back in touch," Hope said. "She seems like a really fun lady."

She'd been *so* much fun. The life of every party. The kind of person who could make Peg laugh till she worried she might pee.

"Have you had dinner?" Hope asked. "It smells good."

There was a casserole in the oven and she'd been waiting for them to come back to eat it.

"Just finished," she lied.

Fourteen

➤TINK➤

Tink woke up the next day pretty excited about the easy life in the cherry-stand business. And so it was a real disappointment when Abel got the harvester to work and they spent the next two days working their butts off in the orchard instead.

But then the harvester started smoking again on the morning of the third day and finally broke down before lunch. Tink felt bad being so happy when Abel looked so upset.

It was great to be in the truck with air-conditioning and a radio and not working in the orchard with the bees and the loud shaker. But the best part was the money. Two stands down and she had another ten bucks in her pocket.

DeeDee used to write her checks every year on her birthday. A dollar for every year she was alive. DeeDee would give her other money, too, like a bunch of change to get candy at the CVS on the corner. But a pocket full of quarters didn't feel anything like the fat roll of ones.

The crunch of car tires over gravel announced the arrival of another customer at the stand by the beach, and Tink grabbed a bag of cherries so she could run it over to where the blue sedan idled a few feet from the stand.

But Mom put a hand on her shoulder, and when Tink tried to shrug it off, she held on tight. Tink glared up at her, only to catch her staring at the blue car. She'd gone real pale. Totally white.

Tink looked back over at the car. It had Missouri license plates, and the sunlight hit the windshield just right so they couldn't see who was driving.

Tink's stomach went cold and her head got fuzzy.

Was it him?

Just then a woman in a green dress stepped out of the driver's-side door. "Do you have any cherries left?" she shouted over the seagulls.

Mom released Tink's shoulder. "Sure," she said with a wobbly kind of chuckle, and Tink walked over, feeling like she suddenly had to go to the bathroom. Bad.

They went to the bakery next, and Swafiya had, like, seven million cherry things happening in her kitchen, including something called chutney that she made Mom try. Mom didn't like it even though she said she did. For such a liar she was actually pretty bad at it.

Tink crossed her legs and made a wide-eyed I-need-to-go-pee expression to her mom, who caught on pretty quick.

"Can Jenny use the bathroom?"

Right. She was Jenny here. She hated that name.

"Sure. Of course." Swafiya was wearing a pretty pink hijab today, but when she turned toward Tink to let her into the bathroom or whatever, her apron looked like it was covered in blood. Tink swallowed and stepped back.

Swafiya stopped, too. "You…?" She looked over at Mom. "You all right?"

"It's from the cherries," Mom said to Tink. "It's just juice."

Yeah. Right. Of course. Tink knew that. Cherries. For such little things, they sure bled a lot.

Sometimes she remembered Daniel on the floor of the hotel room, even when she didn't want to. His blood hadn't looked *anything* like that fake stuff in the old horror movies.

"Here," Swafiya said, and quickly turned on a light in the tiny bathroom between the kitchen and the store part of the bakery.

Tink shut the door and then locked it. She stared at herself in the mirror and wondered what she would even say to Mom, if she did talk to her.

They used to talk all the time, nonstop. DeeDee would get angry and tell them to shut up. But it just seemed like there was so much she wanted to tell her mom—about the new kid in her class with braces and Mr. Borsen's cat with one eye and that dream she'd had where they'd been flying and the stars got tangled in their hair.

Now, she opened her mouth and…there was nothing there.

Mom and Swafiya chatted on the other side of the door, and Tink could hear Swafiya say that once a year, for about three weeks, she went all in on cherries and sold things in bakeries all over the state and on the internet.

"Hey, Swafiya—" a man's voice said.

Tink froze in the bathroom. She even stopped peeing.

"Hope, this is my husband, Matt," she heard Swafiya say.

Tink finished, pulled up her pants and crept up to the door. Carefully, not making a sound, she unlocked it and slowly eased it open just a tiny crack.

Mom got real mad about eavesdropping, but Tink had survived her being mad before. And sometimes a little eavesdropping was the only way to find out what was going on.

"Nice to meet you, Matt. Sorry," Mom said, talking to a tall man with salt-and-pepper hair and glasses, lifting the things she was carrying in her arms as a reason not to shake his hand. Mom was good at that, not touching people she didn't want to touch.

"No problem." Matt gave her a funny wave. He seemed like a nice guy, but that was how the not-nice guys got you. Daniel had seemed nice, too. *Don't trust him, Mom.* "Nice to meet you, too."

"She's delivering cherries," Swafiya said. "And Matt is taking some time off work to deliver pies. There's a joke in there somewhere but I can't think of it."

"What do you do when you're not delivering pies?" Mom asked. She was real chatty today. Mom got chatty when she was nervous. That blue car had rattled them both.

"I'm a lawyer," Matt said. "Family law, but in a town this size you end up doing a lot of things."

"Family law?"

"Yeah, wills and inheritance. A little real estate. Some custody stuff."

"Orders of protection," Swafiya said.

Mom pushed her glasses up high on her face.

"Yep," Matt said slowly. "I do a lot of that."

"Just making sure women are protected legally from people who would hurt them," Swafiya said.

"I know what an order of protection is," Mom said, sharp. If Tink talked to someone like that Mom would say she was being rude.

Orders of protection. Tink liked the way that sounded. Serious and *for real.*

The conversation petered out and Matt cleared his throat. "So, honey, have I got everything you need me to take?"

"Yep!" Swafiya said. She clapped her hands and flour puffed off them.

"Then I'm off," Matt said. He gave Swafiya a kiss on the cheek, waved goodbye to Mom and walked out of the room past the bathroom.

When Tink came out, Swafiya was packaging a shimmering loaf of bread in a bag. "Cherry and chocolate this time," she said with a wink.

Inside the truck, Tink took the bread out of the bag. It was still so warm it hurt her fingers, but she ignored the heat and tore off a huge chunk, releasing steam and the smell of butter and chocolate.

Mom's stomach growled so loud Tink heard it and almost laughed. She handed her some bread.

"Thank you," Mom said and took a bite, chocolate smearing across her upper lip.

"You were eavesdropping in there," Mom said, and Tink shrugged.

"He seemed like a nice guy. Family lawyer," she said quietly.

Order of protection, Tink thought, because she knew Mom was thinking it, too. Serious words and a lawyer man with glasses.

"Do you like it here?" Mom asked.

Tink nodded and handed her a piece of bread.

"We could move to a city. That might be fun. Museums and Starbucks and movie theaters."

Tink shook her head. Those things were okay, but she liked that there was no traffic here. And no neighbors. She liked the way the air smelled. She liked the way her mom was here. Cracking jokes and friendly. Like she used to be.

"Yeah," Mom whispered and put her head back against the seat, like she just couldn't hold it up anymore. "I'm so tired of being scared."

Me, too.

"If I could make it safe for us," Hope asked, her eyes wet, "would you want to stay?"

Tink tore off another piece of bread. A big one, more than half the loaf, thick with chocolate and bright red cherries from Peg and Abel's orchard, cherries they'd helped pick and clean and sort and bag. Cherries they'd delivered to Swafiya so she could make this delicious bread. Tink had never been a part of something so amazing in her entire life.

She handed the bread over to her mom.

"Yeah," Mom breathed. "Me, too."

Mom pulled up in front of the pharmacy/holiday shop, and Tink jumped out, so excited to see if the place was still as weird as it had seemed the other day.

The bell rang over the door as they entered. The kids were there again, the girls with their long hair in perfect slick ponytails. The slickest. And the little boy with his finger up his nose. The baby someplace with his mom. Which was fine. Tink had no use for babies.

The three older kids stood on the tiled side of the floor.

"You've got chocolate all over your face," the boy said and then pointed at the box of stuff she was carrying. "You got any more in there?" He stepped forward to peer in.

Purely as a scientific experiment, Tink stepped deeper into the holiday store, and the boy caught himself on the dividing line, like he'd run into an electric fence.

"You're the girl who doesn't talk," the younger sister said.

In books middle children were always sneaking around unnoticed, because the parents were always too busy with the oldest and youngest. Tink looked forward to studying her habits.

"What's in the box?" the younger sister asked and then, like it wasn't even there, stepped right over the line.

"Maryanne." The mom, Janice, appeared out of nowhere.

She looked extra fancy today with a pretty skirt and high heels. "You know what will happen if she catches you over there."

"Too late." The witch lady, Carole, came up from the back. Her hair was even crazier today, silver, black and gray, all wild around her head. She wore a pair of loose bright yellow pants and a T-shirt that said Fuck The Patriarchy.

Tink gasped with delight at the shirt and looked over at her mom, who stood there like she didn't know what to do.

"Are those for me?" the woman asked, referring to the cherries in Tink's arms.

Mom nodded. "There's more in the truck."

"Well," she said. "Let's go get them."

Mom and Carole stepped out the front door and were back a second later with the cherries.

"Go ahead and take that stuff into the back," Janice said to Tink. "And you guys," she said to the kids. "Go play in the schoolyard."

The kids took off at a run.

"Don't run!" Carole yelled as they burst out the back door.

"You want to go?" Janice asked Tink. "The school is right there."

Her mom would say no, that was for sure. In fact, she could practically feel her saying no from right behind her.

Which might be why she did it.

She took off, and as she hit the door and ran down the stairs, chasing those kids and those slick ponytails across the parking lot and then the street, into the school playground with the spaceship—it was like she was breaking something.

Stretching it so tight that it had no choice but to snap.

➔ HOPE ←

Hope watched Tink run out the door, and if there hadn't been two women watching her, she would have run out, too.

But she was stuck, locked down in some strange place where she didn't want to seem like that overprotective mom, the one who couldn't let her ten-year-old out of her sight.

Even though she had reasons.

"Avery, my oldest, will look after all of them. If you're worried," Janice said.

"I'm not worried," she lied. "Thank you."

Carole came out from a back room with muffins and scones and set the tray down on the counter next to the coffeepot.

"You want a cup of coffee?" Carole asked.

"Don't do it," Janice said. "Your stomach will never be the same."

"Stop your slander," Carole said to her daughter.

"I'd love a cup of coffee," Hope said and pulled out one of the stools. Those tiny thimbles of coffee in the morning with Peg were not enough to get her through a day of cherry season.

Carole poured her a big mug. She smelled like patchouli and cherries and something else…something a little funky beneath it all. "You are the spitting image of Peg when she was your age. The hair's different, but the freckles give you away."

"You guys were good friends?"

Carole nodded. "For a time. A long time actually. We went to school together and she inherited the farm and I inherited this building, and everyone else in this damn town is a fool. So we stuck together."

"You're not friends now?"

Carole pushed away from the counter.

"Sorry," Hope said. "I don't mean to pry."

"No, honey, it's all right," Carole said. "We're two stubborn old ladies, and a long time ago I thought she made a real bad mistake and I said some things I probably shouldn't have."

"Probably?" Janice said. "Saying things you shouldn't have is kind of your thing, Mom."

Carole scowled at her daughter. "But now that I'm old and

wise I can see that she was hurting and I just made things worse. She didn't need my judgment. She needed my support. And I messed that up."

"What was the fight about?" Janice asked. She reached for a muffin and her mother slapped her hand.

"Those are for customers. And you need to stay on your side of the line."

"Not sure if you noticed, Mom," Janice said, "but you don't have any customers."

"What was the fight about?" Hope asked. Peg seemed so alone out there on the farm, choosing to never venture to town and driving so far out of her way just so she wouldn't see anyone she knew.

Carole pursed her lips. "Sorry, honey, that's your aunt's story to tell."

"Did you know my mom?" Hope asked.

"Not very well. Your mom was a little too wild for my taste."

"Oh my god, Mom," Janice said. "Do you even hear yourself?"

"What? She was scary." Carole looked over at Hope with a shrug. "No offense."

"None taken." She smiled thinking about it. "Mom could be a bit…"

All at once it became hard to find a word to describe her mom. Something easy that would make these women smile and understand her to some extent. And what a shame that she felt compelled to do that. That they all did. To classify and categorize each other into roles that everyone could understand. Because it was simpler.

Hope had been overprotected and ignored in equal parts and in unpredictable ways as a kid. She wanted to tell them Denise had been a good mom, the way she had the other day with Peg, even if Hope wasn't entirely sure what she could point to to prove it. But then that felt horrible because Hope herself was such a mess, she had no business judging anyone.

And the truth under all of it was that right now she'd do anything to have a mom. For just a minute. To anchor down one part of her world that was completely out of control.

I want my mom.

Hope put her hand over her face.

"Mom," Janice sighed. "Look at what you did." Janice put her arm around Hope's shoulders and half helped, half pushed her onto one of the stools in front of the coffee counter. "And, yes, I'm stepping over the line, you old bat."

"I'm sorry," Carole said, blinking wide eyes like she didn't understand how they'd gotten there.

"No," Hope said, trying to get them to stop fussing. "It's fine. It's just… My mom… She died a year ago."

"I'm sorry, I didn't know," Carole said.

"I wrote Peg a letter," Hope said, attempting to make a laughing sound. "But I never heard back. The Wright women have a real lack-of-communication thing going."

She lifted the sunglasses carefully to wipe her eyes, trying to keep the fading bruise from showing.

"The sunglasses aren't fooling anyone, honey," Carole said, dry as dirt.

"Yeah," Janice agreed. "You can take them off if you want."

Hope was frozen on the stool. Honestly, who were these women? They were so invasive. She didn't want to take off the sunglasses, thank you very much.

"Here," Carole said, setting a small ginger cookie covered with big chunks of sugar in front of her. Oh, she loved ginger cookies, and Tink hated them, so she could eat this without—

"Are you nuts? Mom!" Janice grabbed the cookie out of Hope's hand, and Carole shrugged. Shaking her head, Janice said, "It's a weed cookie. My mom, in the absence of human emotion, is just trying to get you high. It's how she copes with everything."

Weed cookie? Oh my god. This day.

"Do you want it?" Carole asked.

Sort of. But she shook her head.

"Might help with that eye. Looks like it hurts," Carole said, fishing with real intention.

"No, I better go get Tink. We have a lot of work to do."

"Tink?" Janice asked.

Crap. She was losing the thread all over the place. "Jenny's...ah, nickname."

"How are you liking the farm?" Carole asked. "I helped Peg out with one cherry season when I was younger. Hardest summer of my life. She asked me to come back the next year and I laughed at her."

"It is hard." Hope laughed. "But it's a good hard, you know?"

"That's what Peg always said about it. Too bad you're not sticking around. The old bat could use the help."

That was undeniable. And what was growing more undeniable was how much she would like to stay. Tink, too. Getting her to leave this farm for parts unknown was going to be hard.

Janice nodded and stepped back, giving Hope space to get to her feet.

"I'll walk out there with you," Janice said.

It wasn't much, a walk from the store across the street to the school where their children were playing, but at the moment, threadbare and alone, it felt like more.

"You know," Carole said, "Peg and I had big dreams that you two would be friends."

"Mom, stop being sentimental. It's creepy," Janice said.

"Do me a favor, would you?" Carole said as they walked toward the back door. "Tell Peg I miss her." Carole popped the whole cookie in her mouth and somehow managed to get out, "And if she wants to talk, my number hasn't changed."

Fifteen

→ HOPE ←

That night Hope finally got a moment to open up the bookkeeping. She immediately understood why Peg was so far behind. The old software was glitchy and the spreadsheets were completely out of date, and when she tried to install a new version of the software, the computer locked up.

There were a million easier ways to do this, but she had her doubts that Peg would embrace easier.

Tink walked into their bedroom doing a very suspicious sideways shuffle.

"What's going on, kid?" she asked.

Tink got onto her bed with her back to Hope, awkwardly using only her legs to climb up to her pillows.

A second later Tink hissed.

Hope put aside Peg's laptop and yanked the blankets off her daughter's head, revealing kittens.

"Are you kidding me?" she cried. "You can't bring those cats in your bed. They're outside cats."

That did not persuade Tink one bit, and she kept pushing the kittens under her pillow, or deeper into the folds of the burgundy blanket. They did not suffer this treatment in silence, and from the angry red scratches on her hands, they didn't take it peaceably, either.

"And they probably have fleas. And they're not house trained." Hope looked her defiant, cat-scratched daughter in her narrowed little eyes. "They're gonna poop on your bed, Tink."

That made the ten-year-old pause long enough for Hope to swoop up the kittens. Three of them. A tortoiseshell, a black one with white socks and a calico.

"I'm taking them back to the barn," she said, and Tink threw the covers off her legs like she was going to come with her. "No. Stay here. It's way past your bedtime and we have work in the morning."

Tink fell back on the bed, her face twisted up in that special brand of ten-year-old-girl disgust.

As she walked down the steps, the kittens climbed Hope's shirt and hair. Downstairs was quiet, their hot dog dinner still lingering heavy on the air.

Over hot dogs, watermelon and chips earlier that night, she'd given Peg Carole's message.

"You should call her," Hope had said.

"If she wants to hear my voice she knows my number."

And that had, decidedly, been the end of that.

Outside, the air was still sweet and warm. The glow of fireflies appeared and then vanished in the tall grass around the trees. Shadows pooled, indigo and violet, and the sky painted the dying of the day in a pink so bright it seemed unreal.

Hope liked the way night fell out here, with all its sly

drama, its creeping and crawling. And then the epic last battle of it all—the sky turning outrageous colors as if to call out the shadows for trying to be so sneaky.

A wind blew up from the orchard, bringing the smell of cherries and dust from the road, and beneath that the fecund smell of rot. The barn door was open, a wide slice of buttery light falling out of it, pushing the shadows out wide. Music was playing, and through the large door frame she could see Abel pacing.

She stopped so fast she swayed forward. The feeling was an echo of something old. That sharp electric zap. That bone-rattling thrill of the unknown. From the second she'd turned fourteen and Mom caught her looking twice at Darius Jackson at church, Mom had called her boy crazy. She had taken so much delight in it that Hope had recoiled, refused to look at any boy ever again. So when she'd met Tink's dad, Tony, two years later, she'd fallen into his arms like an overripe peach. Swollen. Hot. Deprived. She felt that way now. It was embarrassing.

One of the kittens tried to jump out of her arms and its claws got caught in her shirt so that it hung off her like an ornament off a tree. At that moment Abel looked up and spotted her. "You okay?" he asked, clearly trying very hard not to smile at the scene.

"Fine," she said fast. "Just…returning the kittens my daughter was trying to domesticate in our room."

"They probably have fleas."

"No. They for sure have fleas. And Tink doesn't seem to care."

Abel laughed and then he vanished from the doorway. Hope stepped into the brightness of the barn. An old Stevie Nicks song was playing from a beat-up radio on the work bench, and the guts of the shaker machine were spread out on a towel beside the tractor.

"The shaker is still giving you trouble, huh?" she asked.

"It is," he said, his hands on his hips. "But I think I've got it figured out."

"Good for you——"

"Human sacrifice," he said, straight-faced. "It's the only solution."

She laughed, and he sat back down on the stool he had pulled up at the edge of the towel. Hope set the kittens down and shooed them off when they tried to climb back up her shoes.

"Peg said you're doing some bookkeeping for her."

"Yeah," she said. "Just cleaning things up and sending out some invoices."

"That seems pretty involved for someone who's leaving after cherry season." His dark eyes glittered as he watched her over his shoulder.

"I don't know if I am," she said. "I mean... I'm trying to figure out how I can stay."

"Don't you just...not leave?" He smiled.

"It's a little more complicated than that."

"Is there anything I can do to help?"

The offer caught her right in the chest for a second.

"Do you know Matt, the lawyer in town?"

"Matt Hageman? Yep," he said. "He's very fair. Very honest. If you're going to him for help, he won't lead you astray."

"That's good to hear."

He nodded, like he, too, had had hard nights making hard decisions. She liked that about him. That the peace and calm he seemed to wear like a shirt had been hard won.

"So, what will it take to convince you to look at my books? If you're staying. Or...for as long as you stay."

"I'd be happy to," she said, pushing aside any reservations.

"I'm warning you, they might be worse than Peg's."

"That is hard to believe," she said. "But I should tell you, in full disclosure, I'm not…official. I have a certificate but I'm not, like, an accountant. I did the books for my mom's salon and a couple of other small businesses—"

He held up his grease-stained hand. "Full disclosure. I don't care."

"Then we're in business."

He told her he would email her his spreadsheet and bring over his shoebox of receipts, and she was both relieved and sort of disappointed that she wasn't going to his house to get them. It would have been interesting to see how Abel lived. If he was messy or tidy. What sorts of books he had on his shelves.

"You know," she said, "I think I solved the mystery of the baby stuff in the basement." He turned to face her. "I think they were for me. I was here when I was one. My mom brought me to visit."

She imagined Peg getting hand-me-downs from friends, or buying that stuff used in preparation for Hope and Mom's visit. It seemed like the sort of thing Peg might do. And then, when she and Mom left, Peg had stored it in the basement, thinking maybe she'd have her own kids someday. Or maybe she'd just kept it because she kept things like old dining room tables and creepy oil paintings.

He blew out a long breath. "I'm glad to hear that."

The radio switched over to an Eagles song that reminded her of driving down Delmar with the windows down in her car listening to KSHE. She felt somehow really young and really old all at the same time.

"You know it's Friday night," he said.

"You're joking."

They looked around and then at each other, like they didn't know how they'd ended up in a barn on a Friday night. "I swear," he said. "I used to have a life."

"Well, I never did so this is all pretty exciting."

"If you like this, wait for apple season. We really go wild."

"Is there ever a time it's not busy?" she asked.

"Winter. No. Actually, I lied, it's like this all the time. If you want a social life you might want to rethink wanting to stay."

"I've been more social at this farm than I've been in years. I'm not sure I could handle much more. What about you, though? Where are your friends or family?"

"My family is in Milwaukee," he said. "My sister had a bunch of kids and that's where the grandbabies are."

"It must get lonely for you then."

"Not really. If I need people, there's a bar in town. It's not great, but it's not terrible."

"Sounds magical," she said, which made him laugh.

"Magical it is not. But people are there, and there's usually a game on." He lifted a greasy finger as if making a point. "And the chicken wings, I gotta tell you, they are kind of magical."

There was a moment, a chance, and she could see him thinking it, too. If she just kept her mouth shut, if she just stood there and let the moment happen—it would.

But before he could ask her out, even as a friend or a co-worker, she remembered that as much as she wanted this place it might not be for her. So she laughed, awkwardly, and said, "Well, good luck with the shaker."

And she left, crossing the lawn, telling herself she'd imagined it all. But secretly hoping she hadn't.

Sixteen

→ HOPE ←

"You want to stay in the car?" Hope asked the next day when they parked in front of the bakery. It was raining and the windshield was an opaque silvery-gray with water.

Tink looked at Hope like she'd lost her mind.

"I figured. But…I'm going to see if I can talk to Swafiya's husband," she said. "Matt. The lawyer." Hope lifted her hand so she could go at that thumbnail she liked to tear apart when she was nervous. Oh god, and she was so nervous. She was sick-to-her-stomach nervous.

Tink reached over and tugged Hope's finger from her mouth, and when Hope grabbed her hand, Tink didn't pull it away.

It was just what she needed to gather her courage. Her daughter's familiar sweaty palm in hers.

"I'm going to talk to Matt about orders of protection. Against Daniel. I'm going to see what I can do to protect us."

Tink was not always a readable kid. Her still waters ran

deep. But that smile—that smile was like the sun coming out behind the clouds.

"I don't know," Hope felt compelled to say. "I don't know what he can do. Hopefully something."

She didn't bother to say that they were going to be okay, that everything was fine—Tink had stopped believing that lie a long time ago. Though sometimes it was hard not to repeat it. Sometimes she had to catch it behind her teeth and hold it trapped in her mouth.

"Let's go see," Hope said. They got out of the truck and grabbed the box of Swafiya's cherries. When they knocked on the door Swafiya answered but without her usual smile.

"You all right?" Hope asked.

"Fine," Swafiya said with a wan smile. "Totally fine. The weather just gives me headaches."

"We have your cherries," Hope said. "But we could come back—"

Tink scowled at her.

"No. No, of course, come in. Do you have them all or can I grab the rest?"

"No, I put them in bigger bags for you."

"Oh," Swafiya said. "I don't know why we didn't do that before."

That's what Peg had said earlier in the day, as if using the two-pound bags had been some kind of creative business solution. Hope couldn't lie—it had made her feel good. They shuffled into the bakery, which after the chill and gray of the outside felt like crawling into a cozy bread-scented movie scene. All that was missing was a fire and some hobbits. Beside her, Tink sighed, her shoulders coming down from around her ears.

What will I do if this doesn't work?

As fast as the thought came, she pushed it away. It was going to work. It had to. Something had to break her way.

They set the bags of cherries on the counter. The bakery was usually a mess, but the kind of mess a very organized person made. Today it looked different; there were a bunch of half-finished projects scattered around.

"I'm sorting out the invoicing," Hope said. "I should have them all to you tonight."

"Peg handed that off to you, did she?"

"Well, I'm a bookkeeper," Hope said. "It's kinda my job."

"Really?" Swafiya put her hand on Hope's arm, her face lighting up. "Oh my god, I need to tell Matt. He's been looking for a bookkeeper for ages. I used to do it for him, but the bakery got so busy and now he's just up there with receipts in shoeboxes and I swear our accountant is going to kill him."

"Well, I suppose I can talk to him," Hope said. "Later or whatever."

Tink elbowed her hard in the side, and Hope glared down at her daughter and her sharp elbows. But Tink only stared, eyebrows raised.

Okay. Okay.

"Is everything all right?" Swafiya asked.

"Actually," she said carefully. "I was hoping I could talk to your husband anyway. I have some legal questions for him."

"Yeah?" she said, all bright eyes and hopeful smiles.

"You don't… I mean, it's not that big a deal—"

"Yes! It is!" she said. She pulled her phone from her pocket and, with floury hands, tapped away. Within seconds she tucked the phone back with a satisfied smile. "He's in his office now and doesn't have a meeting for another hour. He's all yours."

Oh. Well, she hadn't expected it to happen so fast. She thought she'd have a day or two, maybe, to put her thoughts together, to get her story in order. To brace herself. It was one thing to get ahold of her life; it was another thing entirely to do it on a rushed timeline.

"Where is his office?" *Please say somewhere far away.*

"Right upstairs," Swafiya said and pointed toward the door opposite the bathroom.

"Tink—"

"Is going to wash her hands and help me make scones."

Tink honestly looked like she was going to fall down backward with delight.

There were no excuses left. It was happening. Right now. She tried in her buzzing, slightly panicked mind to figure out when she'd last decided to put her feet down in her life. Tink, certainly. Her mom had wanted to take her to a clinic, and when Hope said no to that option, Mom'd pushed hard for adoption. But Hope, who'd been doing what her mother told her her whole life, had been adamant in a way she'd never been before; she was keeping the baby.

Running away from St. Louis had been the opposite of that.

Running away from the hotel and what had happened there? Totally the opposite.

It was time to stop running. Time to stop hoping she and Tink were safe and do something about it.

"Okay," she said. She glanced at Tink and sent her a "be good" look, then climbed the steps to the lawyer's office.

Matt Hageman was a nice guy. Sitting behind his messy desk in front of a wall of diplomas and certificates and legal stuff, he looked pained.

"So what you're saying," Hope said, wanting to be sure she really understood, "is there's not much I can do?"

"No," he said. "There are things you can do—"

"But those things will put my daughter and me in more danger?"

"They will alert your abuser of where you are. We won't use The Orchard House address. But he will know the county the order was filed in."

Alpena was a tiny little county on the edge of the Michigan mitten. If she had to guess, there were probably only a couple thousand people in the whole county. It wouldn't be hard to find her, and for a guy like Daniel, it would be a breeze.

"Doesn't that seem absurd to you?" she asked.

"In your situation, yes. It's not ideal. But, as I said, you are the person who understands your situation best. You don't have to do this. But," Matt said, leaning forward over the desk, "I will alert local law enforcement, and if he's seen here, he can be arrested without a warrant. And violating a protection order is taken seriously in Michigan."

"But he lives in Missouri."

"I know. He'll still be served."

"But the farm is so isolated," she said. "It's ten minutes out of town. If he finds us…"

"They recommend you put a safety plan in place. So if he does show up, you and your daughter, and Peg, for that matter and even Abel, they all have a way to stall for time until the police get there."

She gaped at him. "You're saying I should figure out how to stall him?"

"I know," he said, looking regretful. "It seems inadequate."

"Seems? It *is* inadequate. None of this makes me safer."

"You can press charges against him in Michigan for assault."

"But he can press charges against me, too, for hitting him with the lamp."

"If you believed he had a gun?"

"I don't know that he did."

"But if you *believed* that you did."

"I don't know what I believed!" she cried. "I believed I was scared. I believed he wanted to hurt us. And I believe that he still does."

Matt sat there, quietly.

She didn't want to press charges. There were too many ways that could go wrong. Gun or not. Bruised face or not. It would probably require Tink to testify. It would certainly require her to see Daniel again. And Daniel could, as Matt explained, turn the whole thing around and make it about her hitting him with the lamp.

"What do I do? I mean, how can he get away with this?"

But she knew the world was full of men who'd gotten away with it. Women in the same position as she was, terrified to make a move. It felt very much like the rest of the world didn't understand. Or care.

"You know your situation best," he said. "And that's the truth. If these choices make you feel less safe, then don't choose them."

"What do *you* think?"

"I believe in the legal system," he said. "And I have tremendous faith in the local police and in the state troopers. I can only imagine how terrifying this is for you, but I can appreciate and value the bravery it takes to stand up. If he breaks the order then we have legal recourse. We can see him punished."

"But if he breaks the order—"

"Then you and Tink could also be in danger."

Seventeen

→TINK←

They made cherry scones and put them in the oven, and Mom still wasn't down from the lawyer's office. Tink glared at that door and did Mom's old trick: *You're going to open in three…two…one.*

The door stayed closed.

"Don't be nervous," Swafiya said.

"I'm not," Tink said.

"So you do talk?" Swafiya said, playing it cool.

"Sometimes."

Swafiya pulled an apron out of a drawer and held it out to Tink, who had no interest in wearing it.

"Trust me," she said. "Things are gonna get messy."

That sounded interesting so she put on the apron and Swafiya helped tie it so it wasn't so big. Then she got out two large bowls and showed Tink how to use the cherry pitter. She was right; things got pretty messy.

"So," Swafiya said, dropping a pitted cherry in the silver bowl. "I've never worked with anyone else in my kitchen. What should we gossip about?"

"I don't know any gossip," Tink said.

"Me neither. What grade are you going to be in?" she asked. "When school starts?"

"Fifth," she said.

"Oh, fifth grade was my favorite."

Tink wasn't looking forward to it. Ms. Grayson at her school in St. Louis was a real hard-ass and...

I'm not going to be there next year.

Tink squeezed a pit out wrong and the cherry fell onto the floor.

"Whoops," Swafiya said and grabbed it before Tink could. "Mrs. Jordal is the fifth-grade teacher at the elementary school and she's really nice. She brings her class here for a field trip and we bake bread as a science experiment. You'll like her."

The door opened upstairs and Mom came down. There was a second before she smiled, and Tink saw that whatever had happened up there hadn't been great.

"Well, look at you two," Mom said, her voice climbing up into that octave that made Tink want to hurl the cherries to the ground and run away.

"Scones are almost out of the oven," Swafiya said.

"That's okay," Mom said. "We need to get going. We'll get some scones another time."

Tink took off the apron and felt suddenly vulnerable, which was stupid. It was just an apron; hardly a suit of armor.

"Here." Swafiya slipped another loaf of bread in a plastic bag. "Cinnamon raisin this time." She handed it to Tink with a wink and a smile and walked them to the door. "Hope," she said as they stepped outside. Both Tink and Mom turned to look at her, so pretty in her turquoise head scarf. And so worried, but trying to hide it.

"Yeah?"

"Everything will be okay," she said.

"Of course," Mom said and even managed to laugh. "Everything will be fine."

✦ HOPE ✦

The sun was setting behind the tall trees to the west and the rain had stopped so the air was cool and damp. She and Tink were walking back up from the barn where they'd parked the truck.

"You tired?" Hope asked her slightly droopy daughter. She even went so far as to run her palm over Tink's shoulder. The soft silk of her hair brushed over the back of her hand and Hope lifted her fingers to gather it all in a ponytail.

That Tink allowed this gesture shouldn't have made tears burn behind her eyes, shouldn't have made her throat hurt with a swallowed sob.

But it did.

Tink nodded and pulled away.

"Yeah," Hope whispered, her voice rough. "Me, too. It… ah…it didn't go great with Swafiya's husband," she said.

Tink stopped, turned to face her. She stood there, shoulders back and her face still like she'd just been expecting this, for Hope to fail her.

Again.

"But I'm not done trying," she said.

Tink turned back and kept walking toward the lit-up windows and open back door of The Orchard House. Hope could see Peg at the kitchen sink, her head cocked in the way that told Hope she was talking to Nelson, who was probably begging for food at her feet.

Stop begging, Peg would be saying, while giving the dog a treat from her hand.

The tall grass, damp from the rain, brushed against the skin of her knees so gently it felt like an itch. Or maybe that was her. Her wires were crossed and nothing felt the way it should.

"I'm sorry, Tink," she whispered, but her daughter couldn't hear her, having raced ahead to the back door. Nelson barked in greeting.

There were hours left in the day, hours with nothing to do but try to get her silent daughter to talk to her and think about every single mistake she'd made that had led them here. Despair colored the air around her and she couldn't see clearly. She couldn't go in the house, not like this.

The garden was to her right. Blackbirds flew in and out of the foliage, perching on thin leaves, cawing at her in warning. The back-fence line had been pushed down completely and a watermelon had tumbled out, still attached to its vine, like it had made its bid for freedom but could get yanked back at any minute.

"I'm going to work on the garden!" she yelled toward the house. Peg, standing at the open windows, lifted her hand in acknowledgment. Tink stood with the screen door open, looking back at her. "You want to help?"

Tink shook her head and went inside, the screen squeaking shut behind her.

Good, she thought. It was better this way. Just Hope and the garden. Nothing but the beetles to hear her cry, listen to her scream.

Birds cawed. Bugs buzzed. The garden kept growing without a plan or anyone to care for it, kept growing like the small lives of humans didn't matter to it at all.

Startled by her approach, creatures scattered away through the tall, coarse grass. She didn't even stop as something slithered across her shoe. She stepped down on the bowed edge of the fence, driving it down to the ground, and walked into the garden. It felt like stepping into a green sauna. It smelled like dirt and rot and the vibrant place in between.

She pushed aside some vines and stepped over a fallen corn plant, making her way deeper and deeper inside. Birds departed with a flourish, sending corn stalks and tall, slender weed trees waving and smacking into each other. The rows of plants were overgrown, spilling everywhere, so it was hard to tell where it was safe to walk, and truthfully, she didn't really care. Tomatoes, some green, some red, squished under her feet. Strawberries, too.

The bees came, but she was used to those. The blackflies, too, and she slapped at them as they bit, swore at them with the filthiest words she knew. Kicked at them, smacking weeds in the process, which bounced back and hit her in the face.

"Dammit," she said. Then she put her hands over her mouth and yelled it, the words muffled against her fingers so Peg or Abel didn't come running.

This was going to be a very private breakdown.

She screamed into her hands until even the birds were silent and the flies were gone. Light-headed, she lifted her face and stared up at the sky, bruised and dark over the edges of the plants.

Stop crying. Stop. You did this. You.

The words were the most poisonous venom she had and she let herself have it.

You let that man into your daughter's life. This is all your fault.

There were weeds everywhere with big fluffy seed pods and—she learned the hard way—thorns on the stems, and she used the hem of her T-shirt around her hands to rip them out. They broke, slimy and in chunks in her hands, and she reached down to grab what was still standing closer to the root.

There were thistles, too, and she kicked at them, mashing them down to the ground, and then kicked them some more until the root ball came right out. She hacked and kicked and pulled and pulled and pulled. Sweat burned in her eyes and in a thousand little cuts on her legs and arms. Her hands were red. Blistered and cut.

Sweat ran down into her mouth. And snot.

Tears.

There were some mistakes. Thin orange carrots, dusted with black dirt, joined the weed piles, and at first, she felt bad about the mint she was pulling out by the handful. But then the mint seemed like its own kind of weed, determined to take over every available clump of dirt in the garden, and she went after it with a vengeance. Leaving nothing but tomato plants in her wake, she made it down one row. The weeds she heaved over her shoulder caught on the corn plants and the edge of the fencing. She gave her arms a reckless scratch and then worked her way down another row.

It was mindless and hard and she did not give a damn if she messed it up. Because anything was an improvement for this garden. If she bulldozed it and set it on fire, it would be an improvement. If she pulled out every single vegetable, who would even care?

Not Peg. She couldn't even look back here.

Not her mom. Who never cared about anything she did.

Would Tink? Had she screwed that up so much that Tink wouldn't even care?

She braced her hands on her knees, biting her lips.

"Hey."

She looked up in the direction of the voice. It was Abel at the end of the row, standing on the bent fence.

She wasn't even embarrassed. Sobbing, bleeding, covered in sweat and bugs, her life in worse shape than the garden she was currently destroying.

What? she wanted to yell. *What are you looking at? What do you want to say?*

But she kept her mouth shut and swatted a bug on her forearm.

"You okay?" he asked.

"Fine."

She understood she didn't look fine, that he was in fact being kind. But she'd messed everything up and his kindness now felt like pity.

"I thought this might help." He handed her gloves and a pair of bright shiny shears as long as her arm. "They're really—"

She chopped off the head of one of those thorn weeds in one quick *snick*. So satisfying.

"Sharp."

"Got it," she said, tugging the gloves over her red hands. "Thank you. And…I'm sorry."

"It's not a problem," he said and lifted his hand as he walked away.

She turned on the garden, opening and closing the shears, her heart delighting in that snick and rasp of the blades rubbing together. After that, the garden didn't stand a chance. She went through row after row, chopping down the largest of the weeds so she could go back and pull out the roots.

If that didn't work, she used those pretty, shiny, sharp blades as shovels.

→TINK←

Since Mom wasn't around to ask her where she'd gotten the magazines, Tink pulled the *National Geographic*s she'd taken from Peg's room and read the one about space cover to cover. Still Mom didn't come inside. So, she opened the one about Vikings, which, frankly, was a little disappointing. Turned out Vikings mostly farmed. And they didn't wear horned helmets.

Still no Mom.

Tink didn't hear the muffled sound of Mom's voice downstairs as she talked to Peg, so there was no point in sneaking down the steps to eavesdrop.

Something had happened with the lawyer. Something bad. And now Mom wasn't talking. Tink could handle not talking to Mom, but Mom not talking to *her*, well, that just wasn't right.

At the bottom of the pillowcase her fingers brushed against the bullets she'd taken and then paper so soft it felt like fabric.

The letters.

She'd forgotten about them.

Carefully, she pulled them out, took the fragile paper from the envelopes and read them.

In the first one, DeeDee asked for money to go to rehab, because, she said in the letter, that Peg had been right—the drugs were a problem.

In the second letter, DeeDee was scared. Jacob was selling drugs. And bringing bad guys to the apartment. She asked for more money, for more rehab.

When Tink was in kindergarten, DeeDee fell in the salon and twisted her knee. She'd had to go to rehab to fix it.

But it wasn't the same thing. She was ten but she knew that.

DeeDee had used drugs. A lot of them, according to the letters.

Suddenly, she wished she hadn't read the letters. Or even taken them from Peg's room. She didn't want to know any more secrets she wasn't supposed to. The weight that had been sitting on her chest since leaving the bakery got too heavy.

I want my mom.

The sky was dark outside the window and her room was all murky, so she tucked the letters back into her pillowcase and went down the stairs like a ninja so she wouldn't alert the beast. But when she pushed open the door to the upstairs, the beast was right there, tongue out, drooling everywhere. "Go away," she whispered, her voice all rough from not being used.

Nelson's tail wagged so hard it thumped against the wall. "I never should have given you that cheese."

The monster's ears perked up at the word *cheese*.

"I don't like you," she said and tried to scooch out sideways around the door, only to run right into Peg.

"That's too bad," Peg said, drying her hands on a rag. "Because that dog loves you. Lasagna's ready. It probably won't kill you."

"Probably?" Tink said, tired of being silent.

"You take your chances in this life, kid."

Tink smiled. She liked Peg when she made those kinds of jokes.

"Where's my mom?"

"In the garden."

"Still."

"Yep."

Peg said it like it was no big deal, but it kinda felt like a big deal. It was dark out and Mom had worked all day. And then the thing with the lawyer... Someone needed to go get her and bring her inside.

Peg stood at the sink, cutting an apple into pieces. Every once in a while she dropped a little chunk into Nelson's mouth.

"I've never seen a dog that eats apples," Tink said.

"Nelson eats everything."

"Why do you call all your dogs Nelson?"

Peg looked up, holding a knife in one hand and the apple in another. "Denise started it," she said. "Your grandmother."

"We called her DeeDee. She didn't like Grandma."

Peg laughed, her whole body shaking. "That sounds like her. She had a barn cat when we were young. Alphie. Alphie died and she called all the barn cats Alphie after that. And then the dog we had, Nelson, died, and the next dog she said we were going to name Nelson."

"So you didn't forget the names?"

Peg shook her head and slid that knife through the white apple with a *snick*. She held out a piece to Tink and she took it.

"The first of Abel's honeycrisp," she said. "They're real good this year."

Tink bit into the apple and it was sweet and tart and crunchy and her whole mouth loved it.

"Good, huh?" Peg asked with a smile.

"Really good."

Peg handed her another piece and she gobbled that up, too.

"Denise told me," Peg said, cutting into another apple, "that she poured all the love she had for the old Nelson and the old Alphie into the new ones. So those animals got double the love and the next ones got triple." She waved her knife in a little circle. On and on.

"That's nice," Tink said, but it didn't sound at all like DeeDee.

"It's different, but we went with it." She shrugged. "You want more?"

On the edge of the knife was a piece of apple. Tink took it but didn't eat it.

"You gonna go get my mom?" Tink asked, and Peg seemed startled by the question, like it hadn't occurred to her.

Outside, the lightning bugs were floating in the tall grass. Tink chased one, only to miss it when it went dark and blended into the shadows. She got the second one and held it in her cupped hands, feeling its little bug feet and its little bug body bashing itself against her palms.

Fast as she could, she let it go.

Sorry, bug, she thought, and ran through the grass to the garden, where she could hear her mom grunting and swearing.

There were giant piles of weeds and dirt on the inside and outside of the fence. The big sunflower had fallen over like it was tired. There were two clear rows now, but the plants didn't look like they liked anything that had happened today.

Tink walked around the edge of the fence until she was standing at the entrance, which kinda looked like a cave. She ducked under a bush that seemed like it was growing sideways and stepped into the garden. The air smelled like the color green and dirt.

She swallowed down the *Mom* she wanted to call out that would make all this easier and just followed the sound of rustling. And swearing.

When she found her mom, she was crouched, her knees in the dirt, but she was so focused on whatever she was doing, she didn't hear Tink walk up to her. She was a mess, a total mess. There were smears of dirt and what looked like blood on her shirt. She had weeds sticking out of her hair and was panting like she'd just gone running. Mom used to go running in the mornings. That seemed like a million years ago.

As Tink watched, her mom put a hand on the ground. And then another. And then she just fell down on her side, right in the middle of the plants, her body curled up like she was going to sleep.

"Mom?" she croaked, and ran over to her.

"Mom?" she said a little louder, alarmed by the fact that Tink talking to her had gotten no reaction.

"Mom!" she yelled as loud as she could.

There was more rustling and suddenly Abel was there, ducking through the garden to find them.

"Hey," he said with a quick smile for her. "What happened?"

"I don't know. She just lay down!"

"Go get Peg, would you?"

Eighteen

→PEG←

It was full dark and those girls were still in the garden. Nelson stood at the screen door, keeping watch, with the occasional whimper and glance up at Peg, who was trying to keep herself occupied checking on the frozen lasagna in the oven.

Let me out there, that old dog was saying. *Please let me out there.*

"It's not our business," she told Nelson.

Suddenly the quiet of the night was broken by Tink's husky voice yelling, which in and of itself was something, but she was yelling Peg's name.

The oven door slammed shut, and she and Nelson went running into the yard just as Tink came sprinting out of the garden so fast and hard she didn't even see Peg until Peg grabbed the girl by the shoulders.

"What happened?" Peg asked.

"I don't know. Mom just…lay down."

Abel came out of the garden, carrying Hope, and something inside Peg squeezed up real tight at the sight of how small Hope seemed in Abel's arms. She was barely a whisper of a thing.

Hope stirred and as if Abel knew how distressed she would be to wake up and find herself in his arms, he carefully lowered her feet onto the ground, his arm still around her waist, holding her up.

"She's okay," Abel said to Tink, who ran up to help support Hope. "She just went a little too hard."

Hope lifted her hand to her head. No doubt she had a splitting headache. Too much work, not enough water and certainly not enough food. The woman had been working in that garden like she was possessed.

Or punishing herself.

Tink threw her arms around her mom's waist and Hope straightened slightly, as if the sudden contact had reinforced her spine, made her legs stronger.

"Hey," she whispered. "Hey, I'm okay. Everything's all right." But then her legs buckled and she would have fallen down if Abel hadn't been there.

"Sit down," Peg said. "Just…rest for a second."

"Just a second," Hope said, and carefully got down on the ground. Tink, Abel and Peg all stood there over her for a second like they weren't sure what to do.

"Tink," Peg said. "Run back into the house and fill up the biggest cup of water you can. Okay? And then come back, but don't run, or you'll spill it."

Tink nodded and ran for the house.

"As for you," Peg said, crouching down with protesting knees beside Hope. "Put your head between your knees. Yep. Just like that. You need some water," Peg said. "And food."

"I'm not very hungry—"

"Hope," Abel said. Just her name in that tone.

Peg got to her feet, grateful for Abel in a way she never expected to be. So many years working side by side a guy and you don't really appreciate him until he carries your unconscious niece out of your husband's overgrown garden.

"Abel," Peg said.

"Don't," he said quietly, like he'd read her mind. "You all right?"

"Sure," she lied. "You want to come in for lasagna?" She'd like to have reinforcements, even though she knew he was going to say no.

He shook his head, his voice low. "I make her uncomfortable."

As he walked backward to the barn, Tink came speed walking out of the house carrying a huge glass of water in both hands, being very careful not to spill.

"Thank you, honey," Hope said, taking the glass with shaking hands that made the water slosh down over her fingers. "I'm okay. I'm sorry if I scared you."

Hope drank down the water, barely pausing for a breath.

Something cracked in Peg. Some restraint she'd had in place. Some braking mechanism that she'd gotten so used to that she didn't even know it was there.

"Tink," Peg said, taking the glass from Hope and handing it back to Tink. "Go get some more water, would you? And in the fridge there's a plate with carrots and celery and some of that ranch dip, and I made some garlic bread. Bring out as much as you can, okay?"

"We can go inside," Hope said, like she was about to get to her feet.

"You stay where you are. Tink?"

Tink nodded, took the glass and went running for the house.

"Peg? What—"

Peg got herself down in the grass next to Hope.

"I think it's time we cut the crap, Hope. I know I told you you didn't need to tell me what drove you up here, but I was wrong. You just passed out in my garden. Scared your kid half to death."

Hope flinched.

"Whoever did that to you," Peg said, gesturing toward Hope's eye, "did he hurt Tink, too?"

"No! I mean, I can see why you might think that, but no. He didn't."

Peg just sat there, waiting.

"He never touched her," Hope finally said and then lifted her hand to her face. "He didn't do this to me, except the one time."

"Well, that's something," Peg said, trying to sound encouraging, but Hope only laughed. As she laughed, her eyes filled up with tears, and she blinked them away so fast Peg thought she might have imagined them.

Bend, honey, she thought. *Bend before you break.*

"I met him at the grocery store a few months after Mom died and I was depressed." The word exploded off her lips in those hard *d* and *p* sounds. "Just blank, you know?"

Peg nodded. She knew that kind of blank. She'd felt it for years after Denise left the second time, would undoubtedly feel it again once these two moved on.

"Everything felt so hard, taking care of Mom's arrangements, the apartment. Tink. Getting out of bed was hard."

Again that terrible smack of guilt. *I should have been there*, Peg thought. *I should have helped you.*

"He offered to help me load my groceries in the car and it was just such a relief. To not be alone. To have a little help. And it just snowballed from there. Until he was doing stuff around the house. Taking Tink and me for hamburgers. Asking if he could spend the night." She shook her head and Peg didn't want to ask about what spending the night with him had meant for her. "It just seemed like so much work to say no. And I never understood why he was attracted to me. I was so low. So down."

"Sounds like he took advantage of that."

Hope nodded. "He moved in and I honestly don't remember asking him or telling him it was okay. He was just *there*. I woke up one morning and I didn't recognize my life. I asked him to move out and that was a fight. And then I broke up with him. And that was a fight. It was never violent. He just… wouldn't leave. And he kept making me feel like I was wrong. Like I was a terrible mom for rejecting his help when I was in such bad shape. And so I started to think maybe he was right. That maybe I did need him. But then—" She pressed her lips together, swallowed so hard her throat made a sound. "He picked Tink up from school one day."

The silence after those words was fraught, so thin and breakable Peg didn't breathe in fear of shattering it.

"And he didn't tell me. And he didn't let her call. And so I thought for a while maybe she was at her friend Dinah's house. But she wasn't. And she really only had that one friend, but I started calling around to everyone, everyone I could get ahold of. I called and I called and it was like ten o'clock at night and I was wandering up and down the street, calling every person I could think of and finally I had to call the police and report her missing. They asked if there was someone in her life who would take her. And I realized—" she blinked and two tears streaked down her face "—he had her. And I'd let this monster into our life. And I didn't know if I would get her back."

The truth of that pain, that rip-your-guts-out pain, was that it changed your whole life. Your whole self. On a molecular level. After that kind of pain, nothing was the same.

Peg remembered it well.

"He drove up like fifteen minutes later. I'll never forget that, looking in the back seat of that car and seeing her red face all streaked with tears, this chocolate ice cream she was refusing to eat melting all over the place. The police came and took his statement and he just made it all sound like a misunderstanding. Like I'd asked him to pick her up from school and just forgot. He said—" she dashed the tears away from her face like they were burning her "'—she's been real depressed lately. Real forgetful. We're trying to get her help, but you know how it is.' And all the cops standing there nodded like they knew me. I was so outraged and so angry, but I couldn't stop crying and I sounded like a lunatic and he sounded so calm. So reasonable. I watched those police officers start to believe him. They were *sympathetic* toward him. Like, 'oh no, man, you were just taking your girlfriend's kid out for ice cream and she did this?' I was this *problem*. They drove away and he stood there, smiling at me. This bland beige man I barely even knew and he—" she shook her head, blinking her eyes like she still couldn't believe it "—had all the control. I had just given it to him, handed it over like the keys to a car. I saw what I had done, and I saw what my life would be like, and I didn't know how to stay and fix it. And maybe I didn't *want* to stay and fix it. It was probably one of those decisions they tell you not to make when you're grieving. But I made it. And it felt good. A week later Tink and I just left. Packed up what we could fit in the car, canceled the utilities and left."

"Is that when Tink stopped talking to you?"

"No. You would think, right?" She laughed and all Peg could think was that this girl was the toughest thing she'd ever seen. "But she was excited about the move. We were still this team, Tink and me. I had a friend from high school in Chicago who lived in an apartment above a movie theater. She'd gone on to be an actress and was doing pretty well, and

I talked about her nonstop because she was kind of the only friend I had. Certainly the only one starring in commercials that came on the TV when we ate dinner. Anyway, we went to visit her. I went to a doctor and got a prescription for antidepressants, and I was looking for an apartment and a job and things were going pretty great. Until one morning Tink looked out the window and there was Daniel standing across the street, wearing his goddamn khaki pants, watching the building, like he knew we could see him." Her voice had gotten high and heated and she took a deep breath, calming herself down. "I don't know if he found us because of my semi-famous actress friend or if he went to every single movie theater in the city with apartments above them. I really can't believe I'm telling you all this," she said. "You said you didn't want to know and now—"

"We're family," Peg said. "I'm not great with family, but I think that's what we're here for."

For an awful second Hope's face crumbled, and Peg couldn't believe she'd thought about kicking this girl out, that she'd been angry about her arrival. All she wanted to do was wrap her up in a blanket and keep her safe.

It's okay, Peg wanted to say. *You can cry.*

But instead Hope laughed awkwardly, even as her face crumbled again, like she was working hard to hold the tears in.

"That night Tink and I left. We drove toward Detroit. I remembered the farm, but with him following us, I couldn't risk it. So, I thought we might head to Canada. And then we went to get gas and Tink and I came out of the gas station and he was there. Standing right next to our car." She took a shuddering breath, sucked on her lip. "The lights, you know those lights at gas stations at night?"

Peg nodded.

"They made him look so scary, like he was so pale and his

eyes were so dark. And he was mad. I'd never seen him mad before. He acted like he had a gun. I don't know if he did, but I was too scared to risk it. No one else was there. No one in the parking lot. No one in the store except for the attendant, who was behind bulletproof glass. It was just us and I didn't know what to do, so I told Tink to run. To go inside. To just go inside and have the attendant call the police." She took a breath that shuddered. "I told her to be brave and that I loved her. And… I started walking toward the car. She grabbed on to me and screamed no and 'Mom, please don't leave me.'" She stopped, gathered herself. "I tried to push her away. Really hard."

"Oh, Hope," Peg sighed.

"I didn't know what else to do." Hope's eyes practically begged Peg to tell her she'd done the right thing, like if it was a test she'd gotten the right answer, but Peg didn't know how to tell her that there was no right answer in that situation. There was only survival.

"Tink pulled on my hand so hard she practically sat down, you know? Her little butt was dragging across the asphalt. And she screamed so loud. I mean, I can still hear it. She screamed no so loud I thought the glass might break in the windows. That's the last time she spoke to me."

"And Daniel?"

"He made us get in our car, and he drove us to some hotel."

"But you got away from him. After he hit you?"

She nodded. "I hit him over the head with a lamp."

"Knocked him out?"

"I thought… I thought maybe I'd killed him. There was so much blood. But I've been looking at the news on my phone and there's nothing about the hotel where we were or a dead body."

"You've been walking around with all that on your mind?" Peg asked. No wonder the girl had passed out. No wonder she hadn't been able to get out of bed for the first two days. No wonder she looked so thin Peg could see right through her.

"I went to Matt, the lawyer in town, to see what I could do about an order of protection."

"And?"

She sighed and attempted to smile. "Would you believe the answer is not much?"

"Yeah," Peg said. "Frankly. Yeah. But I'm real sorry."

"Part of me, you know, thinks this is what I deserve. Like how can I expect some piece of paper or court of law to fix the mess I made—"

"Stop it." Peg shook her head. "Just stop that. You don't deserve any of this. A black eye and running scared with your girl. You trusted a bad man. He's the problem, not you. And that our laws are insufficient to take care of you, well, that's criminal."

Hope wiped her face in the heavy silence of the dark yard. "We can leave in the morning."

"What are you talking about?"

"Or now. He's looking for us. I know he is, and if he finds us, he'll come here. To your house. Maybe it would be better if we just left now."

Nelson barked and a plate made a thud against the grass. Hope and Peg both turned in time to see Tink, behind them, open her mouth and yell.

"No!"

Nineteen

The voice that came out of Tink was rough and gravelly, but it was strong. It was fierce. It was a little girl who'd lost her voice finding it all over again.

Hope and Peg leaned back as if blown away by the power of her voice.

"I don't want to leave," Tink said, eyes welling with angry tears, her little body ramrod stiff. "I like it here."

Tink looked right at Peg, and she was so much like Hope and so much like Denise, so much like every part of her family that she'd tried to stop loving and couldn't.

"Don't make us leave. We'll work really hard," Tink said. "You don't even have to pay me—"

"Honey." Hope's breath broke on a sob and she got to her feet and reached out for Tink, but the girl wouldn't have it. She backed away until she was up against Nelson.

"I'm tired of us being all by ourselves," Tink said. "I want to be here. Peg can help keep us safe. Abel. Nelson."

At the mention of her name Nelson barked as if agreeing to the position.

"Mom," Tink whispered. "Let's stay. Let's just stay."

"I agree," Peg said, taking advantage of the indecision on Hope's face. "You should stay. Here at The Orchard House. Whatever happens, we will figure it out."

You're going to have to tell her, Hank's voice said in Peg's ear. If *she stays, she needs to know the truth.*

She'd sort that out later. Right now she just needed Hope to stay.

"What if he finds us here?" Hope asked.

"What if he finds you somewhere else and you're all alone?" Peg kept her eyes on Hope's long past the moment she'd normally look away because it was all too much. She kept her eyes on Hope's until Hope believed what Peg believed.

They were safer together than alone.

There was a long breath and then another.

"Are you sure?" she asked. "Because he's dangerous."

"I'm sure. I'm very sure."

It took another second but finally Hope whispered, "Okay," and Peg's heart took flight.

Tink clapped her hands. "We're staying!"

She wanted to hug that scared woman. She wanted to tell her she'd done the best she could. That sometimes the only metric that mattered was survival. She and her daughter were standing here, mostly whole, mostly healthy. That meant she had won.

But Peg hadn't hugged anyone in a very long time and it was an easy skill to lose.

"Go on, now," Peg said to Hope. "Go get some rest."

"Thank you, Peg," Hope said, and then, like she hadn't done enough tonight, she reached out and squeezed Peg's hand.

"You're welcome."

"Come on, Tink," Hope said. "Let's pick this up."

She crouched down to gather up the garlic toast and vegetables that Tink had dropped.

"I got it," Peg said. "You go on in. There's lasagna in the oven."

"Peg," Hope said, and Peg turned to look over her shoulder. Hope was gazing at the moon struggling its way out from behind the clouds. "You said punishing myself wasn't going to make it right."

"Yeah?"

"How do I?" She looked at Peg. No tears. No crumpled expression. Just an exhausted mother. "How do I fix what I did?"

"You can't," Peg said. "You just have to live with it."

Like she had, for so many years.

"Peg?"

"Go to sleep, Hope. It's cherry season. Tomorrow is another day."

➤ HOPE ◆

They brushed their teeth the way they used to, before everything went so wrong. Tink sat on the top of the toilet, her little bare feet on the closed seat. Hope stood to the side of the sink. They took turns spitting and filling their mouths with clean water.

"Say something," Hope whispered.

Tink tipped her head up so the foamy toothpaste wouldn't drip down her chin. "Something."

Hope smiled slowly. "I missed your voice."

It had been so long since she'd felt this companionable comfort with her daughter. For years it had just been the two of them against the world, a duo with auxiliary aid from Mom. She'd missed her daughter, yes, the bright loving girl she'd been. But she'd also missed her friend.

Hope worked alone as a bookkeeper and mostly dealt with her clients online. There were a few friends from Rosati-Kain, the all-girls Catholic high school she'd attended, who hadn't moved out to the country, and one of them threw a big Christmas party every year that Hope always tried to attend.

She'd had Tink, and her mother. But if she was going to admit it, she'd been lonely. Really lonely.

When Tink had gone into preschool, Hope had looked at all those moms in SUVs unbuckling their kids and brushing the goldfish cracker crumbs off their shirts, and thought, *Now, now I'll have friends.* But then Paulette was there, turning her head away, telling her that single moms had to stick together, which mostly meant drinking rosé in the courtyard of Paulette's apartment and bitching about men and other moms while Tink and Paulette's son, Jesse, played Legos. Their friendship had been pinned to their kids and the hard realities of being moms and being alone. When Mom died, Paulette attended the funeral and she'd called a few times, but as Hope slipped into depression, she'd stopped coming around.

Because, it turned out, they weren't those kinds of friends.

There were plenty of people who had warned her that being a friend to her daughter would get in the way of being a good parent. But Hope had felt that they'd created an island of something in the middle, her and Tink, and they'd lived there happily for a long time. Recent storms had thrown them off, and, god, it was so nice to have a flicker of something familiar between them now, a flicker of hope that they would find some new territory in this wintry and cold no-man's land where they weren't family and they weren't friends.

Hope spit and washed off her brush. Standing upright, she caught sight of herself in the mirror, something she'd been trying to avoid. The swelling had gone down and she could see the whole of her eye, and the bruising was fading from black and blue to a sickly yellow. Past the black eye, her whole face looked different. She was freckled, yes, and sunburned.

Eleven days of cherry season, thirteen days at The Orchard House, and she was thinner, harder somehow. Not in a bad way. Like Peg. The work was whittling off everything extraneous from her, leaving her with only what was essential.

Tink spit and rinsed her brush. "Has it changed?"

"Has what changed?" Hope asked.

"My voice?"

"Yes," Hope said. "You speak with a thick French accent now."

"Mom!" Tink laughed. "Be serious."

"I'm sorry, I can barely understand you."

Tink bounced past her and into their bedroom. Hope turned off the light and followed. In the dark rooms, lit with silvery light from the moon, they got into their separate beds and pulled the covers up to their chins.

Ten seconds later Tink crawled out of her covers and pounced from her bed right onto Hope.

"Oof," Hope said as Tink elbowed her in the ribs. Hope turned on her side, her back to the wall, and Tink fell onto her back, one leg kicked up and over Hope's knees. Hope put her hand on Tink's stomach, felt the rise and fall of her breath, the thump of her heart. As soon as Tink fell asleep she'd be hogging this bed and Hope would be pinned against the wall with an elbow in her face.

Hope couldn't wait.

"Good?"

"Good."

⇥ PEG ⇤

Peg was stuck in the backyard, on the well-worn path between the kitchen door and the barn. The moon lined the clouds in silver and the stars were fighting to be seen. She saw the barn lights blink off and Abel walk out the big doors. He looked up at the house and she lifted her hand in a wave. He stopped, like he might come up and ask how everything was, but then he just waved back and continued walking across the road and through the orchard to his cabin on the other side of the property.

She pressed a hand to her chest, her fist against the hard bone of her sternum. She pressed until it hurt, until it was all balanced. The pain inside and the pain outside. It was the only way she could do what she needed to do. She needed to call Hank.

Thirteen days those girls had been here, and she'd been pretending this moment wasn't going to come, that telling him Hope was at the farm would only prove cruel when she left again. Peg had already hurt him enough.

But now the girls were staying.

She didn't think of his voice, or his hands around the phone. She didn't think of where he'd be when she called. In his truck. Or still at his office. His new home. Maybe he would be alone. Maybe he wouldn't. Hank was the kind of man designed by god to be a woman's partner. He was meant for it, for domesticity and intimacy and love. It was a goddamn wonder he'd spent fifteen years with her.

But she didn't think too hard about any of those things, because if she did, she'd talk herself out of it like she had a million times already. There was no work left to make an excuse of. There was only the moonlight and the weight of the phone in her pocket.

He answered on the second ring. "Hank Pazski."

The South still clung to his voice. Once upon a time Peg had teased him about it, accused him of working to keep the Baton Rouge accent alive and well in his vowels and dropped *ing*s. The sweetness of it, though, that was all Hank. Slow and sweet as honey.

"Hello? Anyone…"

"Hank," Peg said, her voice catching. "Don't hang up."

"Peg?"

"Yeah."

Peg could hear the buzz of the evening news on his end and she wanted to ask if he'd fallen asleep again. The theme song for the ten-o'clock news used to be as good as a lullaby for him.

"What do you want?" Hank asked, not unkindly, just… careful, and Peg understood that. Deserved it.

"She's back."

"I can't hear you, Peg."

"She's back," she nearly yelled.

"Who?"

"Hope. And she has a little girl."

Hank gasped, and Peg closed her eyes, wishing away his pain.

"I thought you'd want to know."

Then she hung up.

Twenty

Peg turned off the hose and rolled it back up on its big metal caddy that Hank had paid too much for.

She'd been going down to the farm to deal with the cats when she got sidetracked by the garden. It was just too pitiful to leave it the way it looked. All those fruits and vegetables had been traumatized last night and were drooping into the dirt, and if Hope came down and saw it in this state, she'd just feel awful.

But a little water and the plants were perking right up.

The peas needed to be tied, so she got some string from the kitchen and some stakes from the barn for the tomatoes. In no time the garden was looking pretty good.

Hope, when she came downstairs, could look at that garden and be proud of herself.

Peg was proud of her. So proud she was standing in the damn garden she thought she'd never go into again.

The phone buzzed in her back pocket. Peg didn't even have to check to know who was calling.

Hank.

Two times already this morning. Three last night after she'd called him and then shut off her phone. She should have expected it, but she hadn't. In her mind she'd say her piece and he would just know. She'd forgotten that Hank always wanted more, rolling over her boundaries and her hang-ups like they weren't even there.

At the beginning of the day, Hank would stand behind her at the sink and press kisses to her neck, above the edge of her shirt. His wide hand with its blunt fingers and workingman calluses would curl around her, cupping her stomach.

As if he'd missed her while they slept right next to each other in the same bed.

There'd been a lot of late starts in the orchard in those years.

"Dammit," she said and grabbed the phone, not sure if she was going to answer or just end the call. But then the buzzing stopped and his name vanished from the screen.

He'd leave another voice mail. The fifth. Each about forty seconds. There was over three minutes of Hank on her phone. She could push a few buttons right now and hear his voice again.

She pulled open the squeaky screen door only to find Tink standing in the middle of the kitchen in a pink shirt turned inside out.

"Hey, Tink," she said, stepping up to the sink to wash her hands. "Tomato sandwiches this morning." She'd already assembled the ingredients. A ripe beefsteak tomato, cheddar cheese and big slices off the loaf of sourdough that was going a little stale in the heat. "We need to get out into the orchard before it gets too hot."

"Mom is still sleeping."

"Well, I imagine she's real tired from last night."

Tink nodded and picked at the hem of her pink shirt.

"She's okay," Peg said, reading uncertainty in the set of Tink's shoulders.

"What if she's not, though?" Tink asked in a soft voice. "She's not been okay before."

"No?"

"She slept," Tink whispered. "All the time. And she didn't come out of her room. And I would make her dinner in the microwave and she wouldn't eat it."

Peg drew in a very careful breath. "After Denise died?"

Tink nodded, chewing on her lip.

"Yeah." Peg sighed. "You know what's different this time?"

Tink shook her head. The poor kid was working so hard not to cry.

"You're not alone," she said, and Tink's little chest shuddered. "I'm here," Peg told her, putting her hand over her shoulder. To her absolute surprise, Tink turned and threw her arms around Peg's waist, burying her face there. It was overwhelming for a second, like her body just couldn't register what was happening.

Just a hug. Nothing to get riled up about.

After a breath, she put one hand on the girl's head and her other hand slipped from her shoulder to her back, holding her warm little body close.

Nelson barked as if hoping to be included, and Peg smiled as the little girl's hand stretched out to scratch the soft spot between the dog's ears.

➤ HOPE ◄

She came awake in bits and pieces, drifting upward out of the deep, deep sleep she'd been in. Disoriented at first, it took her a second to realize what was wrong, what had pulled her awake.

Smoke.

Instantly, her eyes were open and she climbed out of bed. Tink's bed was empty, her pillow on the floor. She ran down the stairs, skidding at the bottom through the open door she'd forgotten to lock last night.

The house was quiet and the smell of smoke was coming from outside.

She followed the smell around the side of the house and at first thought it was the garden that was burning, as if Abel and Peg had taken one look at it and thought, *What a disaster*, and tossed a match right into the mess. But then Abel came around the side of the garden with his arms full of the weed trees she'd pulled out yesterday. "Hey," he said and tossed the trees down on the fire, which smoldered, obscuring him with gray smoke.

Nelson came up from the barn in a long, slow amble. She barked at her once, a cheerful greeting like she was an old friend, and then came over to lean against her legs.

"I thought…I thought the orchard was on fire."

"No, just burning the brush. You sleep okay?" he asked.

"Yeah. What time is it?"

"Almost eight."

"Aren't you supposed to be in the orchard?"

"We're just off to a slow start."

They were slow to start because they were all waiting for her. She looked around for Tink and Peg.

"They're down at the barn, trying to get antibiotic ointment on that cat's eye," Abel supplied.

Beyond the smoldering fire, the garden didn't look at all like she'd expected. The half she hadn't weeded seemed even wilder. But the half she'd weeded…was beautiful. She could see the dark dirt between the rows of tomatoes and corn and peppers, the trailing delicate pea shoots twirling up strings that weren't there last night.

"What happened?" she asked.

"To what?"

"The garden. It looks…good." She walked over to the entrance and wandered into the half she'd weeded. The sunshine was warm on her head. Little yellow butterflies touched down on her skin and bees buzzed around her head. "It's beautiful," she said.

"Peg watered it this morning. Tied up the peas. Staked the tomatoes," he said, following her into the lush, damp green space.

"And you're burning the evidence of all the vegetables I pulled out instead of weeds."

"I don't know what carrots and mint ever did to you," he joked. "Peg and I cleaned up, but you did the hard work."

"I thought I ruined it."

"Nah," he said. "If it's growing it can't be ruined. If it's got roots, it still has a chance."

For some reason those words made her throat tight and her eyes burn with tears, and she had to look away and think of getting the car an oil change to make it stop.

"I should thank you for last night," she finally said, trailing her fingers over the feathery head of the carrots she'd managed not to pull yesterday. "My daughter said you were like a superhero, carrying me around."

"That's a stretch," he said. "I'm just glad I could help. How are you feeling this morning?"

"Foolish," she said, feeling herself blush.

"Nothing to feel foolish about," he said quietly. "Next time I faint in the apple orchard, I'll let you carry me out."

It felt good to laugh, to let down her guard.

Hope bent over to pull a weed from the other half of the

garden. When she stood again, every muscle in her back and legs protested, and she made a sound like a very old lady.

"That's the sound of cherry season right there," Abel said with a laugh.

"What's the sound of apple season?" she asked.

He lifted his arm, turned his wrist and hissed.

She pulled another weed. Beside her, he shoved a fence post back into place.

"Hank would be really proud of the work you did here." He stood with his hands on his hips. "Peg doesn't like talking about him, so she won't tell you that. But Hank would like that someone was taking care of the garden."

"Did you know Hank?" she asked.

"He was gone by the time I came back from the army, but during those summers when I was kid, he was here."

"You liked him?"

"He was just a solid guy. Friendly. Fair. Always, and I mean always, ready to take a bunch of kids for ice cream."

Sounds like you, she thought. They were standing so close to each other she could smell him. Dirt and mint. Part of her wanted to get some distance between them. But she was tired of that part of her.

"Peg is such a solitary person. I'm trying to imagine her with someone and it's not easy."

"She was different back then. Happier. She smiled a lot. Joked around. I don't know what happened between them. I stay out of that kind of stuff. But when he left, all the joy drained right out of the place. Right out of Peg." A long lock of his hair had fallen over his face and he brushed it away with his wrist. The lock of hair fell right back down, and she wanted to tuck it behind his ear for him. "She's been happier since you arrived."

"We're staying," she said, blurted really. "Me and Tink.

We're going to stay. Here. At the farm." There was more she could say, about how Daniel might show up and that maybe everyone was in danger, but she just wanted to be happy for a second. The fear she'd been carrying around for so long was too heavy to pick back up just yet.

"I'm glad to hear it," he said.

"So…you know, I can do your books. And help with apple season." She lifted her arm, twisted her wrist and hissed, like she already had the lingo down.

God. You're a weirdo.

"I didn't want you to stay to help with apple season," he said. "Or to do my books."

He touched her fingers with his, not holding them. Just touching them. His thumb against hers.

The sunshine came in the garden in sheets, gilding everything in its path, making it glow. The peppers, the tender white-and-yellow blossoms of what would be zucchini. The bees. Abel.

Hope.

The garden glittered with possibility.

They heard Peg and Tink coming up from the barn, and Hope jumped back away from Abel, like they'd been caught doing something wrong.

She practically ran out of the garden, blushing so hard she could light the rest of the plants on fire.

"You're up!" Peg said.

"I am. I'm sorry I slept in."

"Didn't bother us any," Peg said, and then stepped with Abel over to the brush to monitor the fire and discuss plans for the shortened day.

"You're in your pajamas," Tink said, eyeing her carefully.

Lovely, she'd had that whole conversation with Abel wearing pajama pants with donuts on them.

"I smelled the smoke and came running," Hope said. She touched the little knobs of Tink's collarbone. "How'd you sleep?"

"Good."

"Me, too."

"You slept a lot."

Worry was clear in the set of Tink's shoulders up by her ears. "I was just tired," Hope said. "It's not like when DeeDee died."

"You sure?" Tink asked. "For sure, sure?"

Hope nodded. "For sure. Come on. Last I checked it's still cherry season. We've got work to do."

Twenty-One

That night, Peg dreamed about Denise. About the storm. When Peg was ten and Denise was twelve, a late-February storm closed the whole family up inside The Orchard House for two days. The snowdrifts got higher than the windows on the first floor of the house, slowly making all the rooms darker and darker as the sunlight became muffled by the snow.

And then the power went out.

Peg had been scared. Scared they wouldn't have enough oxygen. That the snow would break the windows and they'd all freeze. That the kittens in the barn that Dad wouldn't let them bring into the house once the snow started would die of starvation.

That was Peg, though. Always scared.

Mom and Dad paced the house, short-tempered, their

shared stress filling the air with something like a toxic gas that made it harder to breathe.

Peg and Denise stayed in the room they shared, upstairs and out of their path. They'd played a five-hour game of Risk, pulled Solar Quest out of the cupboard even though they'd memorized all the answers. They fell asleep at weird hours and woke up in the middle of the day disoriented by the strange light and the cottony silence.

At one point, Denise made up a game where she sat on one bed and threw stuffed animals like missiles, trying to knock Peg off her bed. An oversized Winnie the Pooh made Peg fall down and she got trapped between the wall and her mattress. Denise laughed so hard she hadn't been able to help it until they heard Dad stomping up the steps. By the time he entered their room, they were sitting silently side by side on Denise's bed, trying their best to look both innocent and sorry.

When the storm finally broke and Mom and Dad shoveled them out, she and Denise had put on all their gear. The world was so bright and white it stunned the brain, burned the eyes. They blinked and held their hands up until they adjusted and could see clearly again. The snow was so high they could jump and touch the eaves.

Dad got into the barn and Peg was relieved to see the cats curled up together, sleeping soundly. She gave them more kibble and felt foolish for worrying.

At the back of the barn, the icicles glittered and dripped in the sun. Peg and Denise made snowballs and threw them at the icicles, trying to knock them down. They hit just about everything *but* the icicles, including the glass windows not covered by snow.

They'd been laughing and so focused on the game that they didn't hear Dad until he was right behind them and had grabbed them by their hoods, yanking them off their feet and down into the snow.

"See what happens if you break that glass," he said, and walked away.

Peg had lain there, feeling the chill of the snow and of her father through her coat and scarf, her snow pants and mittens.

"I hate him," Denise had whispered.

"He's our dad," Peg said.

"Like that means anything?"

It did to Peg.

"All I want to do is leave," Denise said. "The second I'm old enough I'm out of here. And I'm not going to look back."

But what about me? Peg thought. *Are you going to leave me, too? Leave me alone with them?*

Peg started to get up, but Denise began moving her arms and legs, making an angel in the deep powdery snow. Peg joined in, because all she wanted was to stay with her sister.

When Peg opened her eyes this morning, the first thing she thought was *I miss her.* After everything her sister had done, Peg was astounded to realize it was still possible to miss Denise. She did not like this one bit. She liked all her emotions separate. Her anger with her anger. Her guilt with her guilt. Nothing touching. Like vegetables on Tink's dinner plate.

She grabbed her phone. At some point last night, Hank had gotten the message that she wouldn't be answering his calls and upgraded to texts.

Four of them now appeared on the screen.

Peg. Please.

Tell me something.

Is she happy?

I can sleep at night if I just know that she ended up happy.

Peg didn't know how to tell him that Hope had shown up with a black eye, a terrifying story and a daughter who didn't talk.

No, Hank. I can't say she's happy. That was the text she could never send. *But she's resilient. And she loves that little girl. And she's trying. She's trying so hard it will break your heart.*

But that wouldn't be enough for Hank. He'd want more for Hope. He'd wanted the world for her and he would have given it to her.

But I made him stop.

The guilt she'd been feeling was compounding, multiplying. So many mistakes. She wondered, if Hope knew about them, even half of them, would she still be so willing to stay?

Her phone buzzed with another text from Hank. It was, frankly, the one she'd been expecting all along. And maybe, with those daydreams of his hands against her skin, wanting.

Give me answers or I'm driving out there to get my own.

She'd opened this box of trouble with the man, and she needed to deal with it.

With shaking fingers she texted Hank the truth. As close to it as she could get. She doesn't remember us. She doesn't remember anything. It's like she was never here. So take all your memories and all those things you wanted for her and put 'em away. They don't matter.

"Good morning," Peg said a half hour later as Tink came into the backyard scratching a mosquito bite on her ankle. The bugs loved that little girl, the same way they used to love Hope when she was a baby.

"Morning, Peg," Tink said in her croaky just-woke-up voice. The sky was turning dark in the west, over the lake. They'd get rain sometime today.

"Ready?" Peg already had the rifle over her arm and the cartridges in her pocket.

"Yep."

"Let's go," she said, leading them toward the old gray fence.

"Did you know one day on Venus is longer than one year on Earth?" Tink asked, skipping along beside her.

"I did not."

"And there might be a planet made out of diamonds?"

"You're making that up."

"I'm not."

Now that Tink was talking, the trick was to be ready for anything. Any topic. Any change in conversation. Any wild question. For a woman who had spent the last couple of years not talking much to anyone, it was like riding a bucking bronco.

"What happens in rehab?"

Peg stopped, the tall grass brushing against the bare skin of her knee. "What are you talking about?"

"Like I know about knee rehab. But there's another kind of rehab, right?"

"Why are you asking me this?" Peg asked and winced at the angry sound of her voice.

Tink looked vaguely alarmed. "I just…I just heard it is all."

Of course, Peg told herself, relaxing the sudden clench of her jaw. *It's a question from a ten-year-old.*

"People go into rehab to help them deal with problems they have with alcohol or drugs," she said, keeping her voice calm and still.

"Yeah, I know that. But what do they do?"

"I don't know really. Talk, probably."

"About drugs?" Tink seemed dubious.

"About why they have problems with them. Why they can't quit, even when they want to."

For a second there was the old fury, the grief from so long ago, when that first letter had come. Compounded by the second and then the third.

Tink made a worldly sound in the back of her throat. A kind of "yes, sure, I knew that."

But then Peg realized where this girl might have heard of rehab and that she might have questions about it that had not been answered. "Did DeeDee go into rehab?"

"For her knee. She hurt it at the salon. There were exercises."

Was that code for something? A lie Denise and Hope told a young girl to protect her? Or to keep the endless questions at bay? Peg didn't know what to believe and then reminded herself it didn't matter. Denise was dead. The past was the past.

Except, lord, there was something about today that made it seem so close she could touch it.

"What do you say," Peg said, "we do some target practice, with real bullets this time?"

"You said we couldn't!" Tink cried, clearly delighted, if not a little scared, at the prospect after all these mornings of aiming and pulling the trigger on an empty chamber.

Peg was out of sorts this morning. The dream. Hank. Maybe shooting the heads of flowers would make her feel better, and if Hope came running down here angry, well, then they'd have a conversation they needed to have anyway.

"I changed my mind," Peg said. She got down on one knee beside the girl and let her load the gun. "What do we know about this gun?" Peg asked.

"It's a serious tool, and we treat it seriously," Tink responded.

The girl had lifted it to her shoulder and Peg crouched beside her, her arms on her shoulders to brace her for the recoil.

Peg remembered her first shot. She'd been blown back on her butt by the recoil and her father had bent over laughing at her.

Behind them there was the squeal of the screen door opening and then slamming shut.

"Target practice is over," Peg said, taking the gun from Tink just as Hope yelled, "What the hell are you doing?"

Peg emptied the cartridge from the rifle and put it in her pocket. She turned to face Hope, who was laying waste to the tall grass as she marched toward them.

"Uh-oh," Tink whispered.

"I'm right here," Peg said, trying to stop the lecture before it started. "No one can get hurt."

"No one can get hurt?" Hope breathed. "Those feel like dangerous last words. Please don't...don't show my daughter that gun. Don't teach her how to shoot a gun."

"Do you know how to shoot a gun?" Peg asked.

"Don't be ridiculous."

"I'm not. I'm asking a very sensible question." The girls were staying. Daniel might find them, and as unlikely as it seemed, it was worth being ready for. If the police and the law couldn't keep them safe, Peg would do her damnedest.

"Why would I need to shoot a gun?"

"I don't know, Hope. You show up here in the middle of the night with a daughter who doesn't speak and half your face beaten in—"

Hope gasped and even Tink made a sound.

Okay, okay, too far, but, lord! Were we all just going to keep pretending?

Tink stepped closer to her mom like the ten-year-old was going to protect her. There used to be a time when Peg and

Dee had stood together like that, when they held shaking hands in front of their father, a united front.

Good, she thought. *You gotta do that.* Once you stop, it gets easy to turn on each other. To hurt each other to feel safe. To feel better.

"How is a gun going to change anything?" Hope asked.

"Might keep you safe."

"I can keep us safe," Hope said, and Tink looked over at her, her doubt plain as day. "We don't need a gun. Everything will be fine."

➤ TINK ➤

By the time they got to delivering cherries, the rain had started and Mom still hadn't let go of the rifle thing.

"We are not gun people, Tink," she said as they pulled into the cherry stand by the liquor store.

"Peg is."

"Well, that's Peg."

"Abel is."

Mom looked at her.

"What?" Tink shrugged. "He is. Or he was. He shot guns in the army. He said he learned on the farm. His dad taught him using the same rifle that Peg was using to teach me!"

"Have you been talking to everyone but me all this time?" Mom asked.

"Sometimes."

"I'm gonna stop talking to you and we'll see how you like it," she said, and hopped out of the truck, slamming the door real hard behind her.

The cars started pulling in, and Tink went to work, darting from the cars to the back of the truck, delivering new bags.

The last car she got to was a big fancy truck. An old guy was sitting in it, with white hair and a bright plaid shirt.

Tink grabbed a bag of cherries and walked it over to him.

The guy was watching Mom handle the stand and talk to another customer. Tink looked over at her to see what was so mesmerizing. Her eye looked better. She was wearing her favorite green T-shirt that said *weirdo* on it in tiny red letters.

Wait a second, she thought. *Was the guy, like…into Mom?*

As she got closer to the truck, the old guy finally looked at her and she realized he was crying. Before he rolled down his window, he wiped at his eyes, scrubbing his hand over his face.

As a rule, Tink didn't really trust people. Maybe because DeeDee hadn't. Or maybe because Mom sometimes trusted all the wrong people. But Tink had a real eye for knowing when a person was going to be a creep. Daniel could have bought her as many chocolate ice cream cones as he wanted, but it wouldn't hide his creepy, his mean. Not from Tink. This guy, though, with the white hair, staring at Mom and crying, wasn't mean. Or creepy.

He was just sad.

"Hey, kiddo," he said in a bright voice, but his smile was a struggle. It reminded her of Mom's smile after DeeDee died, the way she pretended to still be happy. "How's the cherry business?"

"Not bad," she said. "It's almost over."

"Yeah, I guess so. August is coming up pretty fast. School will be here before you know it."

Tink pulled a face that made the guy laugh, which was the point.

"You know Peg?" he asked. "I figure since you're selling her cherries."

Tink nodded.

"How's she doing?"

"Fine."

"Nelson still around?"

"She farted last night and we almost died."

The old man laughed, a quiet sound that lifted his chest and settled it down again in a sadder shape, like he was shrinking right in front of her. "Word to the wise, do not give that dog bacon or she'll stink up the place."

"That's exactly what happened. We were having BLTs—"

"And Peg gave her bacon?"

"Yes!"

"That dog has always had her number."

"Hey," Mom said, coming up behind Tink, putting her hand on her shoulder and keeping her tight up against her. "Everything all right?"

Tink nodded, and the old man tried to smile again, but it got wobbly at the edges.

Mom stepped forward. "Sir? You okay?"

"I'm fine." He waved her off. "Just feeling a little sentimental." He looked out the windshield. "Must be the rain."

"You get sentimental in the rain?" Mom asked.

"Doesn't everyone?"

Tink shook her head no, and Mom nodded yes and something about that made him laugh.

"You interested in some cherries? They're washed. Real sweet," Mom said.

"Oh, I know Peg's cherries," he said. "I'll take a pound."

Tink handed the cherries up to the man through the window of his big truck.

"I asked your daughter how Peg was doing."

"Yeah?"

"She was a little closemouthed on the subject. Peg all right?"

"Fine," Hope said. "She's doing great. You want me to give her a message? Tell her hello from you?"

"No. She doesn't want to hear from me," he said and winked at Tink. Then he gave a wave and slowly drove away, careful not to splash through the big puddles.

⇥ HOPE ⇤

The next night, after another long day in the orchard, Hope asked them all to come back to the barn after they'd had dinner and showered off the day of work.

"What is this?" Peg asked, entering the barn as the sun was setting behind the trees.

Abel had arrived a few seconds earlier, flipping on the lights as the world got darker outside, the moths buzzing around the bare light bulbs high overhead. It was amazing how they just got used to the bugs.

"Well," she said. "It's kind of a staff meeting."

"A what meeting?" Peg asked.

"Staff."

"We're staff?"

Hope glanced around the barn and settled on Abel leaning up against the shelving in a pair of sweatpants and a clean T-shirt, taken by the sight of him out of his coveralls.

"Yeah," Hope finally said, they were, motley and exhausted as they might be.

"All right, then, what are we supposed to do in these meetings?" Peg asked.

"Well, first I want to solve a problem. Everyone I'm delivering cherries to in town is getting frustrated by your lack of invoicing."

Peg and Abel both pointed at each other, eyebrows raised.

"That's not helping," Hope said. "I've tried to make sense of the system on your laptop, Peg. But it's hopeless. So I'm going to drag you two into the modern age."

"I don't like the modern age," Peg said.

"I don't think that matters," Abel said.

"I just want to show you an app you can get on your phone that will make all of this so easy."

"I thought you were going to handle all this," Peg said.

"I'm going to do most of it. But if we have all the same systems on our phones—"

"I didn't bring my phone," Peg said.

"I asked you to."

Peg shrugged.

"Go get it?"

Peg sighed and turned around, back to the house.

Leaving her alone—sort of, as Tink was off somewhere wrangling kittens—with Abel.

Don't be weird, she told herself.

"She's not coming back, is she?" Hope asked.

"Nope." He pushed away from where he'd been leaning and walked toward her. She fought the instinct to take a step back, flummoxed by his proximity. "But I've got my phone."

"It really is easy," she said.

"It better be." He laughed.

While he downloaded the basic bookkeeping app, she showed him on her phone how simple it was to take pictures of receipts and bills that all went to the same file on all their phones. As they watched her screen, side by side, his shoulder brushed hers. When he would shift back, copying what she'd done on his own phone, his shoulder would retreat, leaving her cold and feeling foolish.

He asked another question, tilting forward, and this time his chest brushed up against her back. She sucked in a breath of air.

"Sorry," he said, leaning away from her. "Don't mean to crowd you."

"No." She shook her head. "You're not." She looked up, catching his eyes. "I'm just a jumpy person."

"I don't want to scare you," he said, his voice low.

"You don't. Really. I'm just…" *Overwhelmed by your sweat-pants?* "Nervous."

"About what?"

Oh, nervous in general was what she was going to say. Those were the words lined up on her tongue. But a different word jumped the line.

"You," she ended up saying and blushed.

"I'm sorry," he said and stepped away.

"No. Not like that," she was quick to add. "I'm not scared of you. I just…" Oh god, she was going to say it. These words were coming out of her mouth. There was no way to stop them. "Like you. Is all. That's weird. I'm being weird. I'm—"

"I like you, too," he said, and she shut up.

The palm of his hand brushed against her elbow and she felt like butter in a hot pan. She didn't flinch; she absolutely melted.

Tink came running out of the back of the barn, a scratch on her cheek, and Abel dropped his hand and practically leaped away from her.

Hope bent down to look at the scratch. "You have got to stop loving those kittens so much," she told her scowling daughter. "Go show Peg. She'll clean you up."

Tink ran off, and the silence in the barn, the warm glow from the light bulbs, the endless night outside, sizzled and crackled.

"Why?" she asked.

"Why what?"

"Why do you like me?" It didn't make sense to her. "I mean, I show up here and I've been beaten up. My kid isn't talking to me. I have more baggage than I can carry. The first few days you have to feed me and fix my car. When I say it all out loud it's—"

"Obvious?" he asked.

"Abel," she breathed. The last guy who'd liked her when she'd been in rough shape just wanted to take advantage of her. Abel didn't seem like that kind of guy, but she'd been fooled before. "Don't joke."

"Well, the bruising has faded, but even when it was bad, I could see you're beautiful. Your daughter is talking and so you two aren't ever quiet anymore, so I know that you're smart. And funny. And loving. You've carried all that baggage and you're dealing with it, so you're a survivor. As for feeding you, that was just a bonus."

He grinned at her and her heart just turned right over in her chest. Like a dog showing its belly.

"You're handsome," she blurted.

"Oh? Go on." He crossed his arms over his chest with a cocky smile.

"You're Peg's friend, even when it's hard."

"Which is all the time."

"You're also funny and smart. And...patient. I like that you made mistakes and you dealt with them."

"More like dealing with them, but I'll take the compliment."

"I...ah...I should tell you something."

"Yeah?" The corner of his lip lifted in what might have been the sexiest smile Hope had ever seen in her life.

"I'm dangerous."

"You are."

"No, that... I mean—" That came out wrong. "Getting involved with me might be dangerous."

"Because the guy that hurt you might come back?"

"Maybe."

"I'm not scared of a guy who hits women and scares little girls."

"I wish I wasn't."

"Do you want to tell me what happened?" he asked.

"Right now?"

She hadn't said anything to anyone except Peg, and part of her understood if anything was going to happen with Abel, she needed to tell him, too. Because it might change things for him.

He shook his head. "You don't have to tell me ever, if you don't want. It's your story, Hope. Your life. But you need to tell someone."

"Peg—"

"Is a start."

"You mean I have to tell a lot of people?" she joked.

"It's easier each time you do it. That load you carry, it gets a little lighter if you share it."

"You learn that in the army?"

"Therapy. After the army." His hands reached for her elbows, ran down the skin of her arms, his fingers curling around her wrists. "There are things I haven't told you, either."

Maybe this was just what it was when you were an adult. When you'd lived a chunk of life. You had mistakes and regrets, things that had made you but no longer defined you.

That was comforting.

"You're dangerous," he said. "But not because of your past."

He leaned in, past all of her words, all of her reasons why this might be a bad idea, and he kissed her. Soft and sweet, his lips slightly chapped against hers. His breath feathered across her face and he was warm—all of him warm—and she realized how cold she was. Her entire life—cold.

Abel pulled back, his hands now on her waist, squeezing her just slightly, and she made a noise, something between a sigh and a squeak, embarrassed and excited and wanting more.

He brushed a long strand of blond hair off her face. "You're dangerous because I never saw you coming."

Twenty-Two

Hope opened the screen door as slowly as she could, hoping to avoid the squeak.

It didn't work.

In the dark she heard Nelson get up, the rattle of her collar and the pad of her feet as she walked across the room to greet her at the door.

"Shhh," she whispered to his panting face.

The dog followed her across the kitchen, where no moonlight fell in through the windows. The storms had returned and it was nothing but dark clouds out there.

What had happened in the barn had her too wired to go upstairs just now. There had to be something between kissing Abel and crawling into bed in the same room as her ten-year-old.

The light of the fridge when she pulled it open made her blink.

"What are you looking for?"

Hope jumped, the door falling open farther to illuminate Peg sitting at the kitchen table.

"Jesus, Peg, you scared me."

"Sorry. You hungry—"

"No, I was looking for a beer or something."

"I got something here." She lifted a square bottle. "Grab a glass. We can go into the other room."

Hope pulled out one of the thimble-sized coffee cups and followed Peg into the living room with all the comfortable chairs they never sat in.

"Can we turn on a light?" Hope asked as Peg fumbled for the cup and poured her a drink of whatever was in that bottle.

"No," she said. "Your eyes will adjust."

"Why don't we ever sit in here?" she asked, curling her legs up on the flowered chair. Peg was on the couch, her legs stretched out on the ottoman. The liquor bottle was on the table between them.

"Too comfortable."

"Oh my god." Hope laughed. "That's the most Peg thing you could say." She took a sip from the mug and whiskey burned down her throat and up into her head. "Wow," she breathed. "You're drinking the good stuff."

"I wouldn't know," Peg said. "The bottle was left here."

There seemed to be a story there, but she didn't press.

"What's got you up looking for a drink in the middle of the night?" Peg asked.

"My life," she joked, but Peg didn't laugh.

"Why are you drinking in the middle of the night?" Hope asked.

"My life."

Well, now that *was* funny, and in the dark they both chuckled.

"You and Abel get the invoicing sorted?"

"Yep." Hope was glad the room was so dark so Peg couldn't see her blush. "I can show you tomorrow. It's really so simple—"

"Can I ask you something?" Peg interrupted, and Hope was beginning to think Peg had been down here awhile, making her way through that whiskey.

"Sure."

There was so much comfort here. The rain against the windows. A sleeping dog by their feet. The faint outline of the other.

"Were you happy?" she asked.

"With what?"

"As a kid. Growing up with Denise."

"I wasn't unhappy," she said. "But you knew my mom. Sometimes it felt like…rebellion to be anything other than cynical. And distrustful. And scared."

"That doesn't sound happy."

"Well, she named me Hope—"

Peg coughed.

"You okay?"

"Fine. Whiskey went down the wrong way. Go on."

"She named me Hope, but it seemed like it was aspirational, you know? Like she wanted to give it a shot, but it was just too hard. And I understood that at a really young age." The wind rattled the windows in their casings. "But I think I turned out okay."

"Your nature was happy," Peg said, and it wasn't a question. "I remember that so clearly, the way you used to wake up in the morning. Never sleepy, never grumpy, only ready. Chubby and freckled and running full-tilt at the day."

Hope was stunned. Not just that Peg remembered her so clearly but with such love.

"I'm sorry I don't remember being here," she said.

Peg put her mug down and stared out the window at a land-scape she couldn't see but must know by heart. "I remember," she said. "And that's enough."

Upstairs, the moonlight came in the window like a flash-light and she could see Tink, sound asleep. Hope watched her for a moment, marveling how a kid could sleep the way she did, sliding, it seemed, half off the bed. The blankets were on the floor and her pillow was in danger of following.

"Come on, kid," she whispered, and picked up her daugh-ter's sleeping body and repositioned her on the bed. She grabbed the blanket and, since it was still hot in the evening, even with the open windows, she covered her with the sheet, leaving the thin burgundy blanket folded at the foot of the bed. She lifted Tink's head and, as she shifted the pillow, her fingers brushed over something slick and cold. She found, tucked inside, what felt like two old magazines. She held them up and saw that they were old *National Geographic*s.

Vikings and Space.

That explained the history lesson on Vikings she'd gotten the other day.

Fossilized poop, honest to god.

Hope set the magazines down on the floor beside her bed and patted down the pillowcase for more contraband. A few pieces of sea glass. Of course.

"Tink," she muttered. "Why are you trying to sleep on this stuff?"

In the bottom corner of the pillowcase she found a cool, slick cylinder. When she held it up to the light, it took her a second to recognize it.

A bullet.

Even knowing it was harmless on its own, it still made her heart stop. Her daughter was sleeping on a bullet. She grabbed the pillow, unconcerned about waking up Tink, who was going to be punished and have a stern talking-to once Hope was able to form coherent thoughts on the subject. The pillowcase was otherwise empty except for some papers, which she yanked out. Holding them up, she saw that they were two letters addressed to Peg.

She sighed and hung her head for a second. Tink had gone into Peg's room.

Hope bent down, picked up the magazines and stacked them up with the letters. Tomorrow, she'd make Tink return them all to Peg and admit that she'd been going places she wasn't supposed to. She walked out of the bedroom and into the kitchen. She turned on the light and opened one of the empty cupboards to put the magazines and letters in. That was when she noticed the handwriting.

The name on the return address.

Denise Wright.

She had one second of indecision, of telling herself that if she read the letters it was worse than what Tink had done, somehow compounding the sneakiness. But even as she thought it, she opened the top letter and started to read.

Peg,
I'm sorry for the way I left. But I knew you would get upset. And taking the jewelry was a low blow—but in terms of our inheritance you came out the winner on that end. So, what's a little jewelry? Besides, you and I both know Mom's jewelry wasn't worth much. I barely got five hundred bucks for all of it.

Jacob and I are in Saginaw. I had a job at a salon. It was shit work and the owner was a total bitch. Said she couldn't trust me. Well, how was I supposed to trust her when she never showed me how to cut hair after she promised me she would? Instead I was just always answering phones and sweeping up. I'll get another job. I'm not worried.

Jacob had a good job at a grocery store but someone stole money and all the cashiers got fired.

But you know Jacob, he got another job right away.

I'm writing because you were right about one thing. The drugs are a problem. I thought I could handle them…that we could handle them. But it's getting bad. Really bad. And I get why you were scared and I'm sorry that I didn't take you seriously. But I am now. I'm taking it all really seriously.

I found us a state-run rehab program that's not as expensive as those private ones you were talking about and I got us on the list. There's a spot coming up in two weeks, but we need three thousand dollars.

It's a lot of money, I know. But I'm in bad shape, Peg. And maybe you could sell off a few acres to that conglomerate that's always sniffing around? Don't be mad. Please don't be mad. I wouldn't write unless I really needed help.

Denise

Hope realized she hadn't been breathing and suddenly pulled in a breath. Another one. Dizzy, she put her hand against the counter and nearly missed, stumbling backward against the window.

The shades rattled and she pressed the letters to her chest. How like her mom. As she read those words, she could see her sitting at some kitchen table, a cigarette at her elbow. Cold and righteous, a willing victim and so hard done by, while at the same time having to swallow the pride that kept her head above the rising waters of her own disaster.

But drugs? Denise Wright liked her white wine and a birth-day bourbon sour, but there were no drugs, not that Hope ever saw, and in the two-bedroom apartment on Euclid there was nowhere for Mom to hide. She didn't have a lot of friends, outside of the girls at the salon, and Hope was often there with them.

It would be so easy to say none of this was true. But the words in her mother's handwriting were the concrete proof.

Her mother had been an addict.

The next envelope was soft and frayed at the corners, like a delicate artifact. The address was for a hospital in Saginaw. The state-run rehab? Probably.

"Mom?" Tink stood in the doorway, rubbing her eyes. "What are you doing?"

Hope turned and held up the letters. "You know," she said. "The better question is, what are you doing?"

✥ PEG ✥

Once Hope went upstairs, Peg's little pity party with Hank's leftover whiskey seemed pathetic, so she put the bottle back under the sink and headed to bed. And because she was drunk, she turned on the television, just in time to fall asleep to the ten-o'clock news. She thought, as sleep dragged her down, of Hank somewhere in Petoskey doing the same thing.

The knock on her door sent her upright in bed.

"Peg?"

The girls, she thought, clearing the cobwebs. *It's the girls at the door.*

She got out of bed and opened the door just a crack and could see Tink standing there, Hope behind her.

"Sorry," Hope said. "We saw the light and heard the TV… We thought you were awake."

"We'll come back in the morning," Tink said, turning around, only to have her mother take her by the shoulders and keep her in place.

"Tink has something to tell you," Hope said.

"Well, this all seems very serious. Give me a second."

She shut the door, grabbed her eyeglasses, thought about a bra, figured what the hell, and then went into the kitchen, shutting the bedroom door firmly behind her. The sound of the news was muffled through the heavy wood.

"Now," she said, joining the girls where they sat at the table. "What's got you girls up in the middle of the night?"

"It's ten," Tink said, and Hope poked her. Peg tried not to smile. She liked their little routines. But then the girls set two magazines down on the table.

*National Geographic*s. Old ones.

A bullet. From the box in the bedroom. For the pistol in the old jewelry box.

And finally two old letters.

Peg grabbed the letters quick, swept them right off the magazines, knocking the bullet to the ground. She pressed them to her chest, leveling a cold gaze on the girl, who stepped back against her mom's legs.

"I'm sorry," Tink whispered. "I went into your room and I'm sorry."

Rehab, Peg thought. *That's why she was asking about rehab.*

"You read 'em?" she asked Tink, and then Hope.

"One of them," Hope said.

She could hear Hank in her head, telling her that secrets always got found out. Always. Hiding them only pushed them out another direction.

"Which one?" she asked.

"Mom asking for money for rehab."

"First time or second time?"

Hope gaped. "Just…the one time. Three thousand dollars for the state-run program."

Well, Peg thought, *there's that, at least.*

"She asked again?" Hope asked.

"She gave that spot to Jacob. Tried to quit on her own but he came out of that state-run program and started using again. She asked again for herself a few months later."

The second letter was bad. Her brave and bold sister had been scared, scared of Jacob and the kind of people now in their lives. They were doing murky things just to stay high. And stay alive.

The third letter… Well, she was never sure why she'd kept the third letter.

Thank god Tink hadn't found the third one.

"I just find this so hard to believe," Hope said.

"Your mom using drugs or me sending her money again and again?" Like a fool. A fool who thought she could change her sister. Could somehow turn back the clock and get that girl who'd made snow angels with her, who'd slept in the same bed as her. Who'd traded chores and took the blame when Peg forgot to feed the chickens.

Until that dream the other night, she'd stopped missing her sister; that soft emotion had calcified under harder ones over the decades. But as she stood in her kitchen with these girls, she wished just a little that her sister was alive to see it, to be here. All of them together in this kitchen. For better or worse.

"She didn't use when I was growing up," Hope said defensively.

"I'm glad," Peg said. Her life had been torn apart by Denise's addiction; she was happy that Hope's hadn't been. "For both of you."

"Did you sell off part of the farm?" Hope asked.

"Both times."

Hope opened her mouth and Peg lifted her hand. "We don't apologize for Denise anymore," she said. "Remember?"

"I wasn't going to apologize," Hope said. "I was going to thank you. Because the money you sent the second time must have worked."

It hadn't. But she wasn't going to tell Hope that, not when she was standing there so carefully in her memories of her mother. She wasn't going to taint any more of them.

"You got any more of my things upstairs?" Peg asked Tink.

"No. I promise."

Despite Tink having sneaked into the room she wasn't supposed to, Peg didn't think she was lying about this. They'd be having a different conversation.

"You," Peg said to Tink, changing the subject, "are in trouble."

"I know," Tink said. "I'm sorry."

"Go to bed. We'll figure out what to do with you in the morning," Peg said, and she waited until the girls were upstairs.

In her room, she opened up the jewelry box, dug through all the pictures she'd been hiding and found the pistol down at the bottom. The third letter was tucked under the gun, scrunched against the bottom. She pulled it out and flattened it in her hands, trying to get out the wrinkles. The words coming back to her through all the years.

Help me, Peg. Please. Help me.

Nelson, who was sitting at her feet, whined in her throat, aware of her agitation in the way of good dogs.

"At least she didn't take the gun," she said out loud. She placed the letters on top of the gun and considered whether she should throw that third letter away.

Because that letter could do just as much damage as the gun.

✦ HOPE ✦

The next day Peg made a big show of locking the door that Tink had used to sneak in to her room.

"What do you think it's going to be, Mom?" Tink asked as they walked toward the orchard.

"What?"

"My punishment."

"Bad. It's going to be bad."

Peg kept the suspense going the whole day, and when they got back from delivering cherries, Peg was waiting with a shovel, gloves and a bucket.

Dog-poop pickup in the field behind the house.

It was unpleasant. For Tink.

But also hilarious. For Hope.

Hope worked in the garden while Peg sat on an old dusty lawn chair she'd pulled up from the basement, watching Tink pick up poop like it was radioactive.

Tink kept gagging theatrically.

"It's a show," Hope said about the gagging.

"It's a good one," Peg agreed.

Twenty minutes later, as the sun was setting behind the trees, Hope came out of the garden with an armful of zucchini. The largest one was as big as her forearm.

Abel was standing next to Peg's chair, holding a box and watching Tink carry on like her life was ending.

Hope felt a giddy little twist in her stomach at the sight of him, his tanned face smiling as she walked up to him.

"What are we going to do with this?" Hope asked about the vegetables. "There are about four more I could pick to-morrow. The garlic is out of control and most of the tomatoes are ripe, too. We can't eat all this."

Peg had them on a steady tomato sandwich diet, but still they couldn't get through all the garden was producing.

"Sell it," Abel said. "At the stands."

"Hank did," Peg said, her eyes still on Tink. "Made a good chunk of change."

"All right," Hope said and stacked the zucchini down on the grass beside Peg's chair. Tomorrow she'd take that crop down to the stand in the liquor store parking lot. It was always the busiest.

"So what brings you here?" Hope asked Abel. He never came up to the house after orchard hours. When they were done at the barn, they usually didn't see him again until the next day. The other night, with the kissing, had been quite an exception.

He handed over the box.

"Receipts. I meant to bring it to you the other day, but I forgot. I emailed you the spreadsheet."

"I got it. Thanks." She took the box, a little bummed that there wasn't more to seeing him after-hours than a big box of receipts.

"And, I don't know." He shrugged. "I thought you guys might be interested in some ice cream."

"Yes!" Tink yelled from across the field. "Yes! We are really really interested in ice cream."

"You're not done yet," Peg yelled back.

"Peg!" she groaned.

"Make her work another twenty minutes," Peg said so Tink couldn't hear. "Then go get her some ice cream."

"You come, too, Peg," Hope said. "We can go to this beach—"

But Peg was shaking her head. "I'm good," she said. "Right here."

Twenty-Three

The smell of the air was changing. Less sweet. More rot. Seventeen days in the orchard with the girls and cherry season was almost over.

Peg and Abel folded up the tarps the way they did every night, checking for holes and wear.

"We're going to have to replace half of these next year," he said.

"I'm too tired to think about next year," she said. "How did it go with the phone app thing the other night?" she asked.

"Yeah, thanks for cutting and running there, Peg."

"I'm an old dog, and invoicing through your phone is a new trick."

"It's pretty straightforward," he said.

"Yeah." She looked at him over her shoulder. "But how did it go?"

Abel, that big old former military man, blushed bright red. "You playing matchmaker, Peg?"

"You two watch each other all the time in the orchard, trying to pretend you're not."

Today his eyes had been all over Hope as she drank from that metal cup of his, and she thought the whole orchard was going to start smoking.

"Is it a problem?"

"Not for me. It's none of my business."

Truthfully, she liked the idea.

The sound of a truck pulling into the driveway caught their attention.

"The girls are back already?" Peg asked, checking her watch. It was way too early for them to have made all the deliveries.

"That's not our truck," Abel said, and they both stepped to the door of the barn to see who was coming on their property.

Abel, Peg noticed, had a tire iron in his hand.

"Who the hell is that?" Abel asked as the big black truck stopped in front of the house.

I should have expected this, she thought, her stomach suddenly in the bottoms of her boots. Telling that man to stay away was like waving a red flag at him.

The big black shiny truck was oversize for the man who owned it, and tricked out, because for all his simplicity, he enjoyed creature comforts. She remembered a time when the sight of his truck would fill her up with bliss. She'd go running out to it, climb into the passenger seat, happy to go wherever.

As long as it was with him.

"Peg?" he asked again, but she didn't know what to say. "Do you know that truck, or do I need to—"

"No." She put her hand on his arm, startling both of them. She was not a toucher and their relationship wasn't the kind of hugs and handshakes. A firm pat on the shoulder around the holidays was about it.

"It's Hank," she said.

Abel's eyebrows went up. "What's he doing here?"

"I called him."

"Peg, that's great." Oh, Abel, he really was such a romantic. She left Abel standing there in the open door of the barn and walked up the grassy hill to the gravel of the parking area, right to where Hank stood.

Ten years hadn't done much damage to him; he looked the same. Mostly. He'd been a big, tall man and he was just as big and tall now. His plaid shirt with the snap buttons was blue and yellow because he'd always been a bit of a peacock. His hair was pure white, a wave up over his forehead. And cowboy boots, always cowboy boots.

All in all, he didn't look much different from the day she'd met him, buying a new tractor in Petoskey. Only, his hair had been jet-black then. He'd asked her out for dinner and a month later he'd moved into The Orchard House.

"Hi, Peg," he said.

"Hank. What are you doing here?"

"You must be joking."

Peg looked away.

"Our girl, Peggy." The nickname was hard to hear and she twitched away, uncomfortable.

"She's not our girl," she reminded him.

Twenty years ago this was all they'd done, worn this conversation out in a million different ways. They'd run a rut with it, right between them, and when they finally broke ten years later, that was the fault line.

As much as it hurt her to see him again, she knew he was feeling it, too.

She could see it in the narrowing of his lips, the way his

hand pressed against his stomach like there was a knot there that had just tightened. She knew that knot, the way it could keep you up late at night, wondering how something you loved so much could just vanish and how you were supposed to live with the pain.

"I saw her," he said.

"Where?"

"Cherry stands."

"You're stalking the cherry stands?"

He shrugged.

"And?" she asked, hands on her hips. "Did she suddenly remember you? Did it suddenly all click into place for her and she went rushing into your arms like the long-lost—" She stopped because he was reaching for her, but she stepped back. "Don't," she whispered, blinking away the tears.

"You didn't tell me she was hurt. Who hit her?" he asked.

"An old boyfriend."

He looked off at the far horizon, the barn and the garden behind it. The moment he saw the garden his face changed. He chewed his lips, opened his mouth and closed it, all of which meant he was choosing his words carefully.

"Is she okay?"

"Better," she said. "She had a bad first week, but she seems to be settling in."

"Are you going to tell her?"

"No."

"Peg—"

"You want to talk to her? Okay. But I'm telling you, you're being selfish."

"*I'm* being selfish."

Oh, he was good and mad about that. And maybe he had the right, but it didn't change a thing that was happening at this farm right now.

"That girl has been through something and you showing up with your memories and all your stories only so you can prove that what she remembers isn't the way things really were... You're going to hurt her. The girl doesn't need to be hurt any more than she's been."

"Is that what you're telling yourself, Peg?" he asked. "That you're keeping all your secrets to protect her? And you're accusing me of being selfish?"

"Judge me all you want."

"I don't want to judge," he said quietly. "But I can't listen to you say you're trying to protect her now when you did nothing to protect her then."

Peg looked over at the sun working its way out of the clouds. It was heating up, and like every early-August rainstorm, the aftermath was just as ugly. Hot and humid like living in a ziplock bag.

"What do you want?" she asked him. "You want to yell at me? Go for it. But it doesn't change anything. You want to wait here so you can rip apart that girl's memories for no good reason?"

"Stop, Peg," he whispered. "Just stop."

"Then tell me! Tell me why you're here!"

"I miss you every day, Peg. I wish it was different and I could just forget you, the way you were able to forget me, but I—"

The words weren't even out of his mouth before Peg was walking away. "I got work to do," she said. "Stay or go, it doesn't matter."

But she knew he would leave.

She was, after all, really good at pushing that man away.

Twenty-Four

The next day they did two days' work in one just so they could put cherry season to bed.

Twenty-three days after it started.

Twenty days after Hope and Tink had showed up, it was over.

Life came rushing back after cherry season; it expanded and filled the corners of the farm. They were just coming in from the orchard under the light of a very full moon and already everything that got pushed aside stood waiting its turn. The lawn, the laundry. Shopping. Bills. Nelson was due a trip to the vet. Peg had a sore tooth.

All of it needed attention and needed it now.

She could see Abel on the other tractor, undoubtedly already thinking about apple season.

Peg, for one, preferred the simplicity of cherry season. It was work without thought. It was straightforward and clear-cut. The sweetness was never tempered by bitterness. Or doubt.

Abel drove the tractor into the barn and cut the engine. "Another season in the books," he said into the deep silence.

"A good one," Peg said. They'd lost seventy-five pounds of cherries to birds and rot—about a tree's worth. Which was actually better than in years past. When it was just the two of them, Peg and Abel, by the time they got to the last two trees, the cherries would be split and soft and they'd lose double that.

"Those girls—" he said and shook his head. They were a big part of why it had gone so well this year. Not just the cherries, but the stands with the garden stuff. It had been a very good cherry season.

"I know," she said.

"I'm gonna check the drainage on the southwest corner," Abel said. "I'm worried about the leaves—"

"Turning yellow?" She'd noticed, too.

"Yeah," he sighed.

Even when the work was over, it wasn't over.

"Peg?" he said carefully. "We're not friends."

Peg turned a dark eye to her business partner and frankly the only friend she had in the world. She would have said they were. Friends. Not great ones. But she cared about him.

"I guess not," she said.

"You know what I mean."

She didn't think she did.

"I'm just saying, we've worked side by side for a few years now and I've offered to buy you out. And I know you've had offers on the house. Which means you can leave. Any time. Buy a condo in Florida so you don't have to stay here all winter."

"I don't mind the winters."

"You hate the winters."

"Well, I hate Florida more."

"I swear to god, Peg, you are the most contrary person I've ever met. I'm trying to make a point."

"Well, get on with it."

He threw his hands up. "Why do you stay?"

In case they came back.

Denise and Hope. Hank, too, for that matter.

In case the family that had left and the love she'd pushed away came back to her.

She gave herself a minute, imagining herself in a new house. A different job. She imagined a place where the air didn't smell of fruit and the bees didn't brush against her skin like old friends. Where the work ended at some normal hour and her fortunes and mood didn't rise and fall with the weather.

"Nelson could never leave," she said, because she couldn't envision herself any other place. She was The Orchard House, and The Orchard House was her, and she'd die there. Be buried out back. Maybe in Hank's garden. She'd let that old sunflower grow right on through her.

"Yeah," he sighed. "That's what I figured. But Peg, I just hope with the girls here now, that maybe you can enjoy it. Hank—"

"Won't be back."

"Oh. I'm sorry to hear that."

"You wanted to double date?" She laughed at his expression.

"I'm just saying," Abel pressed on, not getting the hint at all that she wanted out of this conversation and out of this barn, "homes should be happy. Even yours."

Peg walked in the back door and into the smell of garlic and tomatoes. Hope, flushed over a hot stove, looked over at her, tucking that hair behind her ear. Her face had finally healed. Peg took comfort in the fact that The Orchard House had been good to them.

"You guys are late!" Hope cried.

The clock said nine. "You didn't have to wait."

"Of course we did. Spaghetti tonight. Hope that's all right," Hope said.

"We had it last night."

"Did we?" Hope asked. "God, it's been so busy—"

"It's fine," Peg said. "I'll go wash up and then help."

"I don't need help. We got it under control." She looked over at Tink, who was sitting against the cupboards playing on Hope's cell phone. Peg could hear the long steady trill of bings and boops. Hope gave her daughter's leg a nudge, to little effect. "Seriously, Peg. Let us treat you, would you?"

"Well, I don't know about a treat," she said, and it wasn't until after she'd gone into her room to take a shower that she realized how all of that might have sounded. She glanced over at the door she'd shut, considering an apology, that she hadn't had someone cook for her in...

Well, since Hank.

She just wasn't sure she deserved the meal. The effort. The small kindnesses. They weren't always easy to accept when you lived on a starvation diet.

She showered then stood in front of her empty dresser, trying to remember the last time she'd done laundry. Cherry season was always so intense and fast, nothing else in the world happened. When it was over, it was like slamming into a brick wall at a million miles an hour.

In the back of her closet she found an old dress, a sleeveless blue thing that swung around her body and hung past her knees. She used to love dresses. After working in the fields all day she'd shower and put on a dress and Hank would whistle.

Who is this fancy lady? he'd say and pull her up against his chest.

It's just a dress, she'd say, but inside she was thrilled.

When Hank left, all her dresses got pushed to the back of the closet and the bottoms of her drawers.

It was still hot out, with the dying day putting out its own kind of heat, and the dress felt cool against her skin, so she left it on and grabbed the envelope of cash from the back of the drawer. Over the course of the last few weeks she'd added everything Hope had brought back with her from the fruit stands and the invoice money from Swafiya. All in all there was three thousand dollars there.

If they wanted to set themselves up in town, they could. That would be all right. They needed privacy and she wouldn't mind having hers back. No more early mornings with Tink, being badgered about target practice. No more keeping the door to the bedroom shut, locking herself in every night with all her mistakes.

Yep, if they wanted to get a place in town that would be all right for everyone.

"Smells real good," Peg said as she stepped out of her room and into the kitchen.

"Well, it's nothing fancy. Just some pasta and jarred sauce. But Tink and I made a salad entirely from the garden."

"I hope you like radishes," Tink grumbled.

"It is radish forward," Hope said. "But Tink bought some bread from Swafiya's bakery."

"With my own money," Tink said.

"Which will probably make it taste even better."

The room settled into silence as Hope stirred sauce and Tink put the bread into the oven.

"Cherry season is over," Peg blurted, because she was so bad at this.

"What?" Hope asked, licking sauce off her hand as she turned around. "Just like that?"

"Just like that. Abel's going to be working on the apple harvest and I'm going to do some catch-up work around the place."

She put the envelope down on the table and pushed it over toward Hope, who poured cooked pasta from the colander in the sink into a large bowl.

"Those are your wages," Peg said, and that pulled Hope's head around.

Tink got to the envelope first and when she looked inside her eyes got real wide.

"It's three thousand dollars."

Hope looked up at Peg, shocked. "That's really generous, Peg. I don't think we earned all that."

"It's yours. You can do whatever you like with it. It's enough, if you wanted to get a place in town—"

Tink recoiled. Even Hope looked displeased with the suggestion.

Delight filled Peg, followed by relief. Followed by something she hadn't felt in a really long time. It was surprising how sharp happiness was. Bitter and sweet all at once. She put her hip against the counter, weak in the knees for a moment.

"Or not," she said, and went right for the bowl of pasta.

→TINK←

The next three days they did mountains of laundry and then worked in the garden and took the vegetables out to the stands, but now that cherry season was over, Mom said Tink had to register for school. Well, that was a terrible idea. Tink had spent half the summer working, and it seemed to her that there should be some TV time in there somewhere.

There were things she needed to do. Those Temple Run levels weren't going to win themselves.

"Mom," she said as they pulled into the parking lot beside the big brick building. There was a banner across the front of the school: Registration. "Let's go to the beach. Remember how you wanted to go to the beach and build volcanoes? Let's go do that."

"Nice try, kid," she said, parking the car. "But school starts in two weeks. We need to get you registered."

"Moooooooom," Tink moaned. "This is the worst."

"Tink," she said. "This is a fresh start. A new school. I know you had a hard time last year, but maybe this year there will be some cool kids in your class."

"There won't be."

"You don't know that."

"I do, Mom. There are never cool kids."

"Well." Mom climbed out of the car. "That doesn't change things. We're registering for school."

Tink crawled out of the car as slow as she could, a tactic that would sometimes work, but Mom kept walking, not looking behind her.

"Hey!"

Tink turned and found Avery standing there in a pretty white dress. "What are you doing here?"

"Mom is registering us for school."

"Yeah, me, too."

"Stupid, huh?"

"So stupid."

"We're going to go play in the spaceship, wanna come?"

Well, the spaceship was for little kids, but it was way better than going into the hot school building and sitting there while Mom filled out paperwork. "Sure. Mom!" she yelled, and Mom turned around real quick, her hand at her heart like Tink had startled her.

"What, Tink? You don't need to yell."

"I'm going to go play with Avery in the spaceship."

She didn't even give her a chance to answer, just took off running with Avery, as fast as they could.

✦ HOPE ✦

She stood at the desk in the school's front office surrounded by other moms and dads walking in and out, saying hello to the school secretary. If you'd asked her the name of the secretary at Tink's old school, Hope would have had no clue.

It all felt so good. So warm and friendly. Maybe that was why she didn't trust it.

All she could think was this paperwork was going to be filed somewhere.

And Daniel might be able to use it to find them.

Was that possible? Was she being paranoid for nothing? Probably. But she wasn't about to stop.

"Forget your address?" a voice asked, and she turned to see Janice standing there, holding her toddler while he gummed her necklace.

Hope laughed. "No."

"I did. Had to call my mom. She loved that."

"I don't have Tink's immunization records," Hope said. "The secretary is really mad at me about that."

"I'd imagine. If you need a pediatrician in town I'll give you the name of ours."

"Thanks," Hope said. "That would be great."

Even more forms to fill out. Even more ways to be found.

"You all done here?" the secretary asked, stern-faced and humorless when she'd just been laughing with another mother.

"Hope just moved to the area, and she will have those immunization records for you next week," Janice said, and the secretary smiled like all was forgiven.

"That'll be fine. We look forward to having…" She looked down at the records Hope had filled out. "Jenny at school in two weeks."

Hope mumbled her thanks and she and Janice walked down the hallway toward the front door. "Your daughter excited?" Janice asked.

"No. Not even a little."

"Mine, either." Outside, Janice slipped her sunglasses over her eyes and turned to Hope. "Ready?"

"For what?" Hope asked, because it seemed like Janice wanted to rob a bank or star in a movie about robbing a bank.

"Well, for what I'm hoping will be your half of a bottle of wine at my house."

"Yep," Hope said as easily as she'd ever agreed to anything. She still had plenty of reservations. But she shoved them all aside. "Lead the way."

Janice lived in one of the big houses with the pillars and the bobbing red geraniums. There was a stained-glass window over the front door, and as they drove around the side, there was one room off the back made entirely of windows.

"What are we doing here, Mom?"

"Hanging out."

Tink gave her an exquisite ten-year-old side eye. "We don't hang out."

"Well, we haven't in the past, but maybe we are natural hanger-outers. Maybe we've just been waiting for the right opportunity."

"Let's just go back to the farm."

"And do what, Tink?"

"Not hang out with these people!"

There was something in the Wright family that rejected the company of other people, and Hope didn't want that for her daughter.

She didn't want it for herself.

"I thought you liked Avery."

"Yeah. Avery's fine. But what if there are other kids?" Tink had her arms crossed, scowling at the pretty house like it had deeply offended her. But really, Hope knew, she was just scared.

It's just you and me. DeeDee had said it to Hope, and Hope had said it to Tink. And it was true in a fundamental way. But it was also a trap. DeeDee had said it to keep her close, to keep her from wanting other people in her life. It was one of the ways she controlled her.

Hope said it because she'd been so scared, and so adrift after DeeDee had died, that it was her way of not feeling so alone, blurring those boundaries between parent and friend past what was reasonable.

"We need people," Hope said.

"We have people. We have Peg. And Abel."

Both lovely and wonderful, yes, but Peg was caught in her own trap—scared to leave the farm. And Abel...well, she didn't know what Abel was, at least not yet.

Janice pulled her big SUV around them to park in the drive-way in front of a garage that was easily double the size of every single apartment she and Tink had ever lived in. The little boy who wasn't the baby jumped off the back seat before the car was in Park, racing across the lawn to open a screen door at the side of the house. A small floppy-eared yellow dog came bounding out and the reunion was an ecstatic one.

"Everyone has a dog," Tink sighed.

For so long she'd been telling her daughter that everything

was fine, as if saying it would make it so, that her daughter wouldn't notice their little boat was slowly sinking. Even before Daniel. She'd been talking about choosing a life, rather than just living each day like there was no other choice.

DeeDee chose not to be happy. Hope wasn't sure what Peg was choosing alone out there on the farm, all her memories tucked behind couches.

Hope didn't want any of that for Tink. She didn't want it for herself. This was the hard work they needed to do. If anything in their life was going to change, they had to make it happen.

"Everything is not okay, Tink," Hope said, the truth unsugarcoated spilling from her lips. Tink's head spun toward her, and Hope felt light-headed. She squeezed her hands into fists and then let them go just so she could feel something. "It hasn't been for a while. And it's not just about Daniel. It's about DeeDee and us and how we live. And you're right, we've got Peg now and Abel. School. And maybe—" she looked out at the house with the geraniums and the dog and the blonde woman she'd apparently celebrated her first birthday with "—some friends. I want to live a really big life, Tink. A happy one. And I think going into that house and making friends with people is part of that. It's part of being okay."

Suddenly there was a smack on the door and Avery was there with her mouth pressed up against the glass, blowing her cheeks out big.

Gross, Hope was about to say, but then Tink laughed and got up on her knees and pushed her lips to the glass, too, blowing big raspberries, and they could hear Avery laughing from the other side of the window.

Inside Janice's house was as lovely as the outside. Hardwood floors, a recently remodeled kitchen with black cabinets and a sit-in counter with bright red stools.

"Go," Janice said to her kids, shooing them as she kicked off her high heels. "Be gone. I'll yell when I've got food for you." She pointed at one of the red stools. "Sit there," she said to Hope and then started unloading things from the fridge. A bottle of white wine. Apples. Cucumbers. Cheese strings. Brie.

"First things first." She poured them both a glass of wine.

"Thank you," Hope said. She wasn't much of a drinker but the wine tasted fresh and crisp. "You have a beautiful home."

"It's not her home," Carole said, walking in from the windowed room. "It's mine."

"You want some wine?" Janice asked. Carole seemed to consider it and then declined. Janice narrowed her eyes. "Are you high?" she whispered.

"Yes," Carole whispered back.

Hope could not help her smile.

"Where's Peg?" Carole asked.

"At the farm."

"You should call her, tell her to come."

There had been a tremendous thaw in Peg. She was warmer, and she was sweet with Tink. Her laughter came a little quicker and all that sighing had stopped, but Hope could not imagine her here.

"Yeah," Carole said as if Hope had said all of that out loud. "She's gone feral out there on the farm by herself."

"Why don't you call her?"

"Why do you think I haven't?" Carole asked. "The woman knows how to hold a grudge."

Carole grabbed one of the slices of apple and Janice bumped her away with her hip. "Those are for the kids."

"Fine," she said and went over to one of the sleek black cabinets, stood on tiptoes to reach way, way into the back and pulled out a bag of M&M's.

Janice gasped. "Do not let the kids see that."

"Why do you think they're hidden back there?"

The two women worked in the kitchen together like they'd been doing it a long time.

"Where do you live?" Hope asked. "If this isn't your house?"

"Well." Janice sighed and pushed her hair back, using the wrist of the hand that was holding the long knife. "I was in Chicago. But my husband and I are splitting and it's pretty gross, so I decided to come back here for the summer."

"Summer is over, honey. You'll notice she just registered her children for school," Carole said, shoving a handful of M&M's in her mouth. She grabbed the plate of apples, cucumbers and sliced-up cheese and took it down to the kids in the basement.

"Don't listen to her," Janice said. She slipped a plate with Brie and fancy crackers and apple slices in front of Hope. "She's really settling into her role as the grumpy old lady. The stoner part is a bit of a curve ball, but that's Mom for you." Janice sat on another one of the stools and chopped off a hunk of Brie that could choke a horse. Hope was inspired and took her own chunk. "Triple cream," Janice said. "It's the only way to go. When I found out that Mike was cheating on me Mom drove down, packed me and the kids up, threatened to castrate Mike if he tried to fight her and drove us all up here."

"I'm sorry," Hope said.

"Well, it's kind of a good-riddance situation."

"Still. It can't be easy."

Janice looked at her for a long second and Hope forced herself not to laugh or come up with some excuse to leave or change the subject because it was all getting too personal.

"Today, Avery and your daughter laughing…" Janice shook her head. "It's just been a really long time, you know. And Avery—" she sucked on her lips "—well, she probably saw some things she shouldn't have."

My daughter watched me hit Daniel over the head with a lamp…

"It's just really good to see her being a kid instead of a little adult."

"Tink is the same," Hope said. "And I don't know how to turn her back into a kid."

"Maybe that's not our job?" Janice said. "Maybe they need another kid for that." She laughed and then sighed. "That's probably wishful thinking on my part. It's just so good to see Avery with a friend."

"Cheers to that," Hope said and lifted her wineglass. Janice touched the edge of hers to it and the crystal gave a sweet little ting.

Look at us, she thought. *Two moms trying and screwing up and still trying.* It felt powerful.

"Thanks for coming over today," Janice said in a thick voice.

"You kidding? It's been so long since I've had a friend. Much less triple-cream Brie."

They both laughed and the moment shifted.

"I keep thinking it's getting easier and then I'm hit with this wave of...anger," Janice said. "And grief. We weren't happy. I mean, my therapist is making that clear, if you know what I mean." She laughed as she said it.

"I don't," she said honestly. "I don't know what you mean."

"What I thought was happiness was a lie I was telling myself," she said. "Because he was rich. And because I got to have the four kids I wanted, when he didn't want any. Because I got to do yoga in the middle of the day and work on committees and boards of organizations I was passionate about, I told myself I had to be happy. Because being unhappy with everything I had would pull apart my life."

Hope felt cold in her belly. A ripple of gooseflesh across her arms.

The story sat right there, in the space between their chairs.

In the distance between her wineglass and the cheese. In the turn of her body toward a new friend. She thought of Abel in the barn telling her she had to talk to someone. That the load got easier every time. Maybe she couldn't tell him, not yet, but she could tell this other mother who was trying really hard and messed up sometimes, too.

"My mom died," she said, the words trickling out now like water from a thawing tap. "And I was in bad shape. Depressed. We were complicated, you know?" Again, she felt that strange compulsion to explain that Denise had been a good mom, but she realized it didn't matter. She'd tried, maybe as best as she could, and Hope was exhausted from trying to judge her. Trying to shove her into some hole the world wanted mothers to fit in. *Good mom—what did that even mean?* "But she was the only family I had. And I just fell apart. Barely took care of Tink." She shook her head, the shame of it all still so potent. "And then I met this guy at the grocery store and I should have had warning sirens going right away, because any man attracted to me in the shape I was in wasn't being honest. But at the time Daniel just seemed like a godsend."

"Let me guess…he wasn't?"

"My eye and my lip when I got here? That was him." Janice reached over and squeezed her hand. "Anyway. I thought he was what I deserved, you know? And then I thought all the bad stuff that happened in our lives was what I deserved because I let him in. I convinced myself for a long time that I didn't need to be happy. That being happy was selfish, or ridiculous. My mom wasn't happy. My friend at the time wasn't happy. So, who was I to think I should be happy?"

"Even when I knew Mike was cheating, I was so used to not being happy that I told myself it didn't matter. It didn't change anything. Can you believe that? He was cheating on me and I told myself it didn't matter. But then," Janice said, "I realized I was showing the kids how not to value their own selves. How to compromise and compromise until there was nothing left. How it was more important to have nice things than it was to be happy." Her laughter was sad. "When I say it out loud I can't believe… I can't believe I ever thought that was okay."

"When you're in it," Hope said, "like when you're really in it and you're just trying to survive, you can convince yourself anything is okay."

"Well," Janice said with a shy smile, "here I am, living with my mom, and it's weird, I know, but I haven't felt this good in ages. The kids, too. I mean… I wish I had done it years earlier. But then I wouldn't have the baby. So… I don't know. Sometimes nothing is easy."

"I don't… I don't know if I'm happy," Hope said, as honest as she'd ever been in her life. "Like, I'm worried maybe I just… Maybe I'm just not built to feel that." She thought of Abel and how she wanted him and was scared of him all at the same time. Well, not scared of him, but of the power of wanting him. "But I'd like to be."

Janice stood up and grabbed a card from a cork board beside the oven. She slid it across the counter to Hope. "My therapist," she said. "Todd Ackerman. He sees all of us. The kids and me. It's helped. Swafiya's husband gave me his number and he's been great."

"Matt," she said. "The lawyer."

"He's helped me with some of the legal stuff, too."

"That's lucky," Hope said. "That he was able to make you feel better."

That had been a blocked path for her. But maybe this…the card in her pocket, maybe that was a new way toward feeling whole. Her mom would roll over in her grave to know she was thinking about therapy, but that was undoubtedly because Mom had needed it herself.

There was a knock at the screen door and from downstairs there was a bark and the pounding of dog feet. Hope quickly slipped the card in her pocket.

"Hello?" Swafiya poked her head in just as the dog came up from the basement, tail wagging, tongue out.

"Hey, come in," Janice said. She jumped off the stool and met Swafiya at the door to take the box from her hands. "Glad you could make it."

"Are you kidding?" Swafiya and Janice kissed each other's cheeks as Swafiya took her shoes off. Hope looked down at her own flip-flops and winced. "These Friday-afternoon parties are becoming my favorite things."

"It's Friday?" Hope said, because she'd been blissfully unaware. *This is a party?*

Janice and Swafiya both turned to her.

"That kind of week, huh?" Swafiya said.

"I guess so."

Carole came up from the basement and shooed the dog back downstairs.

"Carole," Swafiya said, and the two women hugged.

"I got that water you never shut up about," Carole said.

"La Croix?"

"It's pretty good."

"Pretty good. Listen to you, it's amazing."

There was hubbub in the kitchen and another woman came in with two older kids, their hair dark dandelion fluff around their round faces. They looked up from their phones to say hello before heading right down into the basement.

"Swear to god," the new woman said. "I thought this week would never end." Hope recognized her from the first day of delivering cherries to the fruit stands, the woman with the braids who'd been so keen to know whether the stands would have Abel's apples. "I recognize you," she said to Hope as she kicked off her heels and handed Janice a plastic pitcher.

"I'm Hope. We met at the cherry stands."

"Yes. Good to see you again. I'm Angela."

More hellos. More hugs. More food was laid out. Vegetables and hummus. Swafiya's muffins.

"Last of the cherries," Swafiya said. "Enjoy them while you can."

"Eat them before the kids find out they're here," Carole said.

"Amen," Angela said and snagged one.

She lifted the pitcher and asked Hope if she wanted a margarita.

"I drove," she said.

"Rookie mistake," Angela said.

Swafiya sat down next to her with a can of fancy fizzy water. There was back-and-forth talk about kids and registering for school, and Carole asked Swafiya if Matt wanted any more of her cookies.

"Cool your jets, pusher lady," she said, dipping a cucumber into the hummus. "He isn't through your last batch."

"Can you believe this is my mother's second career?" Janice asked.

"It was my first career, too," Carole said, and Angela laughed.

"She used to run the pharmacy," Swafiya explained. "Sold the business three years ago but kept half the store."

It somehow all made sense.

Their laughter and conversation all swirled around her and through her. It buoyed Hope up so high she felt like she was floating. She gripped the counter, pinched her leg, all to remind herself that this was real. This was now.

"Mom?" Tink was standing there beside her, forehead creased, lips drawn into a straight line.

"You okay down there?" she asked. It sounded like a party in the basement.

"Yeah. It's…" She glanced behind her at the door. "Cool."

"Cool?" Hope smiled, reached forward to grab her hand. It was damp and small and puffy, and she had to force herself not to kiss it in front of all these people.

"Yeah." Tink smiled again, shrugged like it was no big deal. Like Friday-afternoon parties with strangers and Brie and apple slices were all a very normal thing for them.

"It's pretty fun up here, too," Hope said.

"We're gonna stay?"

"For a little bit. Does that work for you?"

"Sure."

They were both playing it cool, like they didn't want to jinx it by being too glad to be there. How perfectly them.

"Are those Swafiya's muffins?" Tink asked.

Hope nodded, and Tink swiped one before heading back to the basement.

"You better eat that before you go down there," Carole said, and Tink, taking her seriously, put the whole thing in her mouth. Everyone laughed and Tink looked wide-eyed at Hope, who could only shrug.

I'm new here, too, kid.

"Call him!" Janice crowed three hours, a pitcher of margaritas and several bottles of wine later. "Call. Him."

Hope, not used to drinking, had only had a couple glasses of wine. But she could feel them. Especially in her knees. She ran her fingers over the screen of her phone, Abel's number one push of her finger away. "I don't know," she said. "Carole volunteered to drive me—"

"My mom is passed out with the baby," Janice said.

"It's not a booty call," Angela said, the calm voice of reason. "It's just a ride home. It's responsible."

"Is it?" Hope asked.

"Tink is asleep downstairs," Janice said. "You can leave her here for a sleepover and then it will be a booty call."

"No," Hope said. "Tink would…" The idea of her daughter waking up in a strange house without her there… Tink would not like that one bit.

"I get it," Angela said. "My youngest was like that, too. Didn't have a sleepover until the eighth grade."

"I'll just drive slow—" Hope said.

"Enough!" Swafiya said. She reached between all the women, pressed Dial on the phone in Hope's hand then shrugged at everyone's scandalous gasps. "What?" she said with her innocent grin. "Someone had to do it."

"Hello?" Abel's thin voice came through the speaker. "Hope?"

"Hi!" she said, far too bright and cheerful, as if she were calling with an exciting real estate opportunity for him. She stood up from the counter and the women gathered around her and walked to the dim living room off the kitchen. "Am I calling too late?"

"It's eight," Abel said.

"Oh," she said. "I guess that's okay."

"What's happening?" Abel asked. "Is everything okay at the house? Peg—"

"I'm not at the house," she said, and then closed her eyes. "I went to sign Tink up for school and there was this other mom there. Janice—"

"I know Janice."

"You do?"

"It's a small town, Hope. Stay focused."

"Right. Well, she invited me back to her house and then one bottle of wine turned into another bottle of wine…"

His deep laughter practically took her breath away. She was a little drunk, sure, but that…that was a good laugh.

"Is this a booty call?" he asked.

"No! God…no. Well… I don't know. Mostly I need a ride. But—"

"Tell me the address," he said with that low laugh that rang her like a bell. She gave it to him and he told her to sit tight. "Fifteen minutes," he said.

She hung up and turned around to the kitchen. The women who'd been gathered at the doorway listening in scattered like cackling birds.

Tink was passed out in the basement on one end of the couch, Avery on the other end. Two paper plates with pizza crusts sat between them, which the dog was trying his best to get to.

"Wow," Janice said as the two of them stood over the girls. "They're like peas in a pod."

"Literally," Hope said.

"I'm so glad you came over."

"You have no idea," Hope said.

She made plans to get her car tomorrow, and after she carried Tink's heavy sleeping body upstairs, she was given a lot of one-armed hugs. She promised she would be there next Friday.

"Every Friday," she said, and the women cheered.

There was a knock at the door and Hope saw the truck on the street outside the house, the headlights cutting bright slices out of the twilight. Janice opened the door, feigning sobriety that made her seem more drunk, and Abel, standing there in jeans and a flannel shirt, just smiled at all the women staring at him.

"Hi," he said with a wave.

In unison the women waved back.

"Here," he said and reached forward for Tink. "Let me help."

Hope let him take her daughter and grabbed her purse. At the door she turned and waved goodbye one last time.

"So hot," Angela whispered. "I mean. The man is so hot."

Swafiya was nodding in agreement. And Janice, who had

sworn off men multiple times during the night, said, "Get it, girl." They all fell apart laughing.

Hope closed the door behind her and walked through the sweet August evening to the truck, where Abel was clipping Tink into a seat belt.

"You had fun?" he asked, over Tink.

"So much fun."

"That's good," he said. "You need anything? McDonald's?"

She gasped. What a mind reader he was. "Yes!"

Tink woke up in the drive-through and asked for chicken nuggets. Hope got large fries. Abel ordered ice cream.

"My treat!" Hope said, digging into her wallet for some of the money Peg had given her the other night. She was more delighted than she could say to be able to treat her daughter and Abel to a relatively small fast-food feast.

They headed back to the farm. Tink got about one chicken nugget in her before falling back to sleep, but Abel took over and finished the rest.

"I hope you weren't doing anything," she said, "when I called."

"Nothing as good as this," he said.

"Picking my drunk self up—"

"Picking your happy, relaxed self up. Eating junk food." He shrugged. "It's a good night, Hope. Don't try to take it away from me."

The moon traveled with them as they drove down the long county roads.

"Peg wants us to learn how to shoot the rifle," Hope said. "She said that it would help us feel safer."

"What do you think?"

"I would like to feel safer. I guess…that's my answer, huh?"

He laughed. "Sounds like it."

"You think a good guy with a gun can stop a bad guy with a gun?"

"Nothing in the world is that simple. I think the world needs fewer guns, not more. But I also think if there's a gun in the house, everyone should know how to use it safely."

He pulled into the driveway and drove past the farm toward the barn, where he parked and turned off the lights. The dark around them was a cocoon, and she'd never in her life felt so safe.

And sure, part of it might be the wine or the weight of her daughter sleeping so soundly against her. The quiet of the barn that she'd grown to know as well as any other place she'd known in her life.

But it was also him.

"What would you like?" she asked and immediately realized how loaded that question was in the dark. She was about to laugh and take it back, but then she saw the gleam of his eyes.

"Well," he said. "I'd like your daughter to be asleep in her bed right now."

"Yeah," she whispered, feeling bold in the dark. "I'd like that, too."

"I'd like more chicken nuggets," he said. She tilted her fries toward him and he took some. The push of his fingers against the box made her breath catch.

He stretched his arm across the bench seat, his fingers grazing her shoulder.

"I'd like to fix all the things I broke when I was young and stupid."

"What did you break?"

"My mother's heart. My dad's nose." He tried to make it a joke, but she could tell that it hurt him. "Sometimes you look at me, Hope, like I have all the answers. But I'm just trying to figure things out, too."

"His name was Daniel," she said. "And I should have known something was wrong with him at the very beginning." And the rest of the story just came pouring out of her.

Twenty-Five

Well. It wasn't like Hope needed to tell Peg where she was and what she was doing at all times. But it was ten o'clock, and she hadn't heard a word. She was moving between worried and angry and back to worried again, and underneath it all was an energy she hadn't felt in a long time, that indelible attachment. The pleasure and pain of caring.

"I mean," Peg said to Nelson, who was waiting by the front door, "would it be so hard to call?"

She whimpered in response.

"Exactly," she said.

She was about to call Hope's cell again when the front door flew open and in walked Hope and Tink, laughing. Tink was laughing so hard she was sort of falling into Hope, who was trying to hold both of them up, but failing.

"Stop," Hope cried. "Stop, I'm gonna pee my pants." Hope

wiped her eyes and got herself under control, but then looked
down at Tink and the giggles started back up again.

"What's so funny?" Peg asked, captivated by the rarity of
all this joy in The Orchard House. It felt like it was pushing at the walls, lifting the roof, chasing away the darkness
in the corners.

Hope and Tink looked at each other and shook their heads.

"Honestly, Peg," Hope said, flushed and smiling. "I can't
remember."

"Are you…drunk?" Peg asked, taking in the flushed cheeks
and slightly unfocused eyes.

"A little."

"And you drove? With Tink—"

Hope lifted up her hand. "Abel came and got us. Tink was
sleeping and Abel and I were sitting in the barn talking."

"Where have you been?" Peg asked, the edges of that question sharpened by the worry she'd felt over the last few hours.

"Carole's house," Hope said.

"Was your phone out of battery?"

Hope glanced at her phone in her hand. "I'm sorry I missed
your calls. I had it on silent."

"You couldn't call?"

"I could," Hope said carefully, like it had never occurred
to her that someone would be worrying about her. "Did you
want me to?"

"Yes!" Peg cried. "With everything going on, yes. Yes, I
wanted you to call." Hope and Tink looked at each other and
had one of their silent conversations.

"I'm sorry, Peg. Truly, it didn't occur to me that you'd be
worried."

"Your mom wouldn't have been worried?"

Hope shook her head.

"I don't believe that."

"No. If Mom were alive, we wouldn't have been there. I'm sorry," she said. "I really am."

"It's okay," she sighed. "Just call me next time."

"Well," Hope said, bouncing back with her grin. "You should come with us next time. Carole asked about you and Janice was there and a whole bunch of other people, really. Swafiya was there. There were all these kids. It was like…a party. I guess. It was a party." She said it like she'd never been to one before.

"Carole's been having parties on Friday nights for as long as I can remember," Peg said. "There used to be some real wild ones back in the day. I'm glad you had fun."

"We're gonna go back," Hope said. "Next Friday. You should come with."

Tink nodded. "You should. They have a really nice house."

"I think maybe I would just change the mood." She had that effect on people, like her parents had, a cold breeze that made everyone shiver.

"That's the thing," Hope said. "There were, like, twenty different moods. Every woman was complaining or happy or telling some awful story. I almost cried like five times. And I almost peed my pants laughing. Seriously, I've never experienced anything like it."

"There was cheese!" Tink said. "And Swafiya brought muffins."

"And wine," Hope said.

"Well, that's women and friendship for you," Peg said with a laugh. "I don't have a lot of experience, but it usually goes best with wine and cheese."

Peg turned and headed back to the kitchen, ready for bed now that everyone was under her roof, where they belonged. She heard the door to their apartment creak and someone headed up the stairs. Nelson's collar rattled as she lay down in front of the door.

"Peg?" Hope asked, following her into the shadowy kitchen. "Can I ask you something?"

"Sure."

"I was wondering if I could use that money you gave me to buy a laptop. Carole asked if I could help her with her books, and since we're staying I thought I could set up a business, maybe. I mean, nothing fancy—"

"Honey," she said, the endearment sliding right off her tongue. "Of course. The money is yours."

"I know, but it's a lot of money and I just... I guess I wanted your approval."

Peg pulled in a big breath, careful but shaky. "Well, you have it, Hope. I think it's a real good idea."

The girl beamed, glowed like that garden out back after a drink of water and a day of sunshine.

"I was thinking about something else, too," Hope said, and Peg smiled, loving this version of Hope, living in the truest sense of her name.

"What's that?" Peg asked.

"I think we should learn how to shoot that rifle. I think if it's in the house, and if Daniel comes back..." She clearly didn't even want to say it, but Peg knew what was on her mind. "We should know how to protect ourselves."

"I agree."

"And, I think it's just a safety thing, you know? If a gun is going to be out and around then Tink should—"

"Hope, I agree."

"So, you'll, like, give us lessons or whatever?"

"I can give you lessons."

"Okay. Wow." She shook her head and laughed. "Look at me. Getting stuff done."

Yes, girl. Look at you.

"Are you hungry?" Peg asked, pulling open the fridge, the light splashing across the floor and Hope's feet.

"No. We pigged out on cheese and Abel drove us through McDonald's."

"Abel, huh?" The girl's blush was fluorescent. "Well, I'm glad you had fun."

"We really did. You should come next time." Peg nodded but didn't say anything, and Hope leaned up against the brick archway. "What happened with you and Carole?"

"I don't know. People fall out of touch sometimes."

It was difficult to try to hold happy memories when you were unhappy. Like an overfull glass of water you were unable to drink when you were dying of thirst.

"I made a decision years ago," she said. A lifetime ago. "And I lost a lot of people when I did that. Carole was one of them."

"She said she forgot why she was mad."

That wasn't true, but old ladies knew how heavy grudges were—and the relief of letting them go.

"Abel said you don't go into town."

"Not much reason to."

"Peg," Hope said. "You don't have to tell me, but we both know that's a lie. There's a million reasons to go into town."

"Well, maybe for you."

"Okay, stubborn lady, keep your secrets. But you should come to the Friday-night party next week. It's fun."

Hope all but skipped upstairs and Peg stood in the kitchen. Hope, the act of hoping, was brave, really. A kind of rebellious stance, particularly in this house.

When, she wondered, *did I get so scared?*

When did I think this was enough?

Peg went into her bedroom, the place where her relationship with Hank had ended, where they could not fix the insurmountable problem between them. It was more like a waiting room than a bedroom. For so long, all she'd been waiting for was the beginning and end of every cherry season, reliving all her sister's cruelties, her own heartbreaks.

But now—now she saw that life was more than just beginnings and endings.

She called Hank.

"Peg?" he said, his voice rough like he'd been sleeping or just hadn't been talking. She imagined him like her, living a life in which it was possible not to speak for hours, because there was no one to speak to, and that was such a shame. Hank deserved people.

"Everything okay?"

"Yeah," she said. "Sorry if I woke you."

"No, you didn't. I was just watching the news."

"Yeah? How is the news?"

"Depressing. Like you always said." The laughter was a familiar sound, and she closed her eyes to let it in. "Peg, you didn't call to talk about the news."

"No. The…ah…" She took a deep breath and let everything out. "The girls are staying. Indefinitely. And I thought you should know that. And if you wanted to come to the farm and see them, that… I think that would be okay."

"Did Hope remember something?"

"No. And I still don't think there's any point in telling her. She's happy for the first time in a long time, I think. Hank, you should have seen them tonight. They were laughing so hard and I thought Tink was going to just fall down, you know. Just collapse and…" She stopped, words failing her a little. "Well, it was nice. It was real nice."

"Sounds like it."

She could hear his breath over the phone and she had the

urge to shift from the intimacy. To reject it. But the hope had already gotten into her.

"Would you like to come?" she asked.

"You know I would."

"Tomorrow, then," she said. "If that—"

"I'll be there, Peg."

"It's Saturday. So, morning is best," she said.

"I remember and…thanks."

She hung up and pressed the phone to her chest, holding it there nice and warm against her heart, trying to quell the excitement, trying, as best she could, to wrestle her expectations back to nothing.

But hope was running things now and hope had endless expectations.

Twenty-Six

Saturday morning was one of those perfect August days in Northern Michigan. The humidity had broken at some point in the night and there was a breeze blowing through the trees.

Peg was in the back, setting up target practice with cans and bottles along the old fence at the tree line. She remembered being a girl, her father setting up cans along here. Denise and her standing by the roses, clutching each other's hands, terrified they were going to do something to upset their father and knowing it was inevitable. She felt the ghost of her father in this backyard, stern and waiting to be upset or disappointed, to find fault.

Not being angry was a choice. It took conscious effort. It meant clawing back the version of herself she'd grown so used to.

"Peg?"

"Back here!" she yelled.

Hope and Tink came out the kitchen door. Tink was rubbing her eyes; Hope was sipping from a mug of coffee and trying hard not to slosh all over herself as she walked. The two of them looked like incredibly unlikely target shooters.

"Morning," Peg said, allowing the bubble of joy she felt at seeing their messy hair and sunburned faces to lift her.

Tink shaded her eyes. "Mom said we're shooting things."

"Yep," she said, and Tink did a little-girl fist pump.

"First we're going to have some safety lessons," Hope said, putting a hand over her daughter's shoulder.

"I've done those," Tink said. "I've done tons of those."

"I haven't," Hope said.

Peg picked up her father's old rifle from where she'd propped it against the house. The wood was smooth and the metal was warm. She explained where the safety was and how it worked. She took out the bullets and let Tink hold them in her little hands.

"Oh my god," Hope whispered.

"You okay?"

"Am I really going to shoot Daniel? Is Tink? I mean…who are we kidding?"

"Hey," Peg whispered, but Hope was looking up at the sky, blinking back tears.

Peg took the bullets from Tink's hand, put them in her pocket and then set the gun down.

"Hope," she said.

"What?"

Carefully, because she was so rusty, she put her arms around Hope's thin body and hugged her. Hope startled for a second, but then wrapped her own arms around Peg's back, holding on tight.

All those times Peg had hugged this woman as a little girl came flooding back to her. The goodnight hugs. The hugs after she'd tripped on the porch, coming to Peg with a skinned knee. The morning cuddles. After baths. The way she'd slept against her as a baby, heavy and solid, lifted her arms from her highchair, her face covered in peach juice.

It was too much and she flinched, nearly stepped back. But Hope didn't let her go. She held on even tighter.

And they toughed the moment out.

"Are we gonna learn how to shoot guns or what?" Tink yelled.

→ HOPE ←

After the first gunshot split the morning silence, Abel came running up from his cabin, wet from a shower and wearing shorts and his rubber boots. "Jesus," he said, his hands braced on his knees, his breath heaving. "I thought there was trouble."

"We should have told him," Hope said, and Peg grunted in agreement.

"We're learning how to shoot," Tink said.

"I see that."

Peg and Tink both turned back toward the targets, and Abel and Hope shared a long look.

"You okay?" she asked, a little alarmed by how hard Abel was breathing.

"I have not run that fast in years."

"Do you want some coffee? There's some in the kitchen," she offered.

"I think if I had a cup of coffee I'd have a heart attack."

She felt awkward and raw in the morning light without the protection of all the secrets she'd gathered around herself for so long.

Abel glanced over and, seeing that Tink and Peg weren't looking, took her hand in his and kissed the tips of her fingers.

She felt herself go beet red and flustered. "I'm not very good at this," she said.

"You're perfect at this," he said and let go of her tingling fingers.

"Hey, Abel," Peg yelled. "Maybe you can come and give Tink some help. You might have some better tips."

"Sure," he said and winked at Hope as he headed over to help Tink with her stance.

Hope didn't like guns, she really didn't, but she had to admit, his knowledge and his confidence was kinda hot.

"This is hard," Tink said twenty minutes later. It was her third round, Hope's, too, of shooting and missing the targets.

"No one said it would be easy," Peg said. Peg was really working her female Dirty Harry persona this morning.

"Looks easy in the movies," Tink grumbled.

"Those are movies," Peg said, and they set up to do another round. It was fun watching Tink be Tink and Peg handle it.

"Guess what I did this morning?" Hope asked.

"No idea," Abel said.

"Applied online for a business license. Orchard House Book-keeping." It had felt risky, but there was no way for her to apply and keep her name off the paperwork. She'd tried to mitigate the risk by keeping her name out of her business name.

"That is the best thing I've ever heard."

"Don't joke—"

"I'm not," he said, and then despite Peg and Tink being right there, he kissed her. On the lips. Short and sweet. There and gone. But she felt that kiss everywhere.

"One more time?" Peg asked, turning back from where she was helping Tink aim.

"We should go until someone hits something," Abel said.

"That could take all day," Peg muttered.

Tink had been taking the lesson seriously. If she'd been goofy or showing off, Hope would have pulled the pin on the whole thing. But Tink was being very Tink about it and listening to Peg with her whole body, though it wasn't helping either one of them actually hit anything.

"Not bad," Abel said after Hope had missed every single target sitting on that fence one more time.

"You're joking."

"No, I think you were closer," Peg said.

"I appreciate the false vote of confidence."

"My turn!" Tink said. She carefully loaded a new shell, snapping the gun back together.

Peg, Hope and Abel laughed and took a step back as Tink took careful aim.

"You think she's going to hit the can?" Hope whispered to Peg.

"I think I'm going to be in this backyard forever. You're both terrible shots."

And then Tink fired, and the metal ping of a bullet hitting a can startled birds from the far trees.

"Oh my god," Abel breathed. "She did it."

"She did it," Peg said, equally shocked.

"I did it!" Tink cried.

Hope grabbed the rifle from Tink as Tink and Peg ran over to the fence, Tink leaping, arms overhead, whooping like she'd won something.

There was the sound of a car at the front and Hope turned away, peering around the house to try to see who was pulling in. A man with white hair who looked vaguely familiar stepped out of a black truck, wearing a red shirt and blue jeans.

"Holy shit," Abel said with a wide smile. "It's Hank."

"Hank?" she asked.

Peg, as if she'd sniffed him on the wind, popped up out of the tall grasses and started walking their way, patting down her hair as she went.

"Hi, Hank," Abel said with a wide smile when the man got close enough. "Not sure if you remember—"

They shook hands like men who were really fond of each other. "Abel, of course. How could I forget you? Never saw a kid who could eat so much chocolate ice cream. I heard you went and joined the army."

"I did. Served for eight years and then came back here."

"Well, here is a great place to come back to," Hank said. "And I thank you for your service, son."

"This is Hope," Abel said. "Peg's niece."

Hank smiled and then swallowed, seeming a little nervous, and she wondered if he was coming back around looking for a second chance with Peg.

"Hi," she said. "I recognize you from the cherry stands. It's good to see you again." She held out her hand to shake his. He glanced down as if he didn't know what to do with it, then wrapped her hand in his wide palm.

She had another one of those strange memories, the rumble of a tractor through her body and the sound of a man's voice in her ear telling her to hold on tight as they bounced up onto the road from the orchard. She didn't know if they were actual memories or some lingering imprint of a movie. Or maybe just a wish to have had some of the good of this place touch her life when she was a child. For a moment she was furious with her mother for not staying on this farm. Or near it. For living such a solitary life away from these people. She was shocked to feel tears in her eyes. *The father-figure thing*, she thought. She was deeply susceptible to daddy issues.

"Hey," Peg panted as she finally reached them, Tink following behind. "What's... Everything okay?"

Peg looked mildly panicked and Hope was embarrassed by her strange emotion at meeting Hank. "Totally fine," she said, stepping away from everyone for a second. "I'm just going to run to the bathroom. I'll be right back."

⇥ PEG ⇤

"I didn't say a word," Hank told her as they walked through the high grass, gathering up the bottles and cans from target practice.

"I know," Peg said. This was the danger of having Hank here. Hope might actually remember him. "It's all right."

"I didn't mean to upset her," he said. "All I did was shake her hand."

Peg understood how that might be enough. Maybe it jogged some long-buried memory. Was that why Peg had asked him back? To pop this bubble and force all the secrets out of that room and into the light?

"She looks better," he said, glancing over his shoulder to where Tink, Abel and Hope stood by the garden, picking vegetables for lunch.

"She is better," Peg said.

"And that Tink," he said and whistled. "She's a firecracker."

"She's what we thought Hope would be like at that age," Peg said, suddenly relieved to talk about this, to say these words out loud to the one person on the planet who understood. "She's curious and funny. Smart. She's helpful and hardworking and stands on her own two feet. She's everything we wanted Hope to be and more. And more, Hank. Hank—" The sob rumbled up from her stomach, pushing its way through her body like it would no longer be ignored. All the words she'd swallowed since the moment Hope arrived, those pictures she'd hidden in her room, as if she could really forget them…

She sobbed. She sobbed so hard she dropped the cans and bottle from her hand and pitched forward, her hands on her knees. "It hurts. It hurts so much. All those years, Hank. All those years and we missed them. We missed everything—"

"Shhhh," Hank said. "Shhh, Peg. Peggy." He dropped his own cans and, carefully, with his strong arms, pulled her upright and then against his chest. And that hurt, too.

It all hurt. Him being gone. Him being back.

For a second she braced her hands against his waist and tried to push him away. But he wouldn't have it this time. He was stronger and he kept her there, close to him.

"What did I do, Hank?" she said, openmouthed against his shoulder. "What did I do?"

"What you thought was best."

"Best?" It sounded so stupid now.

"What you needed to do to survive."

"Someone hit her. With his fist, he hit her. And Denise stifled all that light we loved in her. And if I'd fought for her the way you'd wanted to—"

"Shhhhh," he whispered against her hair. "Peggy. I know. I know. But she's back and she's here and she's not going anywhere."

"But what if she does?" She whispered her worst fear out loud. "What if she finds out what I did and she leaves?"

After dinner Peg walked Hank to his truck, aware of Tink watching them out of the window in her bedroom. Their boots kicked and slid over the gravel of the driveway and she couldn't even begin to count the number of times they'd done this over the years.

"Thanks for asking me to come out here," he said. "That was a good day."

Peg nodded, unsure of what to say or how to say it. That was the problem with knowing someone so well—it made small talk impossible. All she wanted to do was ask him if he hated her. If she was making another mistake.

"Peg?"

"Yeah."

"You're taking good care of them." She wanted to laugh but was afraid it might come out as a sob. "And I think you're right. Telling her what she doesn't know would not be kind."

Oh, the relief of that. It was nearly unbearable. Like she went numb all over, all at once. "Thank you," she said. The bats were coming out between the barn and the tree line. "That means a lot."

"Can I come back?"

That made her look at him. His earnest handsome face. "You want to?"

He made a fist and set it down carefully on the hood of his truck, like he had to get it in just the right spot. "Yeah," he said. "I'd like to know those girls as much as I can."

She told herself it wasn't about her. That they'd broken up so bad that it would be foolish to try to put their edges back together. But he was *here*. And Hope was *here*.

"The other day you said..." She cleared her throat. "You said that you couldn't forget me the way I forgot you." He was silent and she made herself look at him. "I never forgot you."

He looked up at the stars, his throat bobbing as he swallowed.

"Can you ever forgive me?" she asked.

"Peg—"

"If you're going to be here and I'm going to be here I just need to know."

"I'm trying so hard not to be angry. To not look at that girl and think of all the things we missed." He stopped himself, shook his head and still he didn't look at her. "I can't answer that right now."

She wanted to beg, the way she hadn't years ago, when he was putting all his things in the truck and driving away from her. But it wouldn't have worked then. And it wouldn't work now. Hank was a man who came to things on his own.

She backed away from him. From the truck. And the stupid foolish wish of a second chance.

"Come on back. You're welcome here," she said. "Anytime."

Twenty-Seven

A week later, Hope, Peg and Tink walked through the cherry orchard for the final time, making sure all the cherries that had covered the ground beneath the trees had been cleaned up and everything was draining right. They were saying goodbye to the season. To the bees and the trees, the tarps. The temperamental shaker. To who they'd been when they'd walked into the orchard a month ago.

"Is it weird to say I'm going to miss cherry season?" Hope asked.

"Yes," Tink said.

"No," Peg said. "But you'll get over it when apple season really starts."

Some of the early apples were already coming in, and tomorrow morning Abel was opening part of the apple orchard for the U-pick operation. Abel was going to try to make

cider. As a joke the other night she'd said he should try making boozy cider, and he'd looked at her like she was a genius.

So, she was a genius now.

"Is Hank coming over tonight?" Hope asked.

"Later tonight," Peg said. "He's finishing up a sales thing
over in Boyne."

"I like Hank," Tink said. She wasn't walking through the
rows as much as she was trying to climb every other tree. Her
affection for Hank wasn't news to anyone. Hank and Tink
had taken a real shine to each other, working on their target
practice on the three evenings he'd shown up in the last week.
Abel would be out there, too, the two men standing side by
side with their hands on their hips, taking turns setting up the
cans Tink knocked down.

The last night Hank came over, he'd brought a little charcoal
grill, and after target practice they did up pork kebabs. Hope
made packets of cheesy potatoes with chives and onions from
the garden and she'd been so proud she almost fell apart. Abel
contributed a six-pack of beer and a bottle of sweet wine that
Peg drank most of, and they'd all sat in the sun and laughed
and laughed.

"So," Hope said, carefully trying to figure out how to navi-
gate this conversation as they continued through the orchard.
There were opportunities for both Tink and Peg to get obsti-
nate about what she was going to propose. "I have a favor to
ask. Or a question, really. An idea. I have an idea."

Tink and Peg shared a flat look. "Spit it out, Mom," Tink said.

"I'd like to go to Grayling this afternoon," she said. "And
get a new laptop."

"Sounds fine," Peg said.

"Abel's going to come with me."

"Road trip with Abel, sounds fun! What's the big deal?"
Tink asked.

"Well…you're not," she told her daughter, who sucked in a deeply scandalized breath.

"You're going without me?" Tink asked.

"We were going to get the laptop and have dinner."

"A date?"

"I guess, yes. I guess a date." She could feel the blood pounding in her face.

"It's fine," Peg stepped in. "She'll be fine. Here with me at the farm."

"But it's Friday night, Mom," Tink said. "It's the party at Avery's."

"Oh." When Abel had suggested the trip she'd gotten so excited about her laptop and a night out with him, she'd forgotten entirely about the Friday-night get-together at Janice's. "Well, maybe when I come back we can go."

"But then we'll miss all of it!" Tink cried. "Can't you have your date tomorrow night?"

"Tomorrow we're opening up the U-pick trees and the corn maze," Peg said.

She was right. Tonight was the calm before the storm. But truly they could go on a date any night. In the winter. And Tink loved the night at Janice's and so did Hope, so maybe the sensible thing was to go slow, make sure Tink was happy and then worry about herself.

"I'll take her," Peg said. Tink and Hope turned wide eyes to Peg. "What?" Peg said. "I don't have to go in, do I? I can drop you and pick you up?"

"No," Tink said as Hope said, "Yes," at the same time.

"You need to bring something, though," Tink informed her. "To eat. We didn't have anything last time. And it was a thing."

"It wasn't a thing."

"It was a whole big thing, Mom."

"I think we can find something," Peg said.

The two of them walked on ahead, deciding between meatballs or pigs in a blanket.

It was going to be a good day for every girl in the Wright family.

✦ PEG ✦

There was nothing about this that should be a big deal. Nothing. She was dropping off Tink. That was all. She probably wasn't even going to have to talk to Carole. Maybe not even see her.

She and Tink left Hope futzing around getting ready, and since Hope and Abel were taking the truck, Peg was left with Hope's old hatchback, which actually made her feel better as she drove through town. Like she was invisible.

The plate of pigs in a blanket wrapped in foil balanced on Tink's lap, making the inside of the car smell like hot dogs. They'd unrolled their windows to try to get rid of the smell.

"You know where she lives?" Tink asked for the fifth time.

"Yep," Peg said, turning left on Main Street, heading toward Lincoln, where she'd make a right.

"You know Carole?" Tink asked.

"Yep."

"Janice?"

"I knew her as a baby."

"She's different now," Tink said like she was the authority on these women, and Peg hid her smile.

She pulled up to the side of the house and put the car in Park but didn't turn it off. She wondered if she knew any of the other women in the house. Hope had mentioned Swafiya, whom she'd only talked to through email. A woman named Angela. That might be Angela who ran the bank. She was pretty nice.

"Hello, Peg."

Peg turned to see her old friend standing there beside her car window, looking as wild as she ever did: bright purple pants, a black tank top, her hair a silver-and-black mess upon her head. She wore red glasses and every wrinkle on her face with the kind of grace that came from not giving a single shit about what people thought.

It was the best and worst thing about her.

"Tink," Carole said. "Why don't you go on in? Avery's been talking about you nonstop."

Tink pushed the plate of food onto Peg's lap and was off like a shot, leaving her alone with the only friend she'd ever really had.

And a dozen pigs in a blanket.

"Carole," she managed to say. "Good to see you."

"It's been a while. I thought maybe you'd died on that farm and that dog of yours ate you."

"Poor dog would choke. I'm too tough."

"Ain't that the truth."

"Heard Janice was back in town. How is she?" Peg thought of that pretty blue-eyed child with a scream that could curdle eggs.

"She's got four kids. Each of them worse than the last. The baby's okay, though." The joke was only funny because she knew Carole, and the Carole she knew would probably lie down in traffic for those kids. "She's doing better," Carole said quietly. "Janice had a pretty rough go of it there. But she's acting like herself again. You should bring that plate of food in and see for yourself."

Peg pushed down a side of the foil, letting the edge bite into her thumb.

"Hope's back," Carole added.

"Yep," Peg said past the lump in her throat.

"You must be—"

"Yep."

Carole reached through the open window and grabbed her hand. So hard Peg couldn't pull it away or change her grip.

Here, Carole was saying with that grip. *Take it. Take my friendship and shut up.*

"*I haven't told her,*" Peg confessed.

"*I figured.*"

"*I'm scared she'll leave if she knows.*"

The way Hank did. The way Carole did.

"*I don't know. Hope seems like the forgiving type.*"

Peg squeezed her old friend's hand.

"I heard you're hiring her," Peg whispered.

Carole nodded. "Well, you know me and numbers."

"Thank you," Peg said.

"Stop. It's not charity. The girl knows her stuff and lord knows I need help." Carole lifted her hand from Peg's. "I heard Hank's been around, too, lately."

"I suppose," Peg said.

"'I suppose,' listen to you. Once upon a time you wouldn't shut up about that man."

"He's not… It's not like that," she said. "He's just enjoying spending time with the girls."

"And you? Are you enjoying spending time with him?"

There'd been a minute the other night, when he was saying goodbye, patting Nelson's head for the hundredth time, and she was standing at the door so she could shut it after him, when she'd thought, for just a minute, that he might touch her.

The way he used to. His fingers against her cheek.

But then Tink had yelled, "Shut the door, you're letting in the bugs!" and the moment had passed and she'd felt stupid for wanting more.

"I don't know. Carole, I broke his heart. Maybe…too much to ever forgive me."

"Well, I know," Carole said. "You two were the real deal."

"I wish I had your confidence."

"Well, I'm stoned. If you want a cookie—"

"Oh my god, Carole. You have not changed. Not one bit."

"You want to come in for a drink?" Carole asked. "I have that tea you used to like."

Constant Comment. Tons of sugar. Milk. The two of them used to drink that by the potful, exhausted by toddlers, comforted by each other's presence.

"I missed you," Peg said.

"I know. I missed you, too. Come in for tea."

And she did. She walked in the door and there were kids and a dog. Other women shaking her hand and laughing. There was food and tea. Wine. Friends.

It was like when your ears pop, and everything goes from distant and removed to loud and present. Life, right there in the kitchen.

→HOPE←

"You okay?" Abel asked, looking over at her from the driver's seat.

"Fine."

"You don't have to pretend."

"Okay," she said, checking her phone like she hadn't *just* checked her phone ten seconds ago. The ringer was on. The battery was good. There just weren't any calls coming in. "I'm a little freaked out because Peg was supposed to call me after she dropped off Tink at Carole's."

"Maybe Peg went in, too?"

Well, that was the hope, but still.

"She has a cell."

"But is it on her body and does it have battery?" Abel smiled at her.

"Good point." Peg was notorious for walking around with a phone with a dead battery. "Maybe I should call Janice and just make sure..." She stopped and half smiled, half winced at him. "Sorry."

"Call Janice, Hope. Just get your mind at ease."

Hope quickly called and got confirmation that yes, Tink was there. And so was Peg. Drinking tea by the potful and hogging the cheese. But things were winding down, and everyone was heading out soon.

"Wow," she said after hanging up. "It looks like Peg is making friends. Or making old friends. Or something."

"Maybe she's just buying weed cookies," Abel said, and Hope laughed.

"I'm really happy," she said, the sensation taking her by surprise. She'd felt watercolor versions of this before, but nothing so vivid. So real. Like happiness was a thing she could hold in her hand. Taste on her tongue. She wanted to laugh for no good reason.

Abel put his hand on her knee. "I like your skirt," he said.

She'd worn a skirt today, her only skirt, a swishy thing that made her feel young and pretty.

"You've said that already."

"I know. I just really like it."

Abel pulled over onto the gravel shoulder of the road and put the truck in Park.

"What are you doing?"

He took a deep breath and exhaled.

"Are you okay?" She slid over, putting her hand on his shoulder. "Are you having a heart attack?"

"What?"

"It's just…that's a thing that happens. People have heart attacks while driving. It used to be a fear of mine. Or a stroke. Are you having a stroke?"

He shook his head, smiling at her.

"If you're not having a heart attack or a stroke, why are we stopping?" She looked around but saw nothing but Northern Michigan in August. Which was to say, green and lush and alive and very, very private. Corn like a wall between the truck and everything else.

"Happiness is very sexy on you," he said.

"Sexy?"

"You're familiar with the word?" he asked.

"Yeah, I mean…sure."

"I can't stand *not* kissing you any longer, Hope Wright," he said.

"Here?"

"Yep. And then we're gonna go buy a computer and some dinner."

She was leaning in to his kiss before it even happened, delighted and turned on by the compliment and the heat of his skin and the size of his hands on her back.

Who knew that being appreciated would feel like this? Like being utterly revealed to someone. She'd been so used to keeping so many parts of herself hidden, tucked away in the hope that other people might love her more if she wasn't so much herself.

She was so used to living in the cold shadow of fear, she'd forgotten how warm the sun could feel on her shoulders.

Twenty-Eight

"**Y**our mom is going to be mad," Peg said, which was pretty much stating the obvious. They were breaking the speed limit heading back to the farm, Peg's dead cell phone in the console. "We didn't call."

"She called Janice."

"I know, but we were supposed to call."

Tink rolled her eyes. "Is Hank going to be at the farm when we get there?" That was how Peg had gotten her out of Avery's basement.

The sun was going down behind the cornfields on the left side of the car and the sky was turning pink. The bats were going to come out soon. Hank had shown them to her last time.

She wasn't sure yet how she felt about the bats.

"Maybe. If not, then real soon."

"Think he'll take us for ice cream?" Hank loved taking

everyone for ice cream and Tink was 100 percent in support of that.

"You can't still be hungry," Peg said.

"Oh, but I can!"

"I think if you ask," Peg said, "Hank will do anything you want him to."

Hank was like a grandpa in a corny movie. The kind who made you roll your eyes but wonder what it would be like to have someone who wasn't embarrassed to love you so much.

They got home and Hank wasn't there yet.

"He'll be here soon," Peg said.

Nelson jumped around like Tink had been gone for days rather than a few hours. "You," she said to Nelson as she scrubbed the dog's ears and rubbed her belly, "are gonna have to toughen up. School is starting soon and I'm gonna be gone most of the day. What are you gonna do then?"

Nelson drooled on her foot.

Ten minutes later there was a big knock on the front door. "That's probably him," Peg said, coming out of her room. "He must need help unloading stuff. Come on."

Peg led the way, followed by Tink with Nelson right beside her. But when Peg put her hand to the door, Nelson started to growl and all the hair stood up on Tink's arms.

"Peg," Tink said. Something was wrong. Something just felt...wrong.

"Good lord, dog, what's gotten into you?" Peg asked as Nelson barked and got between Tink and the door. "It's just Hank."

But it wasn't. Something in Tink's gut said it wasn't.

Peg opened the door just as Tink said, "Don't!"

A man stood there in khaki pants and a navy blue shirt. "Hi," he said, cheerful, like he was a normal human, not a monster wearing skin. "Is Hope Wright—"

"Shut the door," Tink said.

"Jenny!" he cried, smiling.

"Shut the door, Peg!" She started backing away. Nelson went wild and lunged at the guy just as Peg slammed the door.

Tink was still backing up, her whole body shaking.

"Tink?" Peg asked. "Who was that?"

"Call Mom," she said. "No, call the police. You need to call—"

The screen door that opened into the kitchen squeaked long and loud.

Nelson went wild again, trying to take off running toward the back of the house, her claws sliding all over the hardwood.

"Hello?" Oh god. Tink felt her stomach roll over, her knees wobble.

Suddenly there he was, standing in the kitchen. His whole face, his body, the whole way he acted, said, *This isn't weird. It isn't weird that your dog is standing two feet away from me freaking out. And it isn't weird that I just walked in the back door of the house after you shut the door on me in the front. I'm smiling and relaxed and wearing khaki pants, so everything must be normal.*

"Excuse me," Peg said, and Tink was relieved she was not buying his calm-and-collected act for even a minute. Peg would be better at this than Mom. Peg could handle this. "What the hell are you doing in my house?"

"I'm sorry," he said, pressing his hand to his chest. "I didn't get a chance to introduce myself. I'm Daniel."

Twenty-Nine

There'd been a change in the air when Dad got mad. Some awful imbalance between electrons and protons, something unfixable, a current that just had to be ridden out.

The air right now had that same feeling.

"You need to leave," she told Daniel. The gun was over the door and only a few feet behind her, and Nelson was baring her teeth. Peg figured with one word Nelson could have this guy running for his life out the back door.

"Actually," Daniel said, still smiling. "I want to congratulate Hope on starting her business. Orchard House Bookkeeping. The name sounded familiar and it took some digging to figure out it was her, but I'm real proud of her."

That was how he'd found them. Son of a bitch.

"You're not hearing me, son," Peg said, and turned around and grabbed the rifle. Because enough with this. This man was not walking uninvited into this home, much less into Hope and

Tink's life. Not again. She turned back around and the man was standing there, arms up. But still smiling. "You need to leave."

"And I will. I absolutely will. I just need to talk to Jenny."

"That's not going to happen." Peg stepped forward, pulling Tink behind her. "Go."

Her words bounced off him.

"Get 'em," she said when he didn't move, and Nelson, growling and barking, lunged at the man. But Daniel kicked the dog, catching her across the face, sending her flying backward.

"Nelson!" Tink cried, reaching for the still-growling dog.

Peg racked the rifle. There wasn't a cartridge in it, but he didn't know that.

"Tink, go get my phone." Even as she said it, she remembered it was dead in the front seat of the car.

"Jenny," Daniel said, and in the blink of an eye, so short it didn't even register, Daniel had his own gun pointed at Peg. "Don't move toward that phone, honey."

Tink went absolutely white with fear.

"You don't want me to shoot her in front of you, do you?" Daniel asked Tink like it was Peg who was causing the problem. She saw in an instant the power this manipulative man had. The evil. It hurt her to imagine Hope living with him.

Tink shook her head no, and Daniel grinned at Peg, knowing he'd won, that the balance had shifted in his favor because he was willing to use that little girl as a pawn.

And unlike her—he probably had bullets.

"Give me the gun, Peg," he said. "Or we'll be traumatizing Jenny more than she already has been."

Like he cared. Goddammit. She knew she didn't have a choice. She lowered the rifle and handed it over. He opened it and saw it was empty.

"Nice bluff," he said.

"You're not leaving with that girl," she said.

"I am, though," he said, so smug. "Jenny is coming with me and then Hope will come back and everything will be the way it's supposed to be. Right, Jenny?"

Back on her feet now, Nelson crept forward, all the hair on her back standing on end.

"Call off your dog or I'll put a bullet in her," Daniel said, and Peg whistled between her teeth. Nelson whimpered, confused, but sat right at Tink's feet.

"Put the gun away," Peg said. "You don't need it."

"I'll decide what I need."

Tink, who, even when she was silent for a week, still managed to convey plenty, was now blank-faced and silent. Terrified silent. Going-into-shock silent.

"Tink," Peg said, beginning to feel afraid herself. "Everything is going to be okay."

Whatever comfort she'd imagined, her words had the opposite effect and Tink began to shake.

"Jenny," Daniel said and straightened out his arm, holding the gun on Peg with such dramatic and malicious intent to scare the girl. Because he was enjoying this. "Come on."

"He won't hurt me," Peg said to Tink. "He's a coward. And a show-off and he won't—"

The front door opened and Hank came walking in, whistling and cheerful. He didn't see what was happening, didn't smell the danger in the air, blinded and made stupid, just like her, by the happiness of the last few weeks.

"Hank," she breathed, gasped really, unable to scream.

"Hey, there, my girls, what—"

Thirty

The gunshot filled the house, so loud she fell to the floor, dragging Tink with her. Her ears buzzed and rang, but she could still hear Nelson barking and growling, her claws on the wood floor as she charged at Daniel, driving him deeper into the kitchen.

Beneath Peg's arm, Tink was shaking. But she was okay. No blood.

Quickly, she prayed to a god she hadn't spoken to in years. *Please let him be okay.*

She turned her head and saw Hank leaning against the door jamb, a big chunk of it taken out by the bullet.

The bullet that had hit him in the arm.

He was bleeding badly, but she could see him gathering his strength to go after Daniel. She knew how that would end: with another bullet. Because after that first shot every bullet would come easier. And easier. Until there were none left.

She made her decision in a split second.

"Call the cops," she whispered at Hank, getting to her feet. "I don't have my phone. Take Tink."

"No," Tink said, clinging to Peg. "No. I'm not leaving."

There was no time to argue. Hank had to go get help. Tink and Peg would stay.

"Goddammit!" Daniel yelled, out of sight behind the brick archway.

Hank gave her that look of his. Utter faith. Complete belief. A split second of fear. A lifetime of love. It had to kill him to leave her and Tink there, but he was their best option. Their only hope.

He turned back out the door and ran to the truck, where he had his cell phone. She shut the door behind him and heard the motor start up.

The police would be here soon. Five minutes.

She just needed to stall Daniel for five minutes.

Before that asshole shot her dog, she called her off. "Nelson," she shouted, and her sweet dog, so trained and so loyal, whimpered. "Come here," she said. "You're okay, brave girl. You're okay."

Nelson ran to her in the living room and Daniel followed.

"Where'd the old man go?" Daniel asked, his mask slipping. She saw fear. Real fear. Oh, the coward, used to his threats and his smile doing all the hard work. But now he was in it. Real trouble.

"You shot him," Peg said.

"Is he dead?" He stormed past Peg, pulled open the front door only to see the truck on the road, kicking up dust as he sped away. "Jesus, he ran?" Daniel asked, laughing as he shut the door. "He left you here. What a hero."

His sarcasm didn't touch her. He didn't know that Hank was heading over to the crossroads of 72 and Flagg Road, so the fire trucks and cop cars coming from town would know where to turn. Because when they'd had that fire a few years back, the fire trucks had gone the long way because their GPS didn't have a satellite signal out here.

Beside her, Tink got to her feet.

"Where's your mom?" Daniel asked Tink. Now that the smile was gone, the real Daniel was showing. Dark and pissy. Bitter and jealous.

"Out," Peg said.

"I didn't ask you," he snapped.

"Tink doesn't feel like talking to you."

"Shut up," he said, his face twisted in ugly lines. "And her name is Jenny, goddammit. Come on." He walked past them and grabbed Tink by the elbow, so rough she whimpered.

Nelson lunged at him and this time when Daniel kicked the dog, he did it so hard Nelson crashed hard against the brick wall and fell to the ground with an awful sound.

"Nelson," Tink cried, pulling herself free to rush to the dog's side.

Peg stared at Daniel, easing her way between him and Tink. "What's your plan?" she asked. "Because things have escalated."

"Jenny is coming with me, and you are going to give Hope a message when she gets back."

"Am I?"

"You are." He smirked at her.

There was a certain kind of man who couldn't imagine himself losing, despite having lost most of his life. Daniel was that kind of man.

"You're going to tell her that she needs to call me or I'm going to go to the police with the hospital report of what she did to me in Detroit. And she can come with us or she'll lose Jenny for good."

"Was that what you threatened her with before?"

"It's not a threat. That woman is a disaster without me. A terrible mother. Jenny, we're leaving." He pushed Peg aside and pulled Tink with him toward the door.

Nelson tried to get to her feet to follow, but she was hurt pretty bad, panting through the pain. Peg felt herself ignite, her old bones suddenly on fire.

So help me. If you killed my dog…

"It's okay," she told her beloved dog. "You did good. You did real good. Stay here."

Daniel headed out the kitchen door, Tink stumbling behind him.

"The police are going to come after you," Peg said.

"I'm comfortable with my head start."

The grass was long behind the house and he made tracks in it around the side, where she saw his car parked, just out of sight of the front window. She trotted a little to keep up with him and he turned around, lifting the gun toward her head again. She would bet a million dollars that the guy was not a good shot, that he had gotten lucky with the one that had hit Hank. But she wasn't willing to push it.

"You seem like a nice old lady. So be a nice old lady and mind your own business. Tell her, Jenny," he said, still pointing that gun at Peg. "Tell her to stay here, or when she gets hurt it will be your fault."

"Peg!" Tink sobbed and then, oh, that girl, that wild brave girl, she tried to smile, as if she could convince Peg to let her leave with this animal. "It's okay," she said. "Everything will be fine."

Peg thought of Hope in the gas-station parking lot, doing the exact same thing.

And then, in the distance, there were sirens, lots of them.

Getting closer, it seemed, from every corner. Peg tried not to smile, but she couldn't help it.

"I'd say you lost your head start."

➔ HOPE ←

Oh, that just-made-out feeling. The giddiness of it made her feel like the teenager she'd never really had a chance to be.

"You make out in a lot of cars?" she asked Abel, pushing back the hair he'd mussed with his hands.

Abel laughed and rubbed a hand over his mouth, like the tingliness of his lips was distracting him, too. "No. Not for a lot of years. Forgot how fun it is."

It was fun. Pure fun.

Except when his hand slid from her back to the skin of her waist, just under her shirt, and she'd flinched. The tiniest flinch. But he'd felt it and eased back.

She didn't want to think about Daniel while she was kissing Abel, but he was there. A ghost between them. His violence against her had never been sexual, but the thought of the times he'd touched her made her stomach turn now.

And apparently flinch.

"I'm sorry," she said.

"It's not a problem, Hope. And I mean that."

He drove back onto the road and his hand covered hers on the vinyl bench seat and squeezed.

Ten minutes later, as they headed toward Grayling, from deep in her purse there was the hum and buzz of her phone. Then his phone, resting on the dashboard, began to rattle. And there was something about the two of them at once that seemed a little dire.

Abel got to his phone first while she dug through her purse. "This is Abel." After a second, he sucked in a breath and glanced over at her. She finally grabbed her phone from the bottom of her purse just as Abel pulled over into one of those median cut-throughs that only police and fire trucks were supposed to use.

It was Janice. "Hey," Hope said.

"Don't freak out."

"What's going on?"

"Mom heard on her scanner—"

"Your mother has a scanner?"

"Honestly, that can't surprise you. But listen, police and fire trucks are going out to the farm."

"What? Why?"

"We don't know. Have you heard from Peg?"

"No. Abel and I were headed to Grayling…well, I think we're turning around. Still, I'm like twenty minutes away." Even as she said that she could feel Abel leaning on the gas pedal.

"It's probably nothing," Janice said.

Hope hung up and looked over at Abel. "Who called you?"

"My friend Ravi at the fire station."

"It's a fire?"

He shook his head.

"Abel. Tell me what is going on."

"It's Daniel. With a gun."

Thirty-One

→TINK←

Daniel pushed them back into the house and, after looking around the first floor, shoved them into Peg's room.

"My bedroom? Really?" Peg asked.

"Your windows have blinds. Cops can't see in."

Tink was so worried about Nelson, all alone out there. She could hear her whimpering at the door.

I'm sorry I was mean to you.

"This is your fault," Daniel said, jabbing the gun toward Peg.

"Yeah?" Peg asked, all defiant, and Tink felt this deep need to tell Peg to be quiet. To not make him angry. "How do you figure?"

Peg crossed her arms over her chest and stared at him, daring him to do something, and Tink reached out and grabbed her hand. *Please*, she thought. *Please be careful.*

But Daniel only sneered at Peg and paced away. There was

a tiny window in the door that led outside, and he went over and looked through it, and then swore and ducked down.

"Holy shit," he said. "There's cops out there."

"What did you think was going to happen?" Peg asked.

"I thought I would get my family back!" he yelled, growing red.

Tink remembered that day he'd picked her up from school. She'd told him she wanted to go home and see her mom and he just smiled at her; the more upset she got the calmer he was. *We're having fun, aren't we? This is a thing that families do. They get ice cream after school. They go to the park. They drive around.*

"Hope and Tink are not your family," Peg said.

He charged over to her. Tink ducked down, collapsed onto her butt, trying to tug Peg down with her, but she wouldn't back down. Peg stood there, and when he hit her, when Daniel punched Peg across the face, it was just like when he'd done the same thing to Mom.

Peg fell forward and then back against the bookshelf, and her nose started to bleed. "Look at you, big man," she said, lifting the hem of her shirt up to wipe her face. "Punching an old lady."

"Shut up!" he shouted.

"You know what, you're just like my father, Daniel. You're a bully. And I stopped being scared of bullies a long time ago."

He leaned down into Peg's face and screamed. Yelled so loud it blew the hair off her face. And Peg didn't even flinch.

Tink put her head down in her lap and wished she was a million miles away. She wished she and Peg and Mom and Nelson were down at the beach, making one of those volcanoes. She should have done that. That day with Mom when she wanted to play at the beach and push Tink on the swing, she wished she'd said yes.

Why didn't I say yes?

From outside came the voice of a man talking through a bullhorn just like on TV. Daniel spun around and headed to a window next to the door, reaching beneath the blinds to slide it open.

Tink was trying to hear what the guy was saying, but Peg grabbed her hand and forced her attention back to her. "The jewelry box," she whispered. "Open it. Get the gun and the bullets."

Tink moved as fast and as quietly as she could, quick, quick, quick. Like it was a game. Like Peg wasn't bleeding and Daniel wasn't even there. She pretended that she and Hank were just going to have target practice. She didn't even waste the time checking to see if Daniel was watching her.

Tink opened the old jewelry box and moved all the old pictures until she saw the small pistol among the letters she'd taken.

"What the hell are you doing?" Daniel yelled, and Tink, acting fast, grabbed the letter on top and turned around, letting the jewelry box shut.

"Getting this?" she said, holding out the letter.

"Why?"

"I asked her to," Peg said, and Daniel walked over and snagged the letter right out of Tink's hands. He ripped the old paper out of the envelope and Peg made a small sound, like the one Nelson had made when Daniel had kicked her.

"Who gives a shit about a letter from a hospital?" he said and tossed the letter. Peg scrambled for it, putting the ripped paper back into the ripped envelope. She closed her eyes and pressed it to her chest.

The guy on the bullhorn started up again, and Daniel went back to his spot, crouching beside the window, yelling through the screen.

Peg shook her head no, but Tink wasn't scared, or if she was, she couldn't feel it.

She opened the jewelry box again, quickly removed the gun

and the box of bullets and scurried back over to Peg, who sat in front of her so Daniel couldn't see what they were doing.

"I just want Hope," he yelled out the window, and Tink wanted to tell him to keep Mom's name out of his mouth.

"Shit," Peg breathed, and Tink looked back and saw that there were only three bullets in the box. "Good thing I'm a crack shot, huh?" She winked, which was a little scary with the blood, and Tink had to stop herself from throwing her arms around Peg.

"She's coming," the man on the bullhorn said. "And you will be able to talk to her, but you need to release the hostages."

"They're not hostages!" Daniel yelled.

"Then let them go."

Daniel popped up onto his feet, crossing the room in three long strides. "All right, old lady—"

But Peg didn't have the bullets in the gun in time. Just as she slid the last bullet in the chamber and was about to click the whole thing shut, point it at him and blow his stupid head off, he was there.

"What the hell?" He smacked the gun out of her hand and it went spinning across the floor, bullets sliding out and rolling out of sight. "Goddammit," he said. "I was going to let you go!"

He grabbed Peg by the hair and pushed her down flat on her stomach onto the floor, holding his gun to her head like he was going to shoot her.

Tink scuttled back on her butt, wishing she was braver and knew what to do. Wishing she was an adult. Or someone else.

Or somewhere else.

Thirty-Two

County Road 72 was jam-packed with cars and police. Sirens blaring. Lights going.

"Oh my god," Hope breathed, her shaking hands over her mouth.

"Let's get some answers," Abel said. "Before we assume the worst."

"This is the worst, Abel!"

This was every worst-case scenario.

A uniformed police officer stepped out in the middle of the road, waving his arms. "Sorry, folks," he said. "You can't go any—"

"My daughter is in there. And my aunt," she cried, practically leaping over Abel.

"It's our farm," Abel said calmly.

"Wait a moment," the officer said, and he turned and spoke into a walkie-talkie attached to his bulletproof vest.

"I should have left," she whispered, too shocked and numb to cry or scream. She could only shake. "When Matt told me there was nothing I could do to keep us safe, I should have—"

"Stop," Abel said. "This is him. This is all him. You can't blame yourself."

"Bullshit, Abel. That's bullshit. If he hurts—"

"No one is getting hurt."

But he didn't know that. Someone might already have been hurt. For all they knew, Daniel could have already killed both of them.

A man approached her window and it took her a second to recognize Hank, pale, his arm all wrapped up and held carefully to his side in a sling.

"Hank," she said, unrolling the window. "What happened?"

"Nothing," he said with a wide smile that she didn't believe at all. "Ran into the door frame, if you can believe it."

She shook her head, blinking back tears. It was a terrible lie, and she wished with her whole heart that she could believe it.

"Listen to me, Hope," he said, grabbing her hand through the window. "There is not a person on this planet tougher than Peg." He smiled again. "I feel bad for that boy in there. He's about to get his ass handed to him."

"But Tink—"

"Will be okay. Because Peg is making sure of it. Because every single person out here is making sure of it."

The officer stepped back up to the truck and leaned in the driver's-side window.

"Sir," he said. "You're going to have to stay here. But, ma'am, you're coming with me."

Abel turned to her and squeezed her hand. "I'll be right here. No matter what happens."

She jumped out of the truck and into a police cruiser that raced her the mile up the road to the farm.

"As far as we know, no one inside the house is injured," he said in what she imagined he believed to be a very calming voice.

"That's good."

"He's asking for you."

"Of course he is."

"They're going to try to convince him to let Peg and Jenny go—"

"Tink," she said.

"Pardon?"

"Nothing," she breathed. "Does he have a weapon?"

"Ma'am?"

"Does he have a weapon?" she practically yelled.

"Yes, ma'am. He does."

They screeched to a stop at the tree line that ran beside the house to the road, where another officer helped her out of the car and into a bulletproof vest.

"Ma'am," he said, and hysterically she wondered who this ma'am was everyone was talking to. "You'll need to stay behind the police line—"

And then a gunshot tore through the world.

Thirty-Three

→TINK←

Peg lay there real still, her nose still bleeding, Daniel's gun pointed to her head.

Then Peg smiled and, with her eyes real wide, looked from Tink to the edge of the chair Tink was sitting in front of. And then she did it again to the edge of the rug by Tink's foot. One and then the other, again and again.

Tink looked behind her, where the gun sat between her and the wooden leg of the chair right behind her. Soundlessly as possible, Tink picked it up, then looked over to where her foot was next to the rug and saw the bullet.

One bullet.

She looked back at Peg. *I can't.*

You can.

With shaking fingers, Tink reached forward and grabbed the bullet, dropping it about an inch off the ground; it made a light *ting* against the wood, but Daniel was ranting so much he didn't even hear it.

She picked up the bullet again, her fingers shaking so hard the chamber seemed like an impossibly small place and her fingers impossibly big. But she got it in, clicked it shut as quiet as she could.

Then she tried to point it at Daniel. That part was hard.

Shooting at cans was one thing. This was scary and she could do it all wrong. What if she didn't hit him at all? Or accidentally hit Peg?

Her breath made a choked sound in her throat and Daniel turned. "What the hell are you doing, Jenny?"

She got to her feet, holding the gun out steady, away from her body. Both hands. "My name is Tink," she said.

Deep breath in, deep breath out. Just like Peg said.

Don't close your eyes. Just like Abel said.

And then, nice and smooth, pull on the trigger. Just like Hank said.

Daniel was lunging for her and then he stopped, almost in midair. The gun fell out of Tink's hands from the recoil and she looked down at Peg, who was pushing herself up to her feet.

"Run!" Peg yelled, and Tink made a big wide circle around Daniel, who was falling down onto his knees, looking down at his leg like he didn't understand why it couldn't hold him up anymore.

Tink ran for the door leading to outside, wrestling it open and sprinting out. She ran around the house and saw a group of police officers trying to hold back her mom, but as soon as Mom saw Tink, she tore past the police and fell to her knees as Tink collided with her, knocking them both to the ground.

"Mom." Tink sobbed and buried her face into the sweet spot of Hope's neck. The two of them, always the two of them, and she felt bad for every silent day. "I'm sorry," she kept saying.

Mom held on to her so hard it hurt.

And then Peg was there, her nose bleeding, sliding into them on her knees.

Mom and Tink opened up their arms, and now it was the three of them.

Thirty-Four

→HOPE←

There were medics and police. A blur. Everything a blur. Tink in her arms. Hope in Peg's arms. Questions. So many questions. They had to go to the police station, where the light made her eyes hurt.

"Where's Nelson?" Tink kept asking.

"I took her to the vet in town," Abel said. "She has a bruised rib and a sore mouth, but she's okay. The vet is going to bring her back to the farm."

"She'll be there tonight?" Tink asked.

"She'll be waiting for you," Abel said, and Tink turned her face into Hope's waist, where she felt her daughter's hot tears through her T-shirt.

Thank you, she mouthed to Abel, who had not left her side. The man was a pure wonder.

Tink's bullet had hit Daniel high in the leg, missing, just barely, his femoral artery. The police officers took turns shaking Tink's hand, calling her a hero. Tink was being very quiet, and there was a child psychologist trained in trauma coming in from Flint to talk to her tomorrow.

Daniel was going to be charged with a long list of things. Matt Hageman had been sitting with her at the police station, listening, and she trusted him to explain it all to her again when her brain was working.

"Okay," she kept saying. "That's okay."

They wanted to keep Peg for the night at the hospital, but she was having none of it. Hope tried to convince her to stay, but Hank, who'd been glued to Peg's side since the moment they were allowed to see her, told Hope to save her breath. If Peg wanted to go home, nothing was going to stop her.

The sun had set and the lightning bugs showed up like it was any other night, and Hope felt wonder and strength at how the world kept moving.

That was how they were going to survive. They were just going to keep moving.

As Abel parked the truck, Nelson came out Peg's bedroom door, which had apparently been left open. A minute later, the vet walked out the front door and came over to talk to Abel.

Peg and Hank pulled in behind them in Hank's truck.

"Nelson!" Tink cried and wrestled her way out of Hope's arms. She fell to her knees next to the dog, petting her and then carefully hugging her.

Nelson licked her face and after a second the two of them went back inside the house through Peg's bedroom.

Hope jumped out of the truck and followed, pausing for a second at Peg's bedroom door, remembering that she didn't want them in here.

But there was Tink, sitting on the floor in the middle of

the room, Nelson in her arms, her tail beating a happy tattoo against the ground.

"She was so brave, Mom," Tink said.

Hope walked in. She would apologize to Peg later if she was upset. The smell of some kind of chemical thick in the room hit her, and she turned on the lamp by the TV, sending shadows scurrying across the old floors.

"You both were," she told her daughter, the tears she'd been crying off and on all night threatening again. "All of you were."

Hope glanced around the room and didn't want to imagine what it had been like in there earlier with Daniel. *We'll burn the rug*, she thought. *All those magazines. Everything he touched, we'll burn.* In the light of the lamp, she made out a mural painted on the wall behind the dresser with the television that had been shoved aside, a vine and little green handprints like leaves, growing up the vine and stopping halfway.

It took a second, adrenaline and exhaustion making her brain fuzzy. But she caught her name written in purple ink and then again, a little lower, in blue. And then again, lower still, black marker. There were a couple dozen marks, and it looked just like the wall between the bathroom and bedroom in Mom's apartment, where Hope would make Tink stand up straight and she'd draw a little line just over the top of her head. A growth chart.

Beside every mark was a date. And there were so many dates, the name Hope written beside each one.

Suddenly Peg was there, her face cleaned up, but her nose in bad shape. She seemed frail. The night had taken away some of Peg, and Hope wasn't sure if she would ever get it back.

Nelson got to her feet and whined low in her throat as she made her way to Peg, who got down on one knee to tell Nelson what a good dog she was.

Hank came in after stopping in the doorway like he was on the edge of something.

"I was here a lot," Hope said. "I mean…" She pointed at the wall. There were no years written down, but months and days and her age. One. Eighteen months. Seventeen months. Two, two and a half, two and ten months. "You said I was here when I was four and then you talked about my first birthday, but I guess I just never put two and two together." She looked over at Peg. "Why didn't you tell me?"

"You didn't remember, and it seemed unnecessary to tell you—"

"Tell me what exactly?"

"We've had a long night," Hank said, stepping farther into the room until he stood between Hope and the wall. "Maybe we can talk about this tomorrow."

"Right," Hope said, embarrassed and off center. "Sorry."

"No," Peg said, struggling back up onto her feet. Hank tried to help her with his one good arm. "No. Let's just…let's just do this. I'm too tired to keep this secret anymore."

Hope felt the way she'd felt driving up to The Orchard House more than a month ago: like she was driving off a cliff but couldn't stop the car.

"What secret?"

"You were here for four years, Hope," Peg finally said. "From when you were first born until Denise took you when you were four."

She reeled back, her knees suddenly weak. *Denise* took *me?*

"Oh my god," Hope breathed. She looked at Peg, so pale. So *familiar.* "Am I…am I yours? Are you my mom?"

Thirty-Five

⇢ PEG ⇠

*O*h, she thought. *If only.*

"No. No, Hope. I'm not your mother."

"Then I really don't understand what's going on."

"Peg?" Hank said, his hand warm on her shoulder. "Are you okay?"

"Fine," she lied. She could feel her heartbeat in her head. The doctors had been serious about keeping her overnight and she'd pitched a real fit about it, but now she was wondering if she hadn't been hasty. The word *concussion* had been thrown around, and that felt about right.

"You are not my biological daughter. But you were mine from when you were just two weeks old."

"Two *weeks*? I don't understand."

"After our parents died, your mom left with your father." Peg shook her head and blinked back tears. "And I never ex-

pected to hear from her again. And then one day I got that
letter—"

"Rehab."

"And the other six months later."

"Rehab again."

"Yeah. And then a year after that, I got this one."

She walked over to the bookshelves, where she'd put the
letter after Daniel had torn it out of the envelope. The paper
was ripped and some of his blood had gotten on it.

In the hundreds of times she'd cleaned this house, purged
the clothes that didn't fit and the coffee cups with chips, this
letter had nearly been tossed out a dozen times. But Peg had
always rescued it from the burn pile at the last minute.

And sometimes when things got really lonely she read it
to remind herself that it had happened. That once she'd had
a child. And a family. And love. So much love.

She handed the letter to Hope, who unfolded it with trem-
bling hands and read it with tears in her eyes.

I'm sorry, girl, she thought. *I'm sorry you have to find out like
this. After everything that's happened.*

Peg knew the letter by heart.

"Peg," it read.

I've had a baby. A little girl. I need you. I really do. I can't
do this by myself. Help me, Peg. Please. Help me. They're
releasing us from the hospital today and I'm so scared.

There was an address written at the bottom. An apartment
outside of Flint.

Hope sat down hard on the edge of the bed, nearly slipping off, but Tink caught her. Sat next to her like an anchor
keeping her in the world.

"I almost didn't go," Peg said, because what was the point

of secrets anymore? "I almost threw the letter in the trash. Denise had left. She'd left the farm and she'd left me and I wasn't going to go save her from herself again."

"But," Hope whispered, "there was a baby."

"That's what Hank said." She smiled, remembering. "He said, 'There's a baby now. And you didn't ask for any of this.'"

"I was rooting for you from the very beginning," Hank said, his smile still sweet.

Her heart squeezed in a terrible fist at the memory, and the edges of the world curled up.

"Peg," Hope said, reaching for her. "Are you all right?"

"Fine," she lied, putting her hand against the dresser. "Just fine."

"What happened?" Tink asked.

"I went to Flint, thinking I would pick up Denise and you. And bring you both back here. But when I got there..." She shook her head. The smell of the apartment still came back to haunt her sometimes. Sour and hopeless. "The door was unlocked and the apartment was filthy. You were crying your eyes out in a crib in the middle of the living room. There wasn't even a sheet on the mattress. It was just that plastic it was wrapped in and it was half torn up. And you had a diaper so full it was leaking everywhere. You were just a little thing, a little tiny baby thing, and your mom and Jacob were passed out in the bedroom. They didn't even realize I was in the apartment."

"Asleep," Hope said.

Oh, she couldn't lie about this, either. Not after all these years. "No, honey. They weren't asleep."

Hope wiped a hand over her face but then left it there. Tink wrapped her arms around her mother's neck and hugged her hard, and it was a real good thing seeing those two like that. But awful that it was happening like this.

Hank put his arm around her and she let herself be comforted. It wouldn't last; she'd ruined that. She'd ruined everything. But he was too good a man to turn away from her in this moment. And she was too weak to let him go.

"I couldn't get them awake. Denise would open one eye and push me away and that—" she shrugged "—that was the best I could get."

"So...you took me?"

"I cleaned you up and changed your clothes. I gave you a bottle and I kept thinking they would wake up, but they never did. I was there for hours. So I left them a note that said I had you, that you were safe, that she knew where we were and I...brought you back to the farm."

"And she got cleaned up and came and got me?" Hope asked. "And we lived here, Mom and me, for a few years. In that apartment upstairs. That's why there's all the baby stuff in the basement. And then when I was four she decided to move to St. Louis?"

Peg took a deep breath and wished she could lie. Wished she could make this part better.

"I'm sorry, Hope."

The internal door opened and in walked Abel, who blinked wide-eyed at the tension in the room.

"She came and got me and we lived in town?" Hope tried again. "And we visited a lot?"

"We didn't hear from her for four years," Hank answered. "You lived here with us for four years. We named you."

Hope gasped and Hank reached for her as if he might hug her, comfort her in some way. Peg knew he had to be just about dying to do that. But Hope jerked away.

Abel, though. Abel sat down next to Hope on the edge of that bed and pulled her close, and that she accepted.

Hank, poor Hank, looked so pained.

Give her a second, she wanted to tell him. *She's living this all right now. We've had years to feel this betrayal and it still hurts. Imagine how she must feel.*

The world was sliding a little and she braced herself against the bookshelf, trying to stay on her feet, wishing that Hank would come put one of those strong arms around her. "We were a family," Peg said. "We celebrated your birthdays. And you learned how to walk. And talk. You were sick in the beginning. The doctor wasn't sure if it was related maybe to Denise's drug use."

"You're saying my mom used when she was pregnant."

"I'm saying we didn't know."

"But," Hank jumped in, "you were such a bright little thing. You learned your alphabet and your numbers so fast. You rode with me on the tractor. You liked that. And you liked bath time. Hated bedtime." Hank and Peg shared a look, remembering those epic battles, how they would tag team halfway through. "You were strong," he said. "You walked early. Talked early. When you were fourteen months old, I swear we never got to sit down. We were chasing you all over this farm."

"Where was my mom all this time?" Hope asked.

"The summer after you turned four, it was the end of cherry season, and she called and told us she was coming. And we thought..." She looked to Hank. Her head was *pounding*. "We thought she wanted to *stay*. And be close to you. It never occurred to us that she wanted to take you. I mean...you were ours. All ours. We named you and fed you and kissed your scrapes and worried when you were sick. We had four years of you and she had none. How could she possibly take you away?" Her voice broke so fast and she lifted her hand to her face. Everything hurt.

"Peg," Abel said. "You don't look well. We need to get you back to the hospital."

"In a second," Peg said. "Let's just…finish this."

"So we did all the work upstairs," Hank said. "Trying to make it homey and private. A place she could make her own."

The second Denise had shown up, Peg knew she wasn't going to stay. She wished more than she could say that she had acted on that instinct instead of merely hoping she was wrong.

"She stayed for two days," Hank continued, his familiar sweet voice rough and chopped. He was deep in his accent, the way he always got when he was emotional. "On the third morning we woke up and you were gone. She left this."

Hank picked up the threadbare stuffed owl, made of patchwork fabric with wings that moved. It was handmade and repaired over and over again. It had been Hope's favorite. Once Denise left, Peg and Hank used to worry that Hope was crying at night for her comfortable old friend. It was easier, somehow, than imagining her crying for them, screaming "mama" until she collapsed exhausted on whatever bed Denise had for her.

"And that was all," Hank said. "We had you for four years and then your mom came and took you and we didn't hear from her again. Not once."

"I can't believe this," Hope said. "I don't even…know what to say." She looked down at Tink, who stared back at her, like she didn't have the answers, either.

"We looked for you," Hank said, generously adding Peg to that sentence with the *we*, but she shook her head. No more lies. This was the great shame she'd been hiding. The secret she knew would drive Hope right back out those doors.

"*Hank* looked for you," she said. "I knew you were gone. And after a month of him driving away every morning like he had a chance in hell in finding you, I asked him to stop. Carole had been calling the highway troopers every day, and I told her to stop. That if Denise didn't want to be found, we weren't going to find you. That's why Carole was mad at me. It's why Hank finally left, because I gave up. I just let you go."

Peg blew out a long breath, every one of her secrets gone, out of her body. Without them, she felt so light. But also empty. Like she'd been made of secrets and guilt and shame and regret and now…now she was made of nothing.

"Let me go?" Hope repeated softly. "How…how did you just let me go?"

"Hank wanted to get a lawyer. And we probably would have had a case. I had those letters and we'd had you for four years—"

"But you didn't? You didn't get a lawyer?"

Peg shook her head.

"My mother was an addict who wasn't around for four years, and then shows up and *takes* me and you just let me go? You didn't even try?"

"Hope," Hank whispered. "Stop. Denise was your mother. We never adopted you. We didn't have—"

"No," Peg said. "Let her say what she needs to say."

"When Tink was four she was reading," Hope cried. "And she chopped off all the hair on her dolls. She had a dream she could fly and jumped off her bed and broke her wrist. And if someone took her from me, I would have burned down the world to get her back and you—"

"Her heart was broken," Hank said, and it was so strange to hear him defending her. "She stopped eating and sleeping. She didn't work."

"Oh, that's how you know things are bad?" Hope asked, wiping away tears as fast as they came. "She can't work the orchards. Good to know the Peg Wright stages of grief."

"Enough!" Hank said. "It's been a long night. We don't need to say things we're going to regret."

"Well, if there's one thing the Wright women are good at it's not talking. So, why break the habit now?"

Peg laughed, a scrape in the back of her throat.

"I think," Abel said quietly into the charged room, "we need to get Peg back to the hospital. She's not looking so good."

Hope stood there, that girl Peg loved so well and so much, stone-faced in her anger.

"This is why I didn't tell you," Peg said. "I just wanted to keep you a little longer."

Hank put his good hand on Peg's shoulder, and she sagged against him. "I'm sorry," she said to him, and finally the tears broke through. "I'm so sorry to all of you." He pulled her into his arms and she rested her head against his chest, where she always had. "I let you all go. We were a family and I gave up. I just gave up on you."

"I'm gonna take her back to the emergency room," Hank said to Hope. "I think she's worse than she let on."

"The hell you are, Hank," Abel said. "You got shot tonight. I'll drive you. Both of you."

Hank nodded and walked Peg toward the door. He was supporting most of her weight, the poor man, doing more than his share of the work.

"I didn't deserve you," she said to him. "Either one of you. That's why I let you both go. Because I knew I didn't deserve you."

Or maybe she had then. But she didn't now. That was for sure. She'd set a series of events in motion that made sure they'd never be a family. And now Hope would leave her. Again.

Thirty-Six

Abel and Hank helped Peg back into Hank's truck, then Abel hopped in the driver's seat.

"Don't leave," Abel said to Hope through the car window.

"Where would we go?" Hope asked, exhausted.

Tink and Hope stood in the driveway and watched them go.

She looked down at her tiny daughter, at the challenges of her, and felt all at once the contradictions of motherhood. The push and pull, the delicate small balances. She knew Denise had not been made for motherhood. She did not have the patience. Or the kindness. She was not forgiving. Every scale tilted toward herself.

She didn't know why Denise had taken her and never looked back. Vindictiveness, maybe. Or maybe she knew if she stayed, she'd always be the sister who messed up. Or maybe she'd just needed to be as far away from Jacob and the drugs as she could be. In a whole other state.

Maybe she'd just needed to be someone new.

Somewhere new.

And maybe Mom had loved her the best she could.

Hope had no idea and never would.

"Mom?" Tink asked.

"Yeah?"

"You okay?"

"I don't even know," she finally said.

"Are you mad at Peg?" Tink asked.

"Yes."

"For not telling you?"

"No. That I understand." Hope, too, had wanted to keep her own secrets, the ones that reflected poorly on her, that revealed just what a flawed human she was. And all Peg had been doing was trying not to relive all that pain.

And protecting herself from new pain when Hope had showed up in the middle of the night with a daughter and a black eye.

Yeah, she got all that.

"You're mad at Peg for not looking for you?" Tink asked.

"Yes," she said, and brushed her daughter's flyaway hair back from her face. She had meant every word she said in there, that if someone had taken Tink she would have done anything to get her back.

But now that the shock had worn off and the anger had burned down she also understood. She understood dark days that messed with your head. That made you numb to your bad decisions. That made you numb enough to live through your bad decisions.

Things could have been bad for Hope had Mom started using again. But those were what-ifs that didn't matter now, because they hadn't happened.

"But I wasn't her daughter. Maybe she could have fought—"

"She should have," Tink said, so fierce. The world was black-and-white to her and maybe she'd grow to understand that really, it was only gray. It was people trying their best and sometimes failing.

Yes, how different Hope's life might have been had they'd stayed, had Peg looked for her and found her and she'd grown up here, in The Orchard House. With Hank and Peg and that growth chart on the wall. Who know who she could have been with all that love?

But then she wouldn't have had the most precious part of her life. Her regrets and mistakes didn't define her. But being this little girl's mother did.

"But if I grew up here, I wouldn't have met your dad and I wouldn't have had you," she said to Tink.

Things had happened just the way they should.

"But still," Tink said.

"Yeah," Hope sighed, because it hurt. Being lied to. Being let go of. It hurt. "A little bit...but still."

⇥ PEG ⇤

In the end, it was a concussion, a whole bunch of tests and a night in the hospital.

"I'm releasing you," the doctor said the next day, surrounded by sunlight that hurt Peg's eyes. "On the condition that you rest and you have someone looking after you."

"I'll look after her," Hank said, and the doctor nodded and left.

Hank had been there the whole night, snoring in that uncomfortable chair beside her bed with his poor arm in that sling. Foolish man. Sweet foolish man. "I'm gonna put that on your tombstone," she said to him.

"What's that?" he asked with a smile.

"I looked after her."

"Did the doc give you some serious pain meds?"

"Hear me out," she said. She wasn't on pain meds, but she was a little unmoored. She'd lived her life for the last twenty-some years bogged down by these secrets and this pain and they weren't anymore. She didn't entirely know who she was without them. Maybe she was silly. Maybe she was sweet. Maybe she could love this man the way he should be loved. "It's the most you thing you could say. 'I'll take care of her.' Or him. Or anyone. It's what you do, Hank. You take care of people."

"You gonna let me take care of you?" he asked.

"Have you forgiven me?"

His handsome blue eyes were sharp, and they were wary. "I keep thinking of those fights we had after Denise left with Hope."

"I wish you wouldn't." They'd been awful fights.

"Yeah," he sighed. "But I think what I was fighting for was for you to get past that decision we made."

"I made it. I made you stop looking."

"But I stopped, Peg. I did that. And trust me, I regret it every damn day. But for ten years you just…tortured yourself. It was like you dug a hole and jumped into it and I could not get you out. But I didn't want to live in that hole with you, either."

That sounded like the pure truth.

"I forgive you, Peg. But you need to forgive yourself. And if those girls are sticking around—"

She sucked in a deep breath. "You think they will?"

He shook his head slowly. "I don't know, Peg. I don't know how deep that hurt goes."

"I have to tell myself they won't be there," she admitted.

"I know you do," he said. "But I hope they are."

The nurse came with the wheelchair, and Peg sat in it, grumbling that it was all unnecessary.

"You ready?" the nurse asked.

"As I'll ever be."

Hank held her hand with his good hand and the nurse pushed the chair out of the room and into the hallway.

The sun was still shining, which seemed so odd; it was a brand-new day. It was—

Hank stopped so fast, the nurse pushing the chair bumped into him. He smiled down at Peg and nudged her with his elbow.

"What are you doing?" she groused. "I'm injured—"

"Peg?"

Oh god, it was Hope. She rose from one of those god-awful chairs outside her room, and Tink was there beside her. Abel, too, putting down a magazine.

"What are you doing here?" Peg asked.

"They let us stay as long as we didn't bother you because the waiting room is so full. Are you okay?" Hope asked and then looked up at Hank. "Is she okay?"

"She's just shocked to see you," Hank explained. "You know Peg."

"I don't know what you're doing here," she said again, sounding grumpier than she wanted to.

"Did you really think I would leave?" Hope asked.

Peg nodded.

"I'm not going anywhere," Hope said, crouching awkwardly to wrap her arms carefully around Peg. "We just got here."

Tink got in on the hug, a little less carefully, and then Hank was there, wrapping his big old arms around everyone. Abel smiled and kissed the side of Hope's head.

"This is a whole lot of fuss for nothing," Peg said, because she had to say something.

"Well," Hope said, taking over the pushing duties from the nurse. "Brace yourself."

Out in the waiting room was…everyone.

Matt and Swafiya with piles of baked goods. Janice and Carole with all the kids.

Peg, when she saw all of them, made Hope stop, and she got up out of the chair. "What are you all doing here?" she asked.

"We're here for you, you old bird," Carole said, and then folded her old friend into a careful hug. The two stood there for a long time, until finally Carole stepped away, wiping her eyes.

Swafiya came over to Tink with a loaf of bread. "I made you something special," she said, absolutely unable to stop crying, just letting go in a sea of people trying hard not to cry. "I'm calling it the Tinkerbell loaf."

"What's in it?" Tink asked.

"Chocolate, peanut butter, caramel and cherries." Those were all of Tink's favorite things. "Basically it's a cake. I made you a cake."

"Thank you," Tink said, and Peg felt like her chest was going to just crack wide-open. Right down the middle. All this kindness.

"Do you feel that?" Hope whispered in Peg's ear.

Yes, she thought. *I feel it.*

I feel everything.

She might have wasted years. Lost people she loved.

But right now she was only grateful to have them here again.

"Let's go home," she said.

Epilogue

THE NEXT YEAR
→ HOPE ←

"This is a whole lot of nonsense," Peg said as Hope tried to pin the daisies into her hair.

But the daisies and the pin and Peg and her hair were not cooperative, Peg most of all. "No, Peg, they're flowers and they're pretty. Now sit still."

Peg harrumphed but sat quietly in her chair in front of the mirror Hope had set up in Peg's bedroom for the day.

Tink came running in, the flowers in her hair already long gone, but she looked lovely in the yellow dress with the eyelet trim that Janice had made for her. "Everyone's here," Tink announced and came to stand next to Peg, looking at her in the mirror. Tink rested her body against Peg's shoulder, and Peg looped her arm around Tink's waist. Tink had only ever been so easy with Hope, and it was beautiful to see her opening herself up to other people.

The bitter and the sweet.

"Who is everyone?"

"My friends," Tink said.

"That's what I figured. Is Hank here?"

"Yep."

"Good. He's really the only one that matters," Peg said.

Hope smiled, knowing she only half meant it.

"He looks really nice in his suit. Not as nice as you," Tink said.

"Well, thank you," Peg said and caught Hope's eye in the mirror. "Am I done?"

"Sure," Hope said, realizing she'd hit the end of what Peg was going to sit still for. Honest to god, Peg and Tink were so much alike sometimes she couldn't believe it.

The ceremony wasn't supposed to start for another twenty minutes and Hope wanted to make sure Abel and the caterers were all set up. "You okay to wait here until—"

The words weren't even out of her mouth before Peg was up out of the chair. "It's my damn farm. It's my damn wedding. I'm not waiting in here."

"But it's bad luck for Hank to see you," Tink cried.

"That man's seen me plenty. The sight of this dress isn't gonna change a thing." Peg wore a pretty blue dress that started darker at the bottom and got progressively lighter as it went up the skirt and across the bodice. Tink, when they'd shopped for the wedding, had said it looked like the sky at the farm in August.

So far there had been nothing conventional about this wedding, because there was nothing conventional about Peg. As the three of them walked out the side door of the house, a cry of joy rose up from the guests milling about with their white wine and shrimp cocktails.

"Oh, come on," Peg said, waving everyone off, but smiling while she did it. "It's just a dress."

"And lipstick," Carole said. "I swear to god, Peg, I don't think I've ever seen you in lipstick."

Hope left Peg in Carole's slightly stoned hands and went

to find Abel and Matt and the caterers. They'd cleaned up the barn and filled it with tables and flowers and a bar in the corner. Swafiya was carefully laying flowers on the cake she'd made while Abel and Matt shoved bottles of champagne into the big metal troughs filled with ice.

"This ice isn't going to last in this heat," Abel said.

"Well, the champagne isn't either, the way this crowd is drinking," Matt said. They'd become good friends, the two men, watching the Red Wings and Pistons games at a bar in town when they could each make it work. Sometimes Swafiya and Hope joined them and other times she and Swafiya and Janice drove out to Grayling to see a movie. Never in her life had she had so many friends.

"Hey," Hope said, coming to stand in front of them.

"My...god," Abel said, his mouth dropping open when he saw her.

Matt took this opportunity to grab his wife and head back into the side yard. Swafiya, as she walked by, gave Hope a kiss on the cheek. "You look stunning."

"It's just a dress," Hope said, embarrassed but delighted all at once. The dress was yellow like Tink's but lighter in color, and it slipped off her shoulders, the bodice and waist clinging to her curves and then fanning out down to her knees. She wore it with a red belt and shoes that matched.

It was the prettiest thing she'd ever worn and she felt like a million dollars.

"It's not just a dress," he said, kissing her cheek and then her lips and then her lips again until she laughed. "You look beautiful."

"Thank you. You're not too shabby yourself." He wore a blue suit and a crisp white shirt with the collar button undone. He had a daisy in the buttonhole, and his hair was loose in that way she loved.

"It's fun playing dress up," Abel said.

"Everything going all right in here with the food?" she asked.

"Pretty good," Abel said.

The cats came out of the grass to twine against her legs. Nelson was snoozing in the shade of The Orchard House, something she did now more often than not. She was getting older, and everyone was preparing Tink for the day she might not get up when she called anymore. So preemptively, when the cats were born, Tink had given them all names that were some variation of Nelson.

"Which one is this one?" Abel asked, picking up the kitten with one blue eye. "Nellie? I can't keep them straight."

"What are we going to do if she wants to name the baby?" Hope asked as casually as possible, watching his face with her heart in her throat.

It took Abel a second, but he turned to her with wide eyes. "Baby?" he whispered. The cat jumped out of his hands and made for the tall grass. "Like...a baby?"

His hands touched her stomach, still flat. But yes. A baby.

"I took the test yesterday and I was going to keep it a secret, but everyone is going to figure it out when I'm not drinking—"

"A baby." He said it again.

"Yes, that is what I'm telling you."

He whooped and pulled her into his arms, where she felt the rumble of his laughter, his joy through her whole body. He was going to be a great father. And Peg and Hank were going to be grandparents like the world had never seen.

"Hey!" Tink came barreling around the corner, leaping through sunshine and tall grasses. A kid on a mission. "Everyone's asking...what's going on? Why are you crying?"

Oh, Tink... This baby didn't know how lucky it was to have a sister like Tink.

"Sweetheart," she said, drying her eyes. "We've got a secret to tell you."

★ ★ ★ ★ ★

Acknowledgments

The Bitter and Sweet of Cherry Season is my fiftieth book. Even writing that seems impossible. And while every book has its challenges, this one seemed to come with some extra-special this-is-your-fiftieth-book problems! And for the people who helped me sort through those problems—I cannot thank you enough.

Stephanie Doyle, who thought of twist after twist—enough for twenty books. And then read an early draft and had the kindness not to laugh at me. She also answers my phone calls, even when she's tired of my whining.

Sinead Murphy, who read an early draft and whose every idea made the story more suspenseful.

Simone St. James, an excellent commiserator and sounding board.

Annika Martin, Skye Warren and Zoe York, who helped me figure out Abel and brought Indian food and wine when it was very much needed.

Maureen McGowan, who read a draft and gave the kind of thoughtful, thorough advice I have come to rely on her for.

Pam Hopkins, my agent of fifteen years, who always has a plan and an idea and compliment when I need it.

But mostly to Melanie Fried, my editor, who walked me through three drafts of this book, carefully nudging me in better directions. Thank you so much for your hard work on Hope, Peg and Tink. They are much much better for it.

Depressive illnesses affect more than 19 million American adults age 18 and over each year. Depression is a treatable medical illness that can occur in any woman, at any time, and for various reasons, regardless of age, race or income. To learn more, visit:

https://endthestigma.org/

https://www.nami.org/stigmafree

Finally, if you are in an abusive relationship or think you might be—there is help. There is a way out. You are not alone. To get help, visit:

https://www.thehotline.org/

THE BITTER AND SWEET OF CHERRY SEASON

MOLLY FADER

Reader's Guide

GRAYDON
HOUSE

1. Hope doesn't remember being at the farm, in part because she'd been so young when she lived there. What are your earliest memories? How reliable do you think those memories are? In what ways might they have been reinforced by family stories?

2. Peg keeps the past a secret from Hope. Do you agree or disagree with her decision? Have you ever kept secrets from your family or friends to save them pain? If so, did they ever find out the truth?

3. How did Peg's and Denise's childhoods shape what kind of people and parents they each became? How does this compare to Hope's childhood and the life she's created for herself and Tink?

4. Cherry season at The Orchard House is the hardest job Hope has ever had, but she says it's a "good" hard. In what way did the work of cherry season help Hope deal with what had happened to her? How do you cope with your own hardships?

5. Hope ultimately chooses not to get a protective order against Daniel. Do you agree with her choice? How can we help women in Hope's situation? What can we change in society to prevent abusive situations for women to begin with?

6. Discuss the ways the farm has affected Peg's life. Do you think she would have been happier away from The Orchard House and its memories?

7. In the novel, old friends reunite and new friends are made. Discuss how these various female friendships empower the Wright women. How do your own friendships lift you up?

8. Who was your favorite Wright woman: Peg, Hope or Tink?

SWAFIYA'S BAKERY CHERRY RECIPES

(as seen in *The Bitter and Sweet of Cherry Season*)

Chocolate Cherry Brioche

Ingredients

2 packets (½ oz) active dry yeast
½ cup warm whole milk
4 cups (1 lb, 2 oz) unbleached all-purpose flour
⅓ cup granulated white sugar
2 tsp salt
4 large eggs, room temperature,
plus 1 egg yolk for the egg wash
1 cup (8 oz) unsalted butter, softened, cut into 16 pieces
1 cup cherries, pitted and roughly chopped
⅔ cup dark chocolate chips
⅔ cup caramel square candies, cut into four

YIELD: 2 loaves

Preparation

1. In a small bowl, dissolve yeast in warm milk. Let stand until creamy, about 10 minutes.

2. In a large bowl, stir together the flour, sugar and salt. Make a well in the center of the bowl and mix in the eggs and yeast mixture. Beat at medium speed and add the butter a few pieces at a time. Beat until the dough has formed a sticky ball. Turn it out onto a lightly floured surface and knead until smooth and supple, about 8 minutes.

3. Transfer to a large bowl, smooth side up, and let rise for 1 hour.

4. After the dough has doubled in size, turn out onto a floured work surface. Knead the dough and form into a ball. Place back in the bowl and let it sit until doubled in size, about 1 hour.

5. Butter 2 brioche pans or 2 standard loaf pans. Divide the dough in half and then divide each half into 8 pieces, for 16 total.

6. Roll each piece of dough into a ball, flatten slightly, and place a small amount of chocolate and chopped cherries and one quartered caramel in the center. Fold the dough over the chocolate, caramel and cherries to seal and form into a ball. Place in the center of the pan. Repeat with remaining pieces, arranging them next to each other inside the pan, with 8 dough balls to each pan.

7. Cover each pan loosely with plastic wrap and rise for about an hour or until doubled in size.

8. Brush the tops with the egg wash and heat your oven to 375°F. Bake for about 25 minutes or until the internal temperature of the bread reaches 195°F. If the bread is turning too dark before it finishes cooking, tent lightly with foil.

9. Let cool on a wire rack for 30 minutes before turning out and serving. Best served warm.

Spicy Cherry Chutney

Ingredients

1 navel orange
4 cups fresh tart cherries, pitted
1 white onion, chopped
⅓ cup brown sugar, packed
¼ cup balsamic vinegar
2 tsp fresh ginger, peeled and minced
¼ tsp dried hot red pepper flakes
½ tsp ground cardamom
¼ tsp ground allspice
½ tsp salt

YIELD: 1 ½ cups

Preparation

1. With a vegetable peeler remove two 2-inch strips of orange zest and cut into fine julienne strips. Reserve orange for another use.

2. In a heavy medium saucepan stir together all ingredients and bring to a boil.

3. Reduce heat and simmer mixture, stirring occasionally, then more frequently toward end of cooking, for about 50 minutes, or until thickened and syrupy.

4. Cool chutney.

*Chutney keeps, covered and chilled, for 3 weeks.

Small-Batch Sour Cherry Jam (With No Pectin)

Ingredients

2 cups sour cherries, pitted and roughly chopped
1 cup granulated sugar
1 tsp seeds from 1 vanilla bean, or 1 tbsp vanilla extract

YIELD: 1 cup

Preparation

1. In a large deep skillet, add cherries, sugar and vanilla. Bring to a rolling boil, stirring often. Once boiling, cook until it thickens, about 10 minutes.

2. Transfer to a heat-proof container. Cool to room temperature.

*Use within 2 weeks. Once opened, store in the refrigerator.

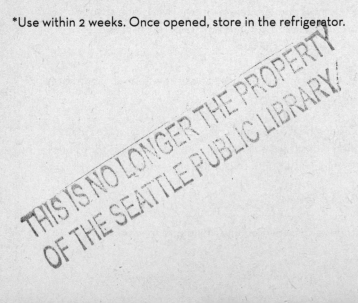